A DEAD RINGER

ROBERT SANDILANDS

Copyright © 2024 by Robert Sandilands

Paperback: 978-1-963883-00-8
eBook: 978-1-963883-01-5
Library of Congress Control Number: 2024903876

All rights reserved. No part of this publication may be reproduced, distributed, or transmitted in any form or by any electronic or mechanical means, without the prior written permission of the publisher, except in the case of brief quotations embodied in critical reviews and certain other noncommercial uses permitted by copyright law.

This Book is a work of fiction. Names, characters, places, and incidents either are the product of the author's imagination or are used fictitiously. Any resemblance to actual persons, living or dead, events, or locales is entirely coincidental.

Ordering Information:

Prime Seven Media
518 Landmann St.
Tomah City, WI 54660

Printed in the United States of America

CHAPTER 1

It was one of those boring moments on a frosty Sunday morning. He was sitting on his parents' sofa, the television on, not paying much attention to it. His father was in his usual chair fumbling with his roll-up cigarettes. His mother was clattering dishes in the kitchen.

Barton was having one of his flashbacks to an incident from his days in the regiment. Sergeant Tommy Marvell had stuck his head around the door of Barton's room. "Do you fancy going down to the mess for a pint and a game of darts?"

Barton had swung his feet out of the bed and attempted to slip his shoes on.

"Hurry up and get your shoes on. Your feet stink," Marvell had complained.

Barton remembered standing up and saying, "Your nose is too near your own arse."

Why this vision had suddenly come to him like so many others lately was a mystery.

"What are you grinning at?" his father said, interrupting his reminiscing.

Not realising he had been grinning, Barton apologised and said, "Just an unexpected memory. I don't know what brought it on. I've been having a lot of them lately—just silly little moments."

"When do you intend moving into your new flat?" the older man asked after a long moment of gazing at the television with the volume turned down, hearing only the constant ticking of the old wooden clock on the mantel, marking time.

"Soon," Barton replied. "I need to get a few things, and then I'll be out of your way."

"You can stay as long as you like as far as I'm concerned. It's your mother. She gets upset when she sees a strange car parked in the street. She frets it could be someone after you."

"What makes her think that?"

Lighting his made-up cigarette and blowing the smoke out the side of his mouth, his father said, "It could be the way you prance about all night from your bed to the window, as if you were hiding from someone."

"That's just the way I am. Don't sleep much these days. Nothing for her to worry about."

"I'm going out the back door to have this smoke before your mother comes in and catches me having it in here. Come out and keep me company," his father said, getting stiffly onto his feet.

Following behind his father through the kitchen to the back door, Barton noticed how thin the older man's grey hair was becoming and how bent at the shoulders he had suddenly appeared.

When the oldster opened the door, the smoke from his cigarette drifted inside with the breeze. Barton could feel his eyes sting and water. He stepped around his father to get to get away from it, wiping the tears with his hands.

At first glance, Barton couldn't believe what he was seeing—thought his eyes were playing tricks on him. It was when his father shouted and the youth stumbled over the fence at the bottom of the garden that Barton realised it wasn't an illusion. Barton charged down the slabbed path and was on top of the youth before he had a chance to recover his balance. "What do you think you're doing here?" he shouted at the young man on the ground, pinned down by Barton's knees on his shoulders.

"It's a mistake," the youngster cried. "I thought this was my mate's house. I've always come in the back way."

"What's your mate's name?" the old man asked as he approached from behind. Tom Barton had been joined by his wife, Jean, and the pair was standing over the two on the ground. The oldster had armed himself with a spade and was holding it ready to strike.

Getting onto his feet, Barton grabbed the youngster's jacket by the collar and pulled him up. "Well, what's your mate's name?" he repeated into the youth's face.

Jean Barton reached out to restrain her son, and Barton relaxed his grip on the young man. She stepped between them. "Where does your mate live?" she asked, staring deeply into the youth's brown eyes.

"I thought it was here. I've been away for a long time. Moved with my parents. I was just twelve at the time."

"What's your mate's name?" Tom asked again, stepping closer to his wife and relaxing his grip on the spade.

Seeing the old man lowering the spade, the youth grinned weakly. "Corrie … Corrie Barton. We were pals at school."

The clatter the spade made when it slipped from Tom's hand made them all stare down at it. Jean stepped back, her eyes staring at the young man. Her lips trembled. "I'm Corrie's mum. This is his dad and older brother. I can't remember you being one of Corrie's pals. Where did you live back then?"

The youth pointed a long finger at the houses a distance from the bottom of the garden. "We used to live in that end terraced house, number thirty-six."

"What's your name?" Jean asked.

"Andy Milton," the young man replied, wiping dirt from his jacket.

"I can't say I recall that name. I'm sure Corrie would have mentioned it if you were one of his pals," Jean said, slowly shaking her head.

"We were all on the football team at school. We were all good pals. Maybe too many names for you to remember."

Satisfied with the youngster's explanation, Jean nodded towards the back door. "You'd better come inside and talk," she said, heading down the slab pathway.

The three men reluctantly followed. They sat at the kitchen table while Jean filled the kettle. Barton sat across from the youth. He leaned on his arms, his chin resting on his clenched fists. "Where do you live now?" he asked.

The youngster leaned back on his chair and shook his head. "I need to live rough. I was tossed out of my flat. Couldn't pay the rent. That's the reason I wanted to see Corrie, to see if he could help."

Tom's chair creaked as he leaned closer to the youth. "I'm afraid Corrie won't be able to help. He's no longer with us, Andy."

Young Andy wasn't convincing Barton. Maybe he was being paranoid, but there was something about this young man's body language sending out signals that he was acting. And the words he spoke sounded like he was reciting from a script.

Andy stared into Tom's watery blue eyes. "Could you tell me where I could get in contact with him?"

Jean placed mugs of tea in front of them. They watched as she placed a jug of milk and sugar containers on the table. "What my husband means," she said as she seated herself next to Tom, "is that Corrie was involved in an explosion; his body was never recovered. That was two years ago. We can only assume he was killed."

Although the youngster offered his condolences to them, Barton could read by his expression that Corrie's death wasn't news to him. "How long have you been living back here?" he asked.

Andy caught that look in Barton's brown eyes; that's when the warning bells started. He could see this big man wasn't swallowing his story. He attempted to get up, but the big man had anticipated his move and was towering over him.

Barton leaned over the table on both hands, glared into the youth's face. "I'll ask you once again. What are you doing here?"

Young Andy stood up, pushing the chair back with his legs, coming level with Barton's eyes. "I told you what I'm doing here looking up an old mate, asking for help."

Seeing tempers rise between the two men, Jean got out of her seat and rushed around the table, gripping Barton's arm. "Calm down, the pair of you," she cried. "I don't want trouble in my house."

"Don't believe a word this little shit is telling you." Barton turned on his mother. "Look at the age of him. He must be five years younger than Corrie, which would put him in primary class when Corrie was old enough to get into the football team. Ask him why he ran when we stepped out the door."

Catching the young man's eyes, Jean said, "Well? Why *did* you run?"

Hunching his shoulders and shaking his head, Andy nervously replied, "I got a fright. I was about to knock on the door when it opened. I don't know why I ran. It just seemed to be the natural thing to do when a big man like your son barged out on me."

Jabbing his thumb at the door, Barton snarled, "Get on your way, shit bag! If I ever catch you near here again, you'll carry the scars for the rest of your life."

The look in her eyes told Barton his mother had been taken in with this young man's story, and he held back from grabbing the youth by the collar of his jacket. They watched the youth stride down the slabbed path of the back garden and climb over the wooden fence. "That guy is up to something," Barton said.

When they got into the living room, Jean remarked, "Why do you always have to look at the negative side of people?"

Fumbling with his tobacco pouch, Tom settled in his usual chair and said, "You've been so involved with thugs and bloody gangsters you think everybody you meet is one."

"It's called instinct brought on by experience," Barton quickly replied. "He didn't even flinch when he was told about Corrie; it was as if he knew."

Slowly getting up off the sofa, Jean headed for the kitchen. "I have work to do," she announced, closing the door behind her.

Picking up the tele remote with the intention of increasing the volume, Tom never got to perform the task. He jumped when he heard the scream. Barton was up there first. They rushed into the kitchen to see Jean standing at the window, her hands on her mouth, her eyes wide open. "He was at the window," she managed to say, gazing out at the garden.

"Who?" Tom shouted.

"That young guy."

The words had hardly left her mouth when Barton darted out the back door. This time, the youth had had enough time to get over the wooden fence and was running along the back alley. Barton gave chase. But by the time he reached the street, the young man had disappeared. At the point Barton gave up the chase, two aged men he knew to be friends of his father were sitting on a bench that seemed to have been there for the millennia. The pair threw him a greeting, and one of them pointed a thumb up the street. Barton read the sign and rushed in that direction.

After a few hundred yards of weaving past oncoming pedestrians, he spotted the youth about to cross to the other side of the street, waiting for a gap in the traffic. Barton took advantage of the same gap and bounded across, catching the youth by the arm and pushing him into a narrow lane between buildings. Two quick punches to the ribs, and the young man collapsed to his knees. Threatening to land another blow, Barton shouted, "What's your game, mate?"

Gasping for breath, doubled over at Barton's feet, the youngster held up his hands in defence and said, "I was told to hide a gun in your parents' garden."

"Who told you? And what kind of gun it is?" Barton said, grabbing his collar and lifting him up.

On wabbly legs, the youth fell against the wall on his shoulder, holding his ribs, his head bent over. "I don't know who the geezer was. Never seen him before. Had the hood down hiding his face." The youngster coughed out mucus. "He gave me twenty quid to go in and plant it. Said it belonged to the man who lived there. And when I did it, he would give me another twenty."

"Did you manage to hide it?"

"No. I was about to when the old man shouted, and you charged at me."

"So, you still have it on you?"

The youth shook his head. "I slung it into one of the wheelie bins when you chased after me."

Still holding the young man's shirt, Barton pushed him out onto the street. "Show me where you slung it."

Barton ignored the looks they were getting from the pedestrians they passed, and the youth led the way back up the lane to a group of wheelie bins. At the first one, he lifted up the lid and stepped back.

"I put it in this one. It was wrapped in an old rag. I don't see it."

"Are you sure it was this one?" Barton shouted and pushed him towards the other bins. "Check the rest. You could be mistaken; you were in a rush."

The lids on all the bins had been lifted, and the gun wrapped in a rag was nowhere in any of them.

"Where have you to meet this guy who gave it to you?" Barton said, pushing the youngster against the open bins.

"In the café up the street." He pointed in the direction he was meant to go.

"Will this guy be in there now?"

The youth nodded. "He said he would wait for me there and to come back when I had hidden the gun."

Gripping the youth at the back of his neck, Barton gave him a push back in the direction of the street. "Lead the way. I'll be behind you. I have a gun in my pocket. So, if you try to run, you're a dead man. Go inside the café and sit at the table and tell this guy the job has been done. When he gives you your money, piss off."

Feeling he was drawing attention to himself from pedestrians, who were all huddled up in heavy clothing—him standing across the street from the café on a cold frosty morning wearing only a short-sleeved T-shirt, jeans, and trainers, his long black hair hanging loose over his shoulders—Barton decided to cross the street into the doorway of the café. That way, he could get away from the curious glances and maybe get a closer look at this guy the youth had been talking about.

Through the misted window on the door, Barton had trouble distinguishing the characters seated at the tables. Luckily, young Andy hadn't had time to get seated and was the only person moving about. Barton watched the slim figure walk the length of the floor between the tables and chairs. At a door that presumably led to the kitchen, he stopped and turned. A few seconds later, he headed back for the exit.

His young eyes widened as he stepped out and came face to face with Barton. He shook his head vigorously. "He's not in there."

Once again gripping the collar of the young man's jacket, Barton pulled him closer. "You'd better not be messing me about. What does this guy look like?"

Young Andy raised his arms as if expecting a blow to his face. "He's not as big as you." He whimpered. "Has a shaggy long beard, had a hood over his head and a long black jacket; that's all I can remember."

"Easy for you to recognise him if you saw him again?"

"I think so," Andy replied.

Still holding the youngster's collar, Barton pushed him onto the street, "We're going to take a walk around the area. He could be hanging about eyeing us."

That long-forgotten instinct had returned to Barton as he tailed the youth down the pavement. The street was crowded with shoppers and traffic, and still he could sense that, somewhere, someone was keeping a close eye on him. If the description Andy had given him was accurate, then this character should be easily spotted. At the end of the shopping area, he caught up with the youngster and took a firm hold of his arm. "Did you spot the guy?"

Andy shook his head. "I noticed a few hoodies, but none of them had a beard that I could see from a distance."

"Do you have a pen or a pencil on you?" Barton asked, patting the pockets of his jeans, realising he hadn't his mobile on him.

"Why?" Andy said and shook his head.

"If you want to make some real cash, you have to get in contact with me if that guy approaches you again."

The youngster fished out his mobile. "Give me your number."

If only Barton had known his instincts were spot-on. He was being closely observed by the character he and the youngster were searching for from only a few metres away. Grinning at them, Walter Lorinna had discarded the black hooded jacket and the false beard in the plastic shopping bag he was carrying. Also in the bag was the pistol wrapped in a rag. He'd recovered it from the wheelie bin where the youngster had ditched it.

The yob had been the ideal target. Lorinna could tell by the way he wandered about the pedestrians looking for a bag or wallet to snatch. He had the experience himself and could easily spot the signs. He had sat in his car watching the young thief looking for a soft target.

The disguise had been perfect—easy and quick to get out of. Now with his black hair groomed and trimmed; clean shaven; and wearing a three-quarter-length grey jacket, white shirt, and red tie, he was confident he looked a long way from bearded hoodie. He passed them so closely he could see the youngster thumbing something into his mobile and guessed the big guy, wearing only a T-shirt and jeans, was giving him his number.

Joining a group of people standing at the bus stop, Lorinna was in a position to see the youngster and the big guy part company. Knowing he could find the yob easily, he decided to follow the man in white T-shirt and jeans. He wasn't surprised to see the big guy opening the door and entering the front door of the house where the Barton family lived. This confirmed his suspicions that this was the oldest son—Richard Barton.

Back at his car standing at the open rear door, Lorinna shed his coat and replaced it with the scruffy black jacket, fitted the false beard, pulled the hood down close to his eyebrows, and headed back to the shopping area.

Locating the yob was no problem. Lorinna stepped into a shop doorway and watched as the youngster headed his way. The youth was following behind an old couple. His actions were obvious to Lorinna. He had played this game many times in his past. Somewhere close behind, the yob had to have an accomplice so as to pass the stolen goods on. Deciding to ignore who this other person was, he stepped out between the couple and the youth. Unaware of what was going on behind them, the oldsters carried on. Lorinna grabbed Andy by the upper arm and dragged him into the shop doorway. "You didn't get the job done," he snarled into the youth's face. "I want my money back."

The grip on his arm happened so quickly and was so painful Andy let out a yelp and his legs gave way under him as he was dragged into the shop door. The hooded man's face was so close Andy could feel his beard touching his face. He gazed up into the dark eyes below the hood. "I tried," he cried. "They saw me and caught me. Twice I tried, and the second time, the son chased me."

"Why did you toss the package into a rubbish bin?"

"I didn't want to be caught with a gun in my possession." Andy whimpered. "That big guy caught me and gave me a doing over. Wants me to contact him if I see you again."

Lorinna grinned and lifted the youth onto his feet, dug into his pocket, and pulled out a thick roll of twenty-pound notes and peeled one off. Stuffing the note into Andy's top pocket, he said, "Call the number after I've left you. Tell him he'll find me in that café we talked about earlier. That should get him out of the way." From the plastic bag, Lorinna pulled out the package wrapped in the rag and rammed it into the young man's chest "Give him time to get out of the house, and you can go and get it done this time."

CHAPTER 2

Picking up his leather jacket on his rush through the house, Barton slipped it on as he darted into the kitchen and out the back door. It wasn't long before he jumped over the wooden fence and raced up the narrow lane between the gardens and came out at the main street. The feeling of being watched had stayed with him all the way back to his parents' house. The description of the man the youth had given him was quite distinctive. But of all the people who were passing, he couldn't find anyone fitting it or anywhere near it.

Leaning on the corner of a building so he could observe movement in all directions, he heard his mobile sound. Cursing at it, he noticed a strange number and guessed it to be the yob with information about the guy with the beard. He didn't get a chance to reply when he pressed the green answer icon. Andy's instructions were quick and simple—to Barton's mind, too simple. But he had to know why this person wanted to hide a weapon in his parents' garden.

This time, the glass on the door of the café wasn't so misted up, and he could see that most of the tables were vacant. A few couples sat at the far end near the kitchen entrance, but he could see no sign of the bearded hoodie. Maybe he hadn't arrived yet. Barton glanced at his watch. It had only been a few minutes since the yob's call. Should he wait or rush back to his parents' house?

Deciding on the latter, Barton headed back the way he had come at a fast jog and caught the youth attempting to climb over the fence. He rushed at the yob on his blind side and, without warning, landed a few punches to the back of his neck.

Young Andy crumpled to his knees, and Barton grabbed him by the collar, lifting him up and pushing him against the fence. The package fell from the youth's hand and landed at Barton's feet. When he picked it up, the weapon fell out. Barton gazed down at it, astonished at recognising it as being his own. The last time he had seen it was when he had left it in his old flat before it had been bombed.

"Where did that guy get this weapon from?" he shouted at the youth. This time, he forced Andy's head against a wooden post, gripping him by the throat.

"I don't know, man." Andy gasped. "I only just met him a few hours ago."

"You're a lying little shit," Barton shouted and squeezed his neck harder. "You must know him well enough to risk planting a weapon in someone's garden." When he noticed the youth's eyes bulging and his tongue hanging out, he relaxed his grip, letting him slip down onto his knees. Barton crouched down beside him, put his fingers to his jugular vein, and felt a strong pulse. At the same moment, a familiar voice came from over the fence. Tom Barton, armed with his spade, was in the process of climbing over.

Barton stood up. "Caught this little shit having another go at getting into your backyard."

"Why is he so determined to get in there? What's he after?" Tom snarled, hefting the spade above his head and threatening to strike it down on the youth.

Grasping hold of the shaft of the spade to prevent his father striking, Barton said, "There must be something in there he wants to steal."

"The only thing in there that's worth anything is this fucking spade. I'm going to smash his head in with—" Tom froze when he noticed the pistol at his son's feet. "What's going on here?" he shouted, pointing at the gun.

Snatching the spade from his father's hand and tossing it aside, Barton said simply, "You don't want to know."

"So, this is all about you and your mobster friends. I can see now why your mother was getting paranoid," Tom complained, bending down and recovering the spade.

Lifting the youth by the arm and leaning him against the fence on unsteady legs, Barton turned to his father. "I don't know what all this is about, but you can be sure I'm going to find out." He wrapped the rag around the gun, pushed it into his jacket pocket, and pulled the youth from the fence. "OK, shit bag, let's find this guy."

"What's going on here?" Jean Barton shouted from the other side of the fence.

Her unexpected approach made them all turn to face her. Taking advantage of the distraction, Andy tried to make a run for it. But Barton was that little bit faster and stuck out his foot, tripping the youngster.

Digging his knee into the back of the yob's neck as he lay facedown on the frosty ground, Barton took hold of his greasy long black hair, pulling it tightly upwards.

The youngster screamed and struggled to get up. Then a flash of light shot through his eyes when the spade blade came down on his head and sent him into total blackness.

"You've killed him," Jean shouted, struggling to get over the fence.

"I didn't hit him that hard," Tom said.

"He'll be OK," Barton said. "He's just unconscious. He'll soon come round." He stood up and stepped away as his mother crouched down to examine the youth, feeling for a pulse in his neck.

"Get him into the house before the neighbours see what's going on," Jean shouted.

—m—

The bearded hoodie stooped down behind the rubbish bins taking in all the action, and he was amused that his plan was near as dammit working out—but for one detail. He hadn't anticipated that the Bartons would carry the youth into their house. Now, a small change of plan and clothing was required. One good achievement was that now the weapon was in the Bartons' hands. All he had to do now was get the youth to make the all-important phone call. At one point, though, when he saw the old man thump the youth on the head with that spade, he thought his plans were over, thinking the young man had been killed. Relief came when he saw him being carried, under arm by the oldster and his son, over the fence and up the garden path into their home, the elderly lady following behind.

—m—

The seating at the kitchen table was the same as the previous incident with the youth. Jean had to bathe his head in cold water and ice to get the swollen lump down on his forehead. "You could have killed this lad." She gazed up at her husband.

"It's what he deserves, sneaking about in our garden."

"I don't understand," Jean replied, "why he's so determined to sneak about out there. What's he after?"

"He's a thief," Barton interrupted. "He must think we have something worth stealing."

"Searching about looking for an easy way into our home more likely," Tom said.

"Nevertheless," Jean said, looking at both her husband and son, "he needs medical attention. We should get him to the hospital."

Barton sprung out of his seat, nodded to his father. "Give me a lift out to my car with him."

Tom looking surprised at his son's sudden agreement with Jean. He hesitated for a moment before nodding and joined Barton as he lifted the youth onto his feet.

"You've no intentions of taking him to hospital, have you?" the older man quizzed when they got the yob fastened into the front seat of Barton's car. All Tom got in response was a grin. He stepped back from the vehicle and watched his son get fastened in and drive off.

Showing signs of recovering, the youngster began wriggling about. Finding himself restricted by the seatbelt, he started to panic. Barton pulled into a layby after only a five-minute drive. He got out and hauled young Andy out. Leaving him seated on a litter bin, he drove off, heading back to his parents' house.

Pulling into a side street, Barton checked nobody was about before pulling the pistol wrapped in the rag out of his pocket and placing it on the passenger's seat. Spreading the rag out, he was careful not to touch the weapon. Using the rag, Barton lifted the Glock 17, released the magazine clip, and discovered there were only three rounds in it. This caused him some concern. He never used it very often and was sure the double stack magazine had been almost full. He had never intentionally shot anyone with it, only fired off a few warning shots.

How could this hoodie have gotten hold of this weapon? Unless maybe he had been scrounging around the debris after the emergency crews had finished. Or, and Barton didn't want to believe it, he was one of the crew, maybe one of the explosive investigators. Wearing a hood could be to hide his identity, as the youngster said he'd had it down almost over his eyes.

His biggest worry now was, where were the missing rounds? What had his gun bee r? Had this weapon been used to shoot people? If so, the police could trace the rounds. Could this be why the hoodie had paid the youngster to hide it in his parents' garden—then to anonymously report it? Doubtless, he would soon have to get rid of it. Starting up his car, Barton decided his priority now was to find this hoodie and get the answers.

"What did they say in hospital?" Jean asked. "Is that young man going to be all right?"

Shaking his head and getting seated on the sofa, Barton replied, "I didn't hang about to get answers. I helped him into A & E and left him with the nurses at reception."

With a look of concern, she gazed at her husband, who wore the same expression. They both turned to look at Barton and, for a long moment, said nothing. Then Jean broke the silence. "I think it's all to do with your criminal friends. We think it would be best if you left—move into your flat as soon as you can."

Barton took a deep intake of breath. "If that's what you want. But I can assure you, he'll be back." This was turning out to be a two-way manhunt—him searching for the hoodie, who would be searching for the yob. "That yob will be back looking for what he originally came here for. Who knows what he'll do to get it if I'm not here?"

"He could be right," Tom said.

"What could he be looking for?" Jean asked.

Nodding to his father, he gave him that look that instructed him not to question him further. "I'll go to the hospital—hope he's still there—and get that info out of him. Also if he is there, I'll know he won't be coming back here frightening you."

CHAPTER 3

Lorinna had discarded the beard and hooded jacket and gotten into his car. As he was about to get it started up, he noticed the front door to the Barton house open. Within a few seconds, they appeared, dragging the youngster out and lumbering him to a car at the far end of the street. Next, they piled him into the front passenger's seat. The old man closed the door and stepped back, and the son got in and drove away, leaving the oldster standing there. It was a big temptation to nab the old man and use him as leverage. But he decided at the last moment, as he drove past him, to abandon the idea for the time being and concentrate on following the son to see where he was taking the youngster.

He had no other option but to drive past when Barton's car suddenly turned into a layby. Because of the following traffic, he had to carry on driving before he found a convenient side street to get turned. He pulled up across from the layby. Barton's car was gone, and the youngster was sitting precariously on the litter bin. He wanted to nab the yob before he got onto his feet.

Taking advantage of a sudden gap in the traffic, Lorinna swerved his car across the road and pulled into the layby as the youngster was about to stagger away. Jumping out and leaving his car door open, he gripped the youth's upper arm and stopped him. Lorinna could see that the youngster didn't recognise him without the hood and beard. "Can I be of assistance?" he said, gazing into Andy's brown eyes and emphasising an upper-class accent.

Not having full control of his equilibrium, Andy fell against the stranger, at the same time trying to focus on this man's face. "Who are you? Where am I?"

"As I was approaching, I noticed you staggering about and thought maybe you needed help."

"That's very kind of you sir," Andy replied, easing himself away from the stranger and, at the same time, dropping this man's wallet behind the litter bin, intending to collect it later. "I'll be OK in a few moments. It's my sugar level—forgot to take my meds this morning."

Very good, Lorinna thought, *very convincing.* "Can I drop you off somewhere?"

"I'm beginning to feel better. I think I'll manage from here." Andy stepped away from the man's reach in an effort to convince this stranger he had recovered so that the man would get into his car and leave. Nicking the stranger's wallet was simple enough, but he was disappointed the guy had nothing else in his pockets.

"Well, if you're sure," Lorinna replied, getting into his car and driving off. He watched the young pickpocket in his rear-view mirror stooping behind the litter bin. Smiling, he drove back to the town centre car park. Here, when he was sure no one was paying attention, he slipped into the scruffy black jacket and beard. By now, he decided, the thief would have looked through the wallet and found the message inside describing the make and model of the pistol and informing him of the reward for anyone finding this weapon or who had information on its whereabouts. The mobile number was a slight cause for concern, not the usual landline the police would use. He was pinning his hopes on the yob being a typical greedy thief—that, seeing more money for the taking and being blinded by the large reward, he would contact the number without thinking.

—⚏—

Skipping a few heartbeats, Lorinna was quick at shrinking below the level of the steering wheel at the sight of the red Volvo passing in front of his car. He instantly recognised the big driver by his designer stubble and long black hair tied at the back in a ponytail. He slowly eased himself up to watch where Barton might park his car. Quickly, he returned to the shrinking position when the Volvo turned around and headed back the way it had come. Now he was regretting having changed into the hoodie disguise. *Are you patrolling this park, chancing your luck?* Lorinna thought.

He remained below the level of the steering wheel but not too low that he couldn't observe to the end of the parking spaces.

Time was now flying in. Lorinna began to panic, should the young thief appear, knowing that by, now, he would be back from that layby. Barton was on the hunt and would spot the youngster and decide to follow him. It was obvious from where the yob had been abandoned, he would have to cross this location to get to the town centre to obtain a mobile phone. Lorinna guessed he would likely nick a mobile from somebody. He'd noted the absence of a mobile when the youth had leaned against him. He had always prided himself as good a pickpocket.

—⁊⁊⁊—

Andy remembered the wallet. *Maybe a few notes in it.* He soon reached over the litter bin and retrieved it. As he was about to investigate the contents, he noticed the stranger was driving away much too slowly and dropped the wallet where he had picked it up from.

In a burst of speed, the stranger's car was soon out of sight. And after a few moments, Andy recovered the wallet. He cursed and swore when he discovered there was no cash or credit cards in it and thought, *What the hell?* The only content was a large piece of white paper. When he read the writing, he could feel one of his panic attacks coming on. "What the fuck have I gotten myself into?" he cried. "Could this be the same weapon that bearded hoodie paid me to plant in the Bartons' garden?" He continued talking at the sheet of paper he held out in his hand. A glance at the reward built up his hopes. *What other weapon could it be?* A frantic frisk at his pockets brought on another outburst of curses when he discovered he had lost his mobile.

With a good fifteen-minute walk ahead of him, he tried thumbing a lift. But all he got in response from the drivers was the turn of their heads. Up ahead, he noticed a collection of bungalows and decided surely one of them must have a car parked on the drive. The only vehicle he found was a mountain bike, abandoned close to one of the front doors. It wasn't long before Andy's legs were pumping the pedals, heading for the town centre in search of another mobile phone.

The first thing that began to play on Andy's mind was where he had lost his phone. If it had been handed in and the police had checked it, it would only be a matter of hours before they picked him up. This rushed through his mind as he cycled along the footpath heading for the town centre car park. He couldn't shrug the feeling that something wasn't right—when things turned out too simple, there was always a deadly catch. In a sudden change of mind, he abandoned the cycle in among the shrubs and, at a fast walk, headed for the back lane leading to the Barton house. It would be a simple job nicking another phone, but this one had all his contacts on it.

Stopping at the collection of wheelie bins, Andy spotted a group of old men standing close to the place where he had been jumped on by that big guy and decided, if this was where he had lost his mobile, surely one of those old guys might have picked it up. Or maybe one of Bartons could have it? He feared the latter idea and decided to retrieve it would mean having to get that big son out of the way. And fuck that.

Abandoning that plan for the moment, he headed for the shopping mall in search of a mobile. It was one of the easiest items to pick from someone, especially from a young girl. Young girls most often carried their mobiles in their hip pockets half sticking out, making it child's play.

Selecting his victim took only a matter of a few minutes. They passed him as he stood at the edge of the parking area. Three young girls of secondary school age pranced and giggled along the street. One was already playing with her phone; the other two, on either side of her, were laughing at something on the centre of the girl's mobile. His target was protruding out of the jacket pocket of the girl nearest him. Andy thought that, if he gave her a nudge on his way past, he could slip it out. That was how simple it was as he edged past them, tucking the pink iPhone into his own hip pocket.

His first attempt at the number on the paper got no dialling tone. Another check at the number, and he tried again—this time with success. He heard a high-pitched effeminate male voice. "The item you are looking for," Andy quickly said. "I know who has it."

"I'm sorry," came the effeminate voice. "Could you be a bit more specific. What item are you referring to?"

Knowing he wasn't the brightest of the batch, Andy still had the presence of mind to know not to describe the item in question and cut the connection. Grinning to himself, knowing that, in a few minutes, his call would be returned, he started walking to the car park, where conditions were less crowded.

The returned call came more quickly than he'd estimated. He hadn't yet reached the car park when the iPhone sounded. This time, it was a different voice, more like a loud whisper, and the caller seemed to be forcing his words out. "We need to meet," the caller said, gasping for breath, "if you want to be paid for the information we want."

Andy gave the caller a location and a time. He got no response and heard the connection being cut. His next call was to the number Barton had given him, informing him where he could locate the hoodie—exactly the same place and time he had given the whisperer. His plan was to get there a few minutes earlier and, hopefully, meet up with this guy offering the reward.

And if his guess was right, he could collect the reward *and* his mobile, which Barton's parents must have found and which their big son would have taken possession of.

Feeling his luck was on a good roll, he was thinking, with all that money, he could give up the pickpocket racket for a long time. His elated mood was suddenly brightened when the three young girls appeared heading towards him. Judging by the way they were acting, he realised they were on the search for something, and he knew what that was. With a broad grin, he approached them, holding up the pink iPhone. "Is this what you're looking for?" he asked.

The girls' eyes widened, and a smile dawned on each of their faces. "Where did you find this?" one of them said and stepped closer, reaching out for the device and inspecting it.

"I spotted a thief nicking it from your pocket and chased after him."

With overwhelming thanks, all three girls gave Andy a hug before heading off and waving back at him. He grinned and returned the gesture, assuming the whisperer would be putting a trace on that device. Keeping a safe distance from them, he let them lead him back into the shopping mall. Luckily, this was a quiet shopping day, and shoppers were sparse. He found it easy to keep an eye on the trio of girls as they pranced and giggled their way out the automatic doors.

Having agreed to meet him at the place he had arranged, the whisperer, Andy guessed, wasn't far away. Had to be within an hour's drive. As for that big guy, he could be anywhere, searching for the hoodie. And in a certain guess, the hoodie would be in the area as well.

Anticipating the whisperer would be, by now, tracing the signal from the girl's iPhone and, hopefully, be closing in, Andy figured he had time to recce the guy and hoped he would be on his own. Andy's hopes crashed when the girls joined another group, and they crossed to the other side of the road and entered through the college gates. Holding back and getting into a position where he could be out of sight, he watched all the students enter into the main doors. This, he made up his mind, was good. It meant that the whisperer would be led to the gates and, no doubt, would hang about there until the person with the mobile phone showed up.

CHAPTER 4

On the assumption that the young thief would have had plenty of time to recover and get back into town centre, Barton drove around the car park, chancing to see this hoodie and guessing he'd have a car. Having finally parked up in a position where he could eye most of the vehicles, he crouched down level with the steering wheel. But soon the cramps started in his calf muscles, and he had to get out to ease them by walking about. He enjoyed his time in the gym, but this was the results of hard workouts. Leaning on both hands against the roof of his car and stretching his legs, he glanced towards the footpath that led to the mall.

Following behind three woman each pushing a trolley, he saw the black jacket with the hood pulled down over most of his face. At that moment, Barton wasn't certain this was the guy he was searching for. It was when the long beard showed as the hoodie had to sidestep to pass the women that Barton's heart jumped a few beats faster.

Realising he had no time to waste, Barton quickly locked his car and followed. He too had to manoeuvre his way past the three ladies, costing him valuable seconds. A lucky last-minute glance caught the hoodie enter the mall. Very few shoppers were moving about, making it easy to follow him. But that could also be a disadvantage, should the hoodie turn round and see him. Barton held back a few seconds, keeping as close to the shop windows as possible. Finding himself quite a distance from the exit doors when he spotted his objective slipping out, Barton had to rush, chancing being noticed by him.

Feeling the frosty breeze on his face as he stood outside searching in all directions, Barton fretted he might have lost the hoodie; the street was jammed with traffic travelling both ways, making it difficult to spot him. A dog walker drew his attention when the large animal tried to chase after something, almost unbalancing its owner. The bearded man in the scruffy black jacket almost got tripped over when he got caught by the leash. After exchanging a few nasty words with the dog owner, the hoodie carried on along the street.

Realising he was much too close to his objective, Barton once again held back and was eventually led to the end of the street across the road from the college. In the blink of an eye the hoodie disappeared, and Barton soon realised why when he noticed young Andy sitting on a bench on the lawn next to the college gates. Having no inclination where the hoodie was, he had no option but to hold back and wait for his next move. That move happened in a few minutes when the youngster got up and ran across the lawn, chased by the hooded man in the black jacket. The youngster was fast and was making ground along the asphalt path; his pursuer was having trouble keeping going.

Finding himself out in the open, Barton had no other choice but to charge up behind, bringing the hooded man down with a stranglehold on the back of his neck. When he tightened his grip, the man's beard came away from his face, and the hood fell off to the back of his head. Two quick right hooks to the man's face put an end to his struggling, and he lay facedown on the frosted grass.

Using the hood, Barton turned him over and stamped a foot on the man's wrist, holding it fast on the ground. "What's your game, mate?"

Lorinna was having trouble focusing on the big man towering over him. "That little bastard stole money from me."

Putting extra weight on his foot and hearing the man yelp in pain, Barton said, "You paid that little bastard to plant a weapon in my parents' garden."

"He's lying," Lorinna pleaded. "All I want is my money back."

Lifting his foot from the man's wrist, Barton dragged him to his feet. "I have that gun," he said. "Now, walk slowly after the little bastard. Put the beard and hood back on. Try and be a hero, and you're dead."

Favouring his wrist, Lorinna led the way along the footpath, Barton only a couple of arm-lengths behind, his hands inside his pocket holding the pistol. The path ended at a busy road. The hoodie stopped and turned. Barton, his mind on the safety of his parents, almost collided into him.

"Now what?" the hoodie asked, stepping out of arms-length from the big man. "Which way?"

Barton nodded. "Cross to the other side of the road."

It was a guess and a good one. Standing a few yards from them, Andy stood at the roadside trying to get the attention of a passing taxi.

Pushing the hoodie's shoulder, Barton shouted, "Get a hold of him, before he gets picked up."

Most of the pedestrians instinctively turned to the direction that the shot had come from. Barton and Lorinna, like the others, had at first thought it was a car backfiring. When they heard females screaming, everybody seemed to freeze. It was then he saw a group of girls in school uniform had gathered in a circle, gazing at something at their feet. That's when Barton realised it hadn't been a car backfiring but, rather, a gunshot. He cursed at himself for not being able to tell the difference. Collecting himself, he turned to the hoodie. "Get hold of that little shit and let's get out of here."

Andy Milton wasn't aware of the gunshot; his attention had been drawn to the hoodie and the big guy heading his way, and his only thoughts were to make a run for it. Without thinking, he dashed onto the busy road.

The driver hadn't deliberately hit the young man. After firing the shot at the girl, his intent was to get away. He was busy tucking the pistol back into his shoulder holster and, at the same time, ramming his foot down on the accelerator pedal.

Stopping dead in their tracks, Barton and Lorinna saw the youngster get hit by the black Range Rover that failed to stop. The youngster lay at the side of the road, crying with shock and pain.

"Carry on walking," Barton ordered.

The hoodie seemed glad to comply and quickened his pace. "How am I going to get my money back?" Lorinna complained without turning.

"He'll need medical attention. They'll take him to a hospital. We'll find out where and pay him a visit."

As if he had just realised something, Lorinna stopped and turned. "That was a shot. I think it must have been one of those schoolgirls who got hit."

"That's what I thought," Barton replied and pushed Lorinna on. "That has nothing to do with us. Just keep walking. Head back to your car."

Getting into the rear seat of Lorinna's car, Barton pulled the Glock from his pocket and pushed it into the back of the hoodie's neck the moment he got in behind the wheel. "You can get rid of the disguise now."

Throwing the false beard on the front passenger's seat, Lorinna said, "Why would anybody want to shoot a schoolgirl?"

"With the speed that Range Rover set off, there's no doubt where the shot came from. Unless it was a mistake, whoever it was must have had a good reason to in a busy place like this."

Starting his car, Lorinna wasn't convinced the shooting of that girl had nothing to do with them. He pushed the hood of his jacket back, knowing that, when the yob had made that call, the mobs ops room would have put a trace on it—that girl's phone could have been the one he nicked. "Where to?" he asked.

"Drive past the incident area to see if the ambulances have arrived. If not, we park up until they do. Then we follow the one that has picked up that young thug."

The entire road was blocked off with blue and white tape, with police cars parked at both ends. Lorinna had to make a last-minute swerve into a side street. "What now?"

"If you want your money back, we need to know where that youngster is," Barton replied. "We need to get out and walk about, ask a few questions. We might just get lucky."

"There has to be more to this than you are helping me to get my money back?"

"Oh, there is," Barton replied, pushing him forward with a hand on the back of his shoulder. "You'll find out when I get the two of you together."

The only piece of information they got was that the youngster had been lifted away in an ambulance. That was from a woman who Barton thought was under the influence of drugs or booze. He knew it would be a waste of time asking her what hospital he had been taken to.

"The coppers are going to suspect that it was the youth who shot that girl," the hoodie said. "That's going to make it tricky to get in to see him."

"That depends on what the witnesses say. And there were plenty of them about. Somebody must have seen that car race off."

At the police cordon, a crowd had gathered, all asking the same question. "Keep your ears open," Barton said. "We might hear something. Somebody must have an answer."

The hoodie was fast. He ducked under the blue and white tape and ran to the other end of the cordon. There was nothing Barton could do but watch two constables chase after him. He couldn't tell if the hoodie had managed to escape and wasn't too annoyed about it. He knew where his car was parked and that he would eventually have to collect it.

The hoodie's car was where they had left it. Barton strolled past it a few times and decided to get to his own vehicle, drive it here, and park a few metres away. That way, he wouldn't look suspicious hanging about the street close to where a shooting incident had happened.

Because of the roads being shut off around the area of the shooting, it took Barton almost half an hour to get into that side street where the hoodie's car had been parked. He didn't need to drive far along the narrow street to discover the vehicle was gone. The place it had been abandoned was now taken up by another car. He couldn't believe what he was witnessing. How could the hoodie have gotten back in such a short time? Barton remembered him being chased by two policemen in the opposite direction from here. And remembering how he'd struggled chasing the youngster, he thought, *Surely, he must have been caught?*

Where the hoodie would be heading was obvious. Driving into the car park of the nearest hospital looking for a vacant bay, Barton spotted the green VW as he passed the lane between the parked vehicles. Chancing that no other driver wanted past, he stopped and ran towards it. With a quick glance inside, he noticed the beard wasn't on the seat.

Finding a parking space where he could observe the main hospital doors was a lucky shot. He swerved in as another car pulled out, blocking and cutting off a vehicle that had been waiting to get in there. This earned him a blast from the horn and a two-finger gesture from the woman passenger. Barton jammed on his brakes and jumped out; the grey-haired driver's eyes widened at the sight of the big man standing there, and he soon shot off, the tyres on his car screaming.

On the assumption that the hoodie was in the hospital searching for the youngster, Barton decided to get in his car and wait for him to step out the doors. People drifted in and out of the entrance, but he was sure he would be able to distinguish that hoodie with the long beard. Time dragged slowly, and there was no sign of the hooded figure among the visitors and staff who entered and left. His only option now was to risk going in there himself.

At the reception, he informed the woman he was here to interview a Mr. Andy Milton. She scanned her computer screen, smiled, and informed him, "Mr. Milton already has people with him wanting to talk to him. I can tell you that police detectives are escorting him."

Barton didn't want to delay a moment longer and told her he would call back later.

CHAPTER 5

Convincing the police officers it was his son who was being taken away in the ambulance, Lorinna confessed, "I know it was thoughtless, rushing through the cordon. Any father would do the same." Putting on his best acting skills he pleaded, "What would you do if you discovered that your only son had been knocked down by a hit-and-run driver?"

The two constables discussed his statement. One stepped away and got on his radio. A few minutes later, they let him go. He made a hasty retreat and spotted a vacant taxi about to turn a few yards along the street. He rushed towards it, waving his arms. His instructions to where he had parked his car were vague. But in the end, the driver got the picture.

Hiding in a thick clump of laurel shrubs that bordered the grounds, Lorinna could observe the hospital car park, confident that Barton would eventually turn up. The blasting of a car horn drew his attention to the parking places nearest the hospital entrance, and he decided it was two drivers contending for the same position. Lorinna grinned when the looser sped off at the sight of the big guy barging out of his car showing aggression. His grin widened when he recognised the aggressor.

Things are looking good for a change. He had guessed right, and Barton was turning out to be predictable.

It came as a shock when he saw the big man rush out the hospital doors on his own. Lorinna had been expecting Barton to be escorting the youngster. About to rush for his own car when Barton got into his, he froze for a moment and ducked behind a nearby shrub when he realised the big guy's car wasn't moving. Lorinna's curiosity was overwhelming him. He wondered why the big ape with the tightly tied black hair in a ponytail had obviously not been able to visit the youngster. The answer came in an instant, when two uniformed policemen and a few suited officers marched the youth out and into an unmarked vehicle.

The scenario meant he had a problem. The police would want to know why Andy had run when that shot was fired. And judging from what he knew about the youth, it wouldn't take them long to make him spill. On the other side of the coin, he knew Barton had the weapon, and as far as he was concerned, that was where he had been paid to plant it. Maybe it hadn't gotten there the way it had been planned, but now there was nothing he could do to change things.

The vibration from his mobile in his breast pocket disturbed him out of his reverie. The voice he heard sent a shiver through his body. "A young girl has been shot," came the roar from Boss Man.

Lorinna had to hold his mobile away from his ear. "Nothing to do with me," was all he could say.

"We traced the mobile the call about the reward was made from," the shouting continued. "The clown we sent to investigate didn't bother. He just let the lead fly at the person using it at the time. How did the phone you gave that piece of shit get into that girl's hands?"

Realising he had made the mistake of not giving the youngster the phone he had been paid to buy for whoever it was he hired to stash the weapon, Lorinna nervously replied, "The thug I hired must have nicked the mobile from that girl and sold the one I gave him."

"You were ordered t to make sure he was left with no other choice but to use the mobile you gave him," the gruff voiced barked. "And that doesn't explain how the phone he nicked got into the hands of a schoolgirl."

Having received the cash, Lorinna had decided to keep the extra expenses, convincing himself surely a pickpocket would have a mobile, so why bother buying him another? That way, he would have to use his own. In Lorinna's view, he was obeying orders. What did puzzle him, though, was why Boss Man had insisted he should supply the thief with a mobile. Maybe he took it for granted the phone the pickpocket would have would have been stolen. That being his way of thinking, then the tracing would lead to the wrong person.

The more Lorinna thought about it, the more panic started to build up in him. He knew, if this job failed, his life wasn't going to last much longer. "Boss Man," he pleaded, "the gun is in the hands of the man you ordered it to be in."

"That doesn't count for anything if that young shit bag gets picked up by the police; he'll land us all in it."

A long moment of silence followed, and Lorinna began to think Boss Man had cut him off. He was about to shut his own phone off when the shouting began again. "You get rid of that young shit bag before that happens."

This time, the connection was cut. All that was left for him to do was to stare at the phone, trying to think of a way round the problem. Strange things happen when the mind is in a state of panic, and he began wondering why the big man, Barton, came to the fore. This set off another fit of alarm. Where was he? Edging himself above the shrubs, he focused on the place where the big man had parked his car. It was still there, but he had to duck back down when the red Volvo's reversing lights came on.

He listened for it to pass before getting up to see it drive out the exit. A quick dash from the bushes, and he was in his car and driving out, intending to follow. A flow of traffic, having been held up by a slow-moving truck, held him at the gates for a time. When he got on the move, he knew the red Volvo was long gone and could be anywhere.

—〰—

Jumping into his car, Barton's intentions were to get away from there as soon as he could. He got the Volvo started and was about to move out when the hassle at the hospital doors drew his attention. Two uniformed constables stepped out first, followed by what Barton guessed was a group of plain-clothes officers. In the centre of them, he could see young Andy, his head bowed, hands cuffed behind his back. The picture came to Barton in a second. Witnesses must have spotted him running when that girl had been shot. Now, the mystery driver of the black Range Rover would be judged a hero for bringing down a killer. Barton hoped that, while the yob was under interrogation, the subject of the gun wrapped in a rag wouldn't come up. But he guessed that young Andy would soon empty his guts.

Surprised that the hoodie's green VW was still parked in the same spot, Barton was confused and wondered where hoodie could be. *Surely not inside the hospital?* He slowed down as he drove past it, searching for signs he may be crouched down inside. Finding no sign of life in or near the vehicle, he drove past and out of the car park.

Feeling uneasy and thinking the hoodie could be close by and could now be following him, Barton made a last-minute turn into a cul-de-sac. He turned at the end and drove slowly, stopping close behind other cars parked there. When a slow-moving truck passed, he guessed the green VW would be at the tail end of the queue, awaiting a chance to overtake it.

His guess was spot-on. Barton grinned to himself. *Predictable little bastard.* He drove out onto the main road, heading in the opposite direction. Pulling into the parking area close to the shopping mall, he sat for a while, wondering how young Andy was coping. He was a little creep, no doubt about it, but did he deserve to be getting interrogated as the suspect of a shooting incident that, Barton guessed, a schoolgirl was the victim of?

He was halfway through stepping out of the Volvo when it suddenly dawned on him he still carried the weapon. Making sure no one was close enough to see him, he tossed it under the driver's seat. In the process of closing and locking the door, he chanced a glance over the car's roof and spotted the youngster chatting to two girls. Barton could only stare at him in disbelief. *How could he have been released so quickly?* Thinking of the seriousness of the charges, he'd figured the police would hold him for at least forty-eight hours. *So, what's he doing here?*

The girls turned and began walking in his direction, the youth trailing behind them and thumbing on his mobile. Barton ducked down behind his car. They passed a few yards from him. He could hear the girls chatting. The youngster behind, playing with his phone, looked like he hadn't a care in the world.

Now, Barton was confused. Just a few hours ago, this youth had been lifted by the law, suspected of murdering a girl. Why was he acting as if nothing had happened? He risked standing up, had to have a closer look at this youngster. Although young Andy was wearing a different jacket, there was no mistaking that long greasy black hair, the long thin nose, and that springy walk. Barton was tempted to rush up behind him and jump him, but a last-moment's decision made him decide to follow them.

A shaven-headed youth approached the two girls. They chatted for a while. The youngster stopped a few paces from them, still concentrating on his mobile. Barton, being caught standing out in the open at this point, was looking for a place of concealment but didn't need to bother when the group started walking away from him again. As long as young Andy was engrossed in his phone, Barton decided he could confidently follow closer. There were a lot of pedestrians moving about the street they led him to. Now, he had no choice but to stay close behind them. In a momentary lack of concentration, Barton lost sight of the youngster. He could still see the two girls and bald head. They carried on as if unaware Andy wasn't behind them.

The hissing sound behind drew Barton's attention. He instantly knew this was the familiar sound of a bus door opening. He turned in time to see the youngster boarding it behind a few other passengers. He knew there was no way he could climb aboard without the youngster recognising him when he stood by the driver to pay his fare. He watched the bus pull away and thought maybe, if he could catch up with the two girls and bald head, they might be able to tell him where Andy could be heading.

Pushing his way through oncoming pedestrians and searching for the group, he wasn't having much luck. A taxi pulled up next to him at the kerbside, letting a plump man out. Barton jumped in and told the driver to follow the bus.

The driver grinned. "That bus is a circular. It runs all day. Do you want me to stay behind it all that time?"

Shaking his head, Barton said, "I want to see where one of the passengers get off. When that happens, I'll get out."

—ɷ—

Stepping out of the taxi at the same place where he had gotten in, Barton paid the driver and watched the cab disappear into the traffic. Confused, he was sure he couldn't have missed the youngster getting off the bus. Only a few passengers had travelled on it, and they'd mostly gotten off one at a time—unless young Andy hadn't been as engrossed on his phone as Barton had thought and the youth had clocked onto him. Had he gotten off the bus while Barton was busy getting into the taxi? This was the only explanation he could come up with. That being the situation, the youngster could still be close by or in the mall.

Deciding to give up the hunt, he headed back to the car park for his car. Barton had only gotten a few yards when he felt a painful jab at his back.

"Don't turn," the voice behind him ordered. "Keep walking slowly."

"Where to?"

"Just keep going. I'll direct you."

Complying with the orders Barton, started to think, *Whoever you are, mate, you must be desperate to push a gun into a person's back in a busy place like this.* He began lengthening his pace but could still sense the gunman at his back. At the double glass doorway into the mall, Barton had to stop and wait for it to open. In the reflection, he recognised the hoodie at his back. "You're not going to fire that thing here?"

"Don't bet on it, pal."

The glass doors opened with a swish. Barton stepped in and jumped to the side and shouted, "Gun! This man has a gun!"

Total panic followed as shoppers ran in all directions. A woman a short distance away screamed. The hoodie about-turned and ran back through the doors, right into the grip of two security officers. Barton didn't hang around to see the scuffle and was soon out the other side of the mall, heading for his car.

CHAPTER 6

"Some clown shouted gun," Lorinna explained to the security men, "and like everybody else, I ran."

"I'm afraid, sir, we have to get the police involved to carry out a body search on you," the officer holding his right arm said, while his mate was talking into his radio.

Lorinna was telling the truth. He didn't have a gun, but he did have a short steel bar. This he pulled from his belt at his back and struck the officer holding his arm on the side of his face. The man stumbled over backwards and fell against his mate. Lorinna took advantage of this short distraction and ran through the open glass door. Thinking that one of the officers would give chase, he bounded up the escalator. Luckily, this was deserted because of Barton's warning. A few paces later, he was out on the street and heading towards the car park and his car. A quick glance behind assured him he wasn't being chased, and he slowed to a normal walking pace. He discarded the steel bar into the back of a pickup truck that had stopped at the traffic lights.

The last thing he wanted was to be seen running. Most people would remember a character barging his way through other pedestrians. But his walking pace was quicker than the people ahead of him, and in some places, he had to nudge them out of his way. Before he reached his car, he had to find a quiet place to remove the disguise. Anyone giving chase would soon describe to witnesses a man with a black hooded jacket and a long beard, and fingers would be pointed at the direction he had taken.

Glancing across to the other side of the street, Lorinna noticed a group of men standing outside a pub smoking and arguing. He asserted the place must be busy and crossed over and entered the bar. Drinkers were packed shoulder to shoulder as he wedged his way to the toilet. The only people taking notice of him were the ones he edged past, and as far as witnesses were concerned, they would swear that the hoodie had gone into the toilet but had never come back out. In the cracked mirror, he combed his hair, wiped down his grey jacket, and shouldered his way out, carrying the plastic bag he had stuffed the disguise in and tucked under his jacket.

He took the footpath that led the long way around to the car park, giving him time to think what his next move was going to be. Also, this route had more hiding places, with overgrown shrubs along both sides. If Barton happened to come along this way, he would have time to dart in out of sight.

It wasn't Barton who came walking towards him. And like Barton, Lorinna was surprised to see the youngster. Although he was wearing a different jacket, there was little doubt it was him. There was no mistaking that shoulder-length greasy hair, the pallor complexion, and the sharp thin nose. The youth had his head bent forward, concentrating on his mobile. Lorinna didn't think it was necessary to jump into the shrubs. And after a quick look around, seeing no other pedestrian, he ran towards the youth.

Avoiding eye contact with the young man, Lorinna barged into him, knocking the phone out of his hand and, at the same time, grasping a handful of greasy hair. The youth screamed, and Lorinna gagged him with his free hand and pulled him into the bushes. After a struggle, the youngster was pinned to the ground. With his hand on the youngster's throat and both his knees on his chest, Lorinna said, "The copper's let you out very quickly. You must have opened your mouth and come to some arrangement."

Realising he was holding the youth's throat too firmly for him to reply, Lorinna relaxed his grip slightly. Staring into the youngster's tear-filled eye, waiting for a reply and getting only the vigorous shaking of his head, Lorinna realised this young man couldn't hear him and wondered if he could be deaf. Being born from deaf parents, he instantly noticed the signs. Releasing his grip on the youth's throat he got up and helped the youngster onto his feet. Facing directly at the youngster's face so he could lip-read, he asked, "Do you have an identical twin?"

Following a selection of puzzled expressions, the youngster replied, "Not that I'm aware of."

"A guy identical to you was arrested earlier and taken to the local police station. Surely, in a small town like this, you must have bumped into him or someone else must have mistaken you for him?"

Still retaining the confused expression, the youngster shook his head and began searching around for his mobile. Lorinna reached out. Grabbing his arm, he pulled him up close. "If you're lying, I'll find you, and you're a dead man." He pushed the youngster away and watched him stagger into a bush.

That was when the two girls and the bald-headed guy appeared a few yards ahead of Lorinna as he was about to walk away.

"Are you all right, Garry?" One of the girls signalled with her hands, and at the same time, they surrounded Lorinna. "What do you think you're doing, you big bastard?" the same girl shouted at him. And without warning, all three of them dived at him.

Lorinna soon realised he was being attacked by a well-organised street gang. He was tripped over from behind, one of the girls having crouched down behind his legs as the bald head had pushed him back. All he could do was lie in the foetal position and brace himself against a barrage of kicks from all directions. The last thing he remembered was Garry looking like a rugby player, running towards him and about to land a kick.

Something was sniffing at his ear. Lorinna couldn't figure out what it was or, for that matter, where he was. The sniffing continued; a long warm wet object slid across his face. He forced his eyes to open but only one reacted. The shimmering figure towered over him, its face a few inches away. In a moment, it was gone from his view. And soon it was back. This time, it wasn't the face he gazed at. Soon, he realised it was the hind leg of a dog. He made a painful effort to turn away from what he knew was about to happen, but his movement was too slow, and the hot wet fluid squirted onto his face.

Excruciating pain ran through his ribcage as he attempted to wipe the urine from his eyes. That's when a man's voice sounded, calling out some strange name he couldn't understand. The bloody owner of that pissing dog. Lorinna cursed and cursed louder when he attempted to get up. It felt as though every bone in his body had been broken. All he could do was to lie still; this way the pain subsided. He could no longer keep his eye from closing and could feel himself drifting into a deep black dreamless sleep.

Something was gripping his shoulders and shaking them, causing pain to ripple through his upper body. He attempted to strike out at it but somehow couldn't sum up the energy. All he wanted to do was lie there, enjoying this peaceful tranquillity, drifting into a mystical world of wonderful colours. The shaking persisted. Again, only one eye would open. As before, the features that stared down at him were shimmering and out of focus. "You're lucky I decided to come back this way," a voice from a distance said in a hollow echo—like a dirty piece of clear plastic had suddenly been pulled away from his sight. The face that looked down at him came into focus, as did the barrel of the pistol a few inches from the point of his nose.

Focusing more on the pistol pointing at his face, Lorinna, in spite of the agony he was going to go through, attempted to move back away from it. But the hand on his shoulder held him fast. This was when the face of his assailant came into true focus. He saw the dark glasses shielding the man's eyes, reflecting the sinking sun. A black baseball cap with a long skip was down over his eyebrows. The collar of his black jacket was fastened close to his neck. Lorinna decided this character was intending to kill him.

—∭—

Finding his parents' full attention on the television when he entered the living room, Barton asked, "What's the big attraction?" He got seated beside his mother on the sofa.

His father pointed to the screen. "A young girl has been shot, only about half a mile from here."

"Still in her school uniform," his mother interrupted. "Who would do a thing like that to an innocent child?"

"The world is full of wackos; some idiot trying out his new weapon," Barton said.

"It seems the police have a suspect in for questioning," Tom said, rolling himself a cigarette.

Knowing that couldn't be true, Barton could only shake his head. He remembered seeing the police's suspect walking down the street playing on his mobile about an hour ago. The broadcaster had changed the subject and moved onto another report. "What have they been saying about the shooting?"

"Not a lot," his father commented, getting out of his seat and placing his roll-up smoke between his lips. "Only that witnesses saw the guy running away when the girl was shot. He didn't get far. He ran out in front of a car and got knocked down. The police managed to pick him up."

Barton got out of his seat and followed his father out to the back door, where the old man soon got his cigarette lit. "Did they say they had identified the suspect?" Barton asked.

Tom shook his head. "You seem to be interested in this. I hope you're not involved. Are you?"

"Relax." Barton grinned. "I happened to be passing by when that shooting happened."

Shaking his head and blowing cigarette smoke up into the air, Tom said, "You always seem to be where there's trouble."

"Just my luck. I don't go looking for it."

"Nevertheless, you don't seem to go out of your way to avoid it."

"There are some things in life you just can't avoid."

"You can try."

"How?"

"Move away from here. Start a new life somewhere else." Tom grinned and dropped his cigarette, stamping it under foot and opening the door. Leaving Barton standing alone, he entered the kitchen to find his wife standing there and suspected she had been listening.

Barton followed and found his parents staring at each other. He walked between them and stopped, looking at both of them in turn. "What's the problem now?"

Jean tore her attention away from her husband and stared into her son's brown eyes. "Your father's right. You should move away from here. We don't want you to, but we're getting too old for this kind of life."

The last thing Barton wanted was to spend time living with them. His reason for being there was to protect them from this kind of life. But how could he tell them that? He was convinced that, if he deserted them, things wouldn't change for them, might even get worse now that the crims in the area know where they lived; and if he wasn't there as a deterrent, hell knew what could happen to them.

"When do you think you'll be moving into your flat?" Tom asked.

His wife turned on Barton, searching for an agreeable reply. "I don't want you to think we don't want you. But the sooner the better," she said softly. "I can't take any more of this life." She about-turned, her head bowed, and walked slowly into the living room.

Barton watched as his father jerked up his shoulder at the sound of the living room door closing. "I still haven't finished decorating, but I'll try and speed things up," he said.

Tom stepped over, placing a hand on his shoulder. "My advice is for you is to get out of this area and find a new life."

Reaching out and pulling a chair from under the kitchen table, Barton eased his bulk onto it. "I would, but I need to know why that youngster was so determined to get into your back garden."

Although he could make a good guess at the answer to that question, he had no intentions of disclosing it to his parents. But the answer to the bigger question was something he had to find. Why would someone go to the trouble of hiding his weapon in his parents' property? How would that person have known he was living here? And how did said person come across the weapon he thought had been destroyed in the explosion at his last house?

Indicating for his son to join him in the living room, Tom whispered, "She's probably gone to bed, so keep your voice down. She has ears like an elephant." Getting settled into his seat, he waited for Barton to get seated and then went on. "I think that youngster was paid to plant that gun."

"What makes you think that?" Barton asked in a lowered voice.

Fishing his tobacco pack from his pocket, Tom replied. "Oh, come on! You know as well as I do, if a creep like that got hold of a weapon, he'd use it to commit robberies or sell it."

Avoiding his father's eyes and gazing at the television, the volume turned low, he replied the only way he could think of. "I don't know." Barton shrugged his shoulders. "There's a lot of guns going about. Maybe he's committed a serious crime with it and decided to ditch it on you." Without looking, he could sense his father wasn't swallowing his explanation.

"That doesn't make a lot of sense. Why pick on us? He doesn't know us."

"Well! He said he knew Corrie and would know his reputation, guessed he had a record. Maybe he was out to get back at him for something."

The older man scoffed. "Then why would he come back when he learned Corrie had been killed?"

Shaking his head, Barton picked up the remote and turned up the volume on the television, hoping to end this interrogation.

"Turn that bloody thing down, or she'll be in here shouting at us."

Finally, after a few sharp glances at his father, Barton turned the television off and jumped up off the sofa. "I'm off up to my room for some quiet."

Before heading up to his room, Barton took a final gulp of the tea his mother had earlier handed him. As he lay awake in bed, his thoughts drifted back to earlier when he'd tried to grab that youngster.

The two girls—were they a part of his team, along with the bald-headed youth who'd joined them? This brought on a picture in his mind of the hoodie. Where was he now. Had the security team handed him over to the police? An overwhelming feeling of tranquillity came over him, and his eyelids became heavy. Soon, he had to give up the fight of trying to stay awake.

37

CHAPTER 7

Pains shot through his entire body as he was forced onto his feet by sets of hands from behind. Lorinna resisted as much as he could, but this caused more agony. "What's going on?" he yelled.

"The boss sent me to ask you that same question," the muscle-bound gun man said.

Two others, similarly built men, took up position at either side of him. They gripped his upper arms and pushed him out of the shrubs onto the footpath, heading towards the car park. Pedestrians heading for the shops stepped aside and gawked at him being escorted by the three muscle men.

Lorinna was surprised when they pushed him past his green VW and out the exit and into a waiting black Range Rover. Being an ex-pickpocket, the first thing he looked at on a vehicle was the number plate. Mentally recording reg. had saved him from being caught in the past. This private registration sent a message to him, telling him this was no strange number; he had noticed it before. And at that moment, it dawned on him. This was the vehicle that had sped past the scene where that shot was fired and knocked over the youth. These must be the clowns that Boss Man had been talking about.

Excruciating pain shot through his entire body as they bundled him into the rear seat. Although he did his best to stifle his cries, one of the clowns gagged him with a big hand. With one on either side of him and the gun man driving, the vehicle shot off. Lorinna knew where his next call would be, and if things didn't go well, this could be his last call.

It wasn't the peak period for traffic in the city centre, and too soon, the big vehicle pulled into a dark narrow lane that was very familiar to Lorinna. This time, he couldn't control his screaming. The pain was beyond his barrier when the two clowns dragged him out and pinned him to the ground, securing his hands behind his back.

Even for a fit uninjured body, the treatment would have been rough. Being lifted by the upper arms from the kneeling position with hands secured behind the back and face on the ground, the pains on the shoulders would make the toughest person scream. Lorinna was no tough guy, and the muscle men rushed him through the door, lest anyone who was nearby should hear.

He was no stranger to walking the length of this sparsely lit corridor and knew what faced him at the other side of the door the driver was now opening. He almost stumbled onto the long table by the force the two muscle men put into shoving him inside. The chair at the top of the table saved him, and he regained his balance. Having sat in this room many times, he knew how many chairs were placed down both sides of this long slab of highly polished mahogany. On idle moments during the seminars, he had counted the amount of shaded lamps placed down its centre. These were the only means of light. The intent of this, he realised, was to distort the identity of the other members. They appeared as dark silhouettes across from where he normally sat. The persons sitting next to him were no more than a shadow, so well placed out was the seating. Lorinna knew, however, who was sat at the top. And under these circumstances, he would be the only other person in the room.

"Ah! Glad you could come," came the hoarse voice from the far end of the table.

I had no other fucking choice! Lorinna wanted to shout back, but he knew better. "Purely my pleasure," he replied, gritting his teeth at the pains jarring through his body. Bad as it was, this agony wasn't his main concern. He had witnessed in this very room what happened to members of the mob when they mess3e up. Three or four black bin liners tucked inside each other and then pushed onto the head of the offender—the idea was to prevent blood spatter when the bullet entered the skull of the victim. It didn't always work. Sometimes, the round went all the way through, depending on what weapon the little Boss Man or one of his thugs used.

"I'll listen to your story," the loud hoarse voice shouted from the top of the table.

The strength of the man's voice always marvelled Lorinna. How could such a roar come from that little frame? A stranger who hadn't seen this man but had only heard him would expect to be confronted by a six-foot-odds giant. "I carried out your orders to the letter," Lorinna pleaded. "Sometimes, thing don't always work as planned."

"It was a simple straightforward job."

"I agree." Lorinna whimpered. "But don't forget that little thief was a stranger to us. We weren't sure how he would react."

"You were given enough money to make sure what his reactions would be."

"As I told you on the phone, the guy, Barton, has the weapon. I thought that was your intentions—to get it into his possession."

Banging his hand on the table, Boss Man shouted, "My intentions were to inform the police of the whereabouts of that gun and for them to find it and charge Barton for multiple murders that weapon has been used for. I want him to spend time in the can like I did. When he has suffered as long as I did, then I will arrange for him to be put out of his misery. Now that he has it, he will get rid of it as soon as he can."

Shaking his head, knowing the Boss Man couldn't see him, Lorinna said, "If you had explained that to me, then I would have made sure the weapon was hidden in that garden even if it meant I had to do it myself." So far, Lorinna hadn't heard any movement from the men standing behind him. Could this mean he might survive another day? There was no sound of the shuffling of plastic bags. "If Barton has the gun, why can't we report him to the police and let them find it on him?"

Another loud slap on the table. "Who do you think you're dealing with? do you think for a moment that Barton would be caught out that simple?"

Bowing his head, Lorinna had no answer to that. Only the sound of the three men behind him breathing could be heard as a long period of silence passed. He could sense the little Boss Man thinking. Lorinna was racking his brains to come up with words of appeasement.

"Well, I have another way to make him suffer," the rough voice from the top of the table interrupted. "We know he has family. I take it you've eyeballed them. So, now you can bring them here. Fuck up again, and you know what will happen."

—w—

Realising it was the toilet flushing that woke him, Barton swung his legs out of the bed. The room was still in darkness. He couldn't remember turning the light off and was quite shocked to discover he hadn't taken his clothes off. Although he had dropped off into a dreamless sleep, he still felt groggy. Finding his shoes, after groping about in the dark, it dawned on him he couldn't remember taking them off. One of his parents must have come in while he was asleep. Almost knocking the bedside lamp over, he snatched his jacket up from the chair, panicking that his pistol had been discovered. Letting out a deep sigh of relief when he felt it was still in his inside pocket, he was about to slip his arms into the sleeves when he felt another object in his other pocket. Letting his jacket fall onto the bed, he carefully fingertipped around the bulge and finally pulled out the object. Barton almost chocked when he extracted it—a bundle of twenty-pound notes secured by an elastic band. *Must be about three grand,* he marvelled. *How did it get there?* He was astonished by his discovery. But at the same time, panic was building up.

Attempting to keep his calm, he eased himself out of the room. The toilet light was still on, and the door was wide open. After a quick glance into his parents' bedroom and finding it empty, he slowly descended the stairs. The first door led to the living room—no signs of them in there. The kitchen offered the same results. Now, concern was beginning to build up. The mantle clock showed six thirty. *They can't have gone out at this time. End even if they did, why leave all the lights on?* Finding the outside kitchen door unlocked, he felt his concern now evolving into panic. A charge down the slab path to the wooden fence offered no signs of life anywhere close.

Deciding that the back door being left open was a decoy, an attempt to make him waste time, and with the discovery of the bundle of cash, he could think of only one answer. His parents had been abducted. Or was this his paranoia taking over? But what would be the point of the abductors leaving all that money? Normally, on a kidnapping, the kidnapper would be demanding money. He became even more confused when he paid attention to the condition of the rooms, finding no signs of a struggle. The front door lock was undamaged. How could he have slept through this, knowing that his mother would have screamed the place down had a stranger entered the house uninvited. Tom would have picked up the nearest thing to a weapon and had a go at whoever it was. The clue came to light when he returned to the back door and discovered it had been jemmied open, very carefully.

All this must have happened in the time he'd spent searching his jacket pocket and gawking at that bundle of notes and putting on his shoes. Remembering the flushing of the toilet, he realised only a few minutes would have passed. He concluded that the intruder had entered by the back door, must have been armed with a gun to silence his parents, and had forced them out of their bed and to leave through the front door and possibly into a waiting car. Had this person entered his room and rummaged through his pockets and left that bundle of twenty-pound notes? Surely, his weapon would have been taken in case he woke up before the abductor had managed to get his parents out.

To begin thinking straight, Barton knew he had to calm his emotions. Deciding it would be a waste of time rushing out to his car in search of the abductor, he settled on the sofa to think. *Who is good enough to accomplish this while I slept through it?* Maybe some of his comrades from the services or a good burglar who had been paid to do it? He decided on the former, and there were too many to point a finger at. He was no stranger to this kind of operation and knew the only thing he could do was to postpone action until the abductor made contact.

Thinking that it was going to be a waste of time—nevertheless, what else was he going to do until the contact was made—he got up from the sofa and began searching the living room. Surely, his father would have left some kind of clue. Giving up, he searched the kitchen. Still nothing. The upstairs search proved to be fruitless—until he entered his own room. Lying just under his bed lay old Tom's tobacco pouch. Cautiously, Barton picked it up. It bulged in his hand as if it was packed full. When he unzipped it, wrapped in the centre of the bundle of tobacco, he found a small piece of white paper with a mobile number written on it.

Having zipped up the pouch, he returned to the living room with it in his hand and sat on the sofa for a while, staring at the number on the paper. Was this the contact he had been expecting? Or was this the clue his father had left? The only way to find out would be to call the number.

It took a long time before he got an answer from a sleepy female voice, asking, "Who's calling?"

"That doesn't matter," Barton yelled back at her. "I got this number handed to me. It concerns my patents."

A sudden rasping angry male voice came on next, demanding to know who was calling this number, saying this mobile belonged to his daughter.

"Who's your daughter?" Barton cut in.

The communication seemed to have been cut off and Barton was about to ask if they were still there when the female voice came on. "The number you called belonged to my sister." Another long moment of silence. "She was killed yesterday—a gunshot, the police say. They have a suspect in custody. They want to talk to all her associates. You having her mobile number means you must have known her. The police will want to interview you. She was very secretive with her mobile number."

The words had hardly left the lips of the caller when Barton disconnected. The last thing he needed was a trace put on his mobile. Not being 100 per cent sure this could be done, he nevertheless didn't think the chance worth taking. Hastily he unzipped the pouch, replacing the note in search of maybe another clue, but there was nothing there. He remembered the words of his instructors back in the days of his recruitment into the special services—*no matter how good you are, you always leave a trace behind.* That meant traces sedentary people wouldn't find, traces only an expert would spot. Although he was no expert, he had gained a good deal from the advice and training. Before beginning a more thorough search, he was certain the intruder was alone and had entered the back door, leaving through the front.

Studying the almost invisible signs on the back door, he decided it had been eased open with a knife similar to the ones he used in combat. That was the only trace left that he could find close to the kitchen. At the end of the short corridor, the edge of the runner carpet had a slight wrinkle. That was not normal. His mother was constantly correcting this carpet. Lifting it up cautiously, he found one of his father's cigarette butts. Studying it, he discovered there was no tobacco inside. He opened it up to find writing inside. The words had been quickly scrawled, and all he could decipher were three words—*an old mate.* Barton was convinced that this had been planted there by the abductor. No way could old Tom have had the time to set this up or, for that matter, to put the tobacco pouch under the bed.

Back in the living room on the sofa, he stared at the small piece of cigarette paper. In the regiment, he'd had hundreds of mates, had known most of them personally. Which one would be most likely to get mixed up in a criminal gang?

Remembering how easily he had been recruited into this criminal life, he realised the choice was unlimited. Had the dapper little man approached others? His problem now was he had learned that Crow was no longer around to maybe give him a hint as to who this old mate could be. That left him with only one choice—the bearded hoodie. Where could he be? Barton pondered. Had he evaded the police, maybe escaped from the security guards?

He jumped up off the sofa when an idea suddenly dawned on him. Having decided that the abductor had made his contact through the obscure clues, there was only one other way now. And he was aware of the risk it posed.

He had to approach the guards. Having being one himself in the past, he knew how little they got paid. Maybe with this cash, he could find out if the hoodie had been picked up by the cops.

Two security officers stood just inside the revolving glass-plated doors when Barton entered. One was studying papers on a clipboard; his mate, a good six inches taller, grinned when Barton approached.

"What can we do for you, sir?" the tallest officer asked, taking a step closer.

"I would like to make enquiries about a client of my company." Barton adjusted the tie on the collar of his white shirt, finding it pinching, but he was glad that his old blue suit still fitted after all those years of being hung up in the wardrobe in his old room.

"What client? And what company are we talking about sir?"

"At this stage in our enquiries, I can't disclose his name," Barton went on and began to step between the two officers. "If you both were on duty yesterday, I'm sure you will remember the incident that took place here."

"What incident would that be, sir?" the officer with the clipboard asked.

Barton described what had happened, describing in detail what his client looked like and, because he had placed himself between them, preventing them from cooperating in their replies—an old trick he'd perfected in his past life. At the same time, he pulled a few twenty-pound notes from his pocket, holding the notes in such a way that the one with the clipboard wouldn't notice.

"I remember that incident," the tall officer at his back said.

Looking at the clipboard officer Barton said, "Do you mind if I have a word in private with your colleague?"

Holding out his hand and grinning, the officer took his hand and the banknotes that were held there.

"Your ID seems to be in order, sir." The clipboard officer grinned and walked away.

<u>CHAPTER 8</u>

Having been given £2,000 from Boss Man, Lorinna was in a desperate state of mind. He knew there was no way he could get his hands on Barton's family on his own. He needed help. But that kind of help came at a price. After he'd been roughly dragged out the building and left standing on the street, those thoughts lingered. He watched as the three muscle-bound goons returned to the big four-by-four. As the big vehicle drove past him, even though the windows were tinted, he had visions of the goons laughing at him when the driver swerved into a deep puddle, drenching him.

Wiping the dirty water from his grey jacket and cursing at them, he couldn't drag his thoughts away from his dilemma. What had Barton done to the Boss Man to make him go to all this trouble to get back at this big guy? He estimated he had about three miles to get back to his green VW, and he stepped out and waved a passing taxi. The driver pulled up next to him. He was about to step inside when the river shouted, "Fuck off, mate. You're not getting in my cab in that state." Instantly, the vehicle shot away.

Not being used to walking great distances, Lorinna was glad to get into his rented flat and get his shoes off. After a warm shower, he settled down on the only padded seat in the small lounge. The only way left for him to raise more cash was to sell his car. It had to be a quick sale, and he realised he wouldn't get anywhere near its value. Filling out the details of the vehicle and posting the information on the internet to agents that might be interested, he sat and waited for a reaction. His first task in the morning was to go and get the car washed and valeted.

Driving into the washing bay, Lorinna recognised the paunchy bald man standing and holding a high-pressure water lance. He knew him only by the nickname of Guppy and that he was one of Boss Man's thugs. Guppy, in turn, recognised Lorinna when he got out his car. Guppy approached.

"Have you taken up honest employment?" Lorinna quizzed, grinning.

"The fuck I have. This is one of the Boss Man's money-laundering scams. I'm ordered to keep this place running. They were going to bump me, but he gave me a second chance, put me in charge of this shit-hole."

"I'm trying to sell this car," Lorinna said, pointing at the VW. "I need to get it cleaned."

"How much are you looking for it?" Guppy asked, dropping the lance and walking towards the car.

"It must be worth about ten big ones."

Grinning and shaking his bald head, Guppy skipped around the green VW. "That might be what it's forecourt value is, but you'd be lucky to get half that." Opening up the driver's door, he quickly glanced and sniffed the interior. "Why do you want to sell it? Is something wrong with it?"

"Nothing wrong with it. I just need to get some quick cash."

After closing the car door, Guppy stood for a moment looking into Lorinna's grey eyes. "Why don't you ask the Boss Man for a loan?"

Lorinna grimaced. "He's the reason I need the cash. And he's already given me some but not enough."

Picking up the lance and handing it over to a youth clad from head to foot in black oilskins, Guppy waved Lorinna into a small office at the back of a corrugated steel building. He got seated behind a rough wooden bench and said, "As you can guess, there is no love lost between me and Boss Man. If it's cash you want, I can sell your car, but I need to know why."

Picking his words carefully, Lorinna went through the details, all the while watching Guppy nodding and grinning. It was at the mention of the name Barton that Guppy's expression changed, it seemed as though a bolt of electric had been shot at him.

"What's wrong? Have I said something or what?"

Jumping up and knocking over a five-litre carton of detergent, Guppy leaned over the bench. "Did I hear you right? Did you say Barton?"

Surprised at the bald man's reaction, Lorinna stepped forward. "Yes. That's what I just said."

"I might be able to get you some help. I know a guy who may have the right qualifications you're looking for."

"How much is this guy going to cost me?"

Holding up his hands, Guppy smiled. "Don't worry. We'll come to some arrangement over your car and what Boss Man has given you."

"I would like to have enough cash left to buy an old banger to get around in," Lorinna said.

—m—

The tall security officer willingly filled Barton in on the details of what had gone on when the police took charge of the hoodie. "The police just let him walk away. They did a quick body search; that was all."

Nodding his thanks, Barton watched the tall officer join his colleague, all the time wondering where the hoodie could be. He was also puzzled why the police let him go. Could it be that this guy didn't have a record? He could feel his paranoia setting in, could feel himself fighting against it. Nevertheless, before moving off, he had a good look around. Not only was he searching for the hooded figure, he was also searching for him without the disguise. Although Barton had a close up look at the guy without the beard and hood, it had been for only a few moments, and he wasn't 100 per cent sure he could pick him out in a crowd.

So preoccupied was he with the thought that the hoodie could be following him that he almost missed seeing the youngster walking behind two girls and a shaven-headed youth. They were strolling in the opposite direction from him, seemingly heading into the shopping mall. Barton estimated they were about a hundred metres from him, making it difficult to follow without being spotted at a time when shoppers were sparse. He was sure the youth had spotted him yesterday. That was why he'd boarded the bus and tricked Barton by jumping back off when the bus moved away.

Turning around and deciding to keep a distance from them, he also had another thought. If he could find this youth so simply, it could mean that the hoodie might be close by, trying to get his money back. At one point, the group of youngsters stopped, and Barton found himself just a few yards away. That was when he noticed the youngster's jacket had a rip at the back and there was mud on the seat of his pants. Had the hoodie already nabbed the youth?

That being the case, then his chances of getting a grip of the hoodie were slim, as were his chances of getting to know who abducted his parents. The girls and bald head stepped into a shop, leaving the youth standing at the door playing with his mobile. Barton rushed up, grabbing him by the upper arm and forcing him down a corridor and out of the fire exit. In spite of his cries for help, nobody paid attention.

"Where's your hooded friend? Barton barked into his face, holding him against the wall by the throat.

All he got in response was a frantic shaking of the head from the youth.

Threateningly, Barton balled his fist when the fire door burst open. Leading the charge was bald head, the girls at his back. Guessing what was about to happen next, he pulled the youth from the wall and sent him staggering towards his friends. Bald head tripped over him, and the girls in turn fell over bald head. Their struggles to get back onto their feet gave Barton time to dive back inside the fire door and close it, making sure the bar locked into place.

After taking a casual stroll through the mall and out to the car park, Barton heard his mobile sounded as he was about to get into his vehicle. He quickly whipped it out from the pocket of his leather jacket. The caller's number was restricted. A cold shiver rushed through his body. This could be the abductor. He froze on the spot when the female voice announced she was a Detective Constable Jones, and at his convenience, could she interview him in connection with an incident he might have witnessed.

"I think you have the wrong number," Barton promptly replied and cut the connection, jumping into his car and getting away from the area in case the police might trace the location he was in through his phone.

He pulled into an area where an old building had been pulled down. The ground was rough and bumpy, cluttered with debris from the condemned house. His plan, and it was the only one he could think of in short notice, was to dump his mobile where it would be impossible to trace. He got out his Volvo and was on the verge of dropping it and stamping his heel on it when it sounded. A strange number showed on the fascia.

For a long hesitant moment, he gazed at it, uncertain whether to respond. When he did, the familiar voice that greeted him shocked him and, at the same time, sent a wave of relief through him.

"Where are you, Dad?"

"We're at home. Where do you think we are?"

Barton thought he detected a nervous quiver in his dad's voice. "Where did you and Mum disappear to at six this morning?"

"We had to rush out, didn't want to disturb you."

Was this his paranoia? Something wasn't ringing true; it was the strange number that alerted him. He knew his father had an old phone and refused to get an updated one. It was also the way his father hesitated before replying, as if he was being told what to say by someone close to him. "I'm on my way over. Stay where you are."

A much longer delay passed before his father responded. This convinced Barton that his parents weren't alone.

"Can I have a word with Mum?" he asked.

"She's not here. She darted out for something out the shop coffee I think it was."

That was the warning. Barton knew his parents never drank coffee and never bought it. "I'll be there in half an hour," he replied and cut the call.

He was climbing over the backyard fence five minutes later. The back door was still unlocked. Silently pushing it open, he creeped into the kitchen. Finding no one there, he stepped out into the short corridor, avoiding the creaking board his father had promised to fix many years previous, and burst into the living room, hoping to catch the abductor by surprize. Like the kitchen, the room was empty of occupants. Upstairs, he searched the bedrooms and the toilet—all void of life with no sign of anyone having been there recently.

CHAPTER 9

Lorinna entered his small flat. He was about to make himself a hot drink when his mobile sounded. Guppy's name came up.

"All has been sorted," Guppy reported. "I sold your car, and I have a guy to do the job."

"Is there enough money left for me to get a cheap car?" Lorinna asked.

"That's all been sorted," Guppy replied. "I have a car when you want to come and collect it."

"Is there any chance I could meet this guy?"

"That'll not happen," Guppy quickly replied. "That was the agreement we made, or this guy won't get involved."

Lorinna had already forecasted this, but there was no harm in trying. "When is he going to do the job?"

"You should know better than to ask," Guppy cut in and ended the call.

Continuing to make his drink of hot chocolate, his favourite—he was almost addicted to it—he sat on the padded seat, holding it between his hands and thinking back on how much that green VW had cost him. *That bald-headed crook Guppy's going to make a fortune off of it.* What troubled Lorinna most was not knowing if and when the job got done and how this guy Guppy had hired was going to get the old couple away without alerting that big ape of a son. He thought back to the way Barton had protected them from the young thief—to the extent of chasing the youngster and catching him and fucking up his chances of getting that gun planted in the garden.

If Boss Man's assumptions were correct, then by now Barton would have gotten rid of the gun. But if by a strange chance of fate, that big ape still had it in his possession, would reporting it to the police put an end to Boss Man's obsession with making Barton suffer? He placed his cup on the floor by his feet and pulled his mobile from his pocket? This decision was too big for him to make on his own. He punched in the private number.

Before he got a chance to say a word, Boss Man shouted, "This better be good, Lorinna."

After he'd explained his suspicions, the phone went silent for a long moment.

Thinking that he might have been cut off, Lorinna said into it, "Are you still there?"

"For starters," came the rough voice, "you need to be sure that Barton has that weapon, which I doubt he still has. How do you propose to do that?" Another long silence followed before Boss Man came back, saying, "Just get hold of the parents and get them here."

His mind was reeling with Boss Man's words as he lay in the single bed trying to sleep. He doubted there was double glazing in the small windows of the attic bed-sit come flat. Although the motorway was a good distance away, he could hear the rumbling of juggernauts. His mobile sounded. He jumped up and scrambled for his jacket and grabbed it out his pocket. Guppy's name appeared on the fascia. "What now?" he shouted. "It's bloody half five in the morning."

"The job's been done," came Guppy's high-pitched voice.

"Where do I pick them up?" Lorinna asked trying to get his sleepless brain to take in this information.

"You don't. You stay put until I contact you."

"I'm to take them to Boss Man."

"I've spoken to the Boss Man," Guppy said with a snigger. "I'm to hold on to them."

"Where?"

"You'll know when I contact you."

Knowing that he would get no more information out of Guppy, Lorinna cut the call and lay back down on the bed. He knew sleep was out of the question. As he stared at the ceiling, thoughts that he didn't like drifted through his mind. He had just given Guppy a way to get back on the Boss Man's good side, the results of which could end his life. The only way he could see to save himself was to find out for sure if Barton still had that weapon.

Jumping out of bed, Lorinna knew that, to save himself, he had to find Barton. A time check told him it was seven o'clock. Where would Barton be? He guessed the big guy was living in his parents' house. And if that was the case, where was he when Guppy's man had gotten in and nabbed the old couple? Guppy's call had come in at half past five in the morning saying the job had been done. Could Barton have been asleep or maybe not in the house?

Following a breakfast of a hot chocolate drink, he phoned Guppy about the car he was to pick up. He was told to go to the carwash, where Guppy would meet him and take him to the vehicle.

The black Fiat looked like it had been used in a stock car race, with dents all over the body. There was no lining on the doors, and the seats were ripped. When Guppy tried to open it, the driver's side window fell down. "You have to be joking," Lorinna scoffed, "if you're expecting me to drive that thing."

"That's all I could get with the money I had left to spend," Guppy replied, struggling to place the window back in the groves.

"How much did you pay that guy?"

"You don't want to know," Guppy said and gave up trying to reset the window.

"My car must have been worth £10,000."

Guppy, the sweat glistening on his bald head, threw the key at Lorinna, saying, "When you need a quick sale, you can't expect its forecourt value." He edged himself into his own car and quickly drove off, leaving Lorinna standing there gazing in awe at the key in his hand.

The old fiat looked in bad shape. But that wasn't the worse that was to come. When he stepped into it, his foot went through the floor. The only thing between him and the ground was the rubber mat. After resetting the mat on the footwell, he was surprised when the engine started at the first turn of the key, although it sounded rough and blasted out a cloud of black exhaust smoke. He drove out of the yard and onto the busy main street, crunching and grinding the gears as he went.

He sighed with relief when he pulled into the shopping mall car park that he hadn't encountered a police patrol car. Parking in a space as far away from the shops as possible, he sat for a while listening to the banging of the old engine. When he had had enough of breathing in the fumes, he turned it off. A hint of panic rushed through him when the engine continued firing. "What the fuck next?" he yelled and slapped the steering wheel. When he jumped out and slammed the door, the window on the passenger's side slid down with a loud bang.

Listening to the engine throbbing away noisily as he walked towards the shopping area, he heard a sudden yell of voices and turned to see the old Fiat had burst into flames. Ignoring this excitement, Lorinna walked on, heading for the glass revolving doors. Just inside the doors, the two security officers who had collared him previously grinned when they recognised him and approached.

With a grin, the tallest of the two said, "We had a big guy in here yesterday asking questions about you."

"What kind of questions?"

His colleague interrupted, saying, "We're not at liberty to answer any questions concerning any incidents that may have happened during the time we were on duty." At the same time, he was winking with his left eye and nodding with a wide grin across his pallor features.

Getting the message, and knowing he hadn't a lot of cash on him, Lorinna fished out the few banknotes he had, hoping it would satisfy them.

"As I said," continued the tall officer, "he was a big guy in a suit he didn't look comfortable in—the kind of guy who is more used to wearing casual clothes. He said he was from a legal firm and wanted all the details of what went down."

"Can you describe him?"

His colleague's eye had stopped winking, and the grin had gone when he looked at the few notes he had been handed. "I think you've had your money's worth."

Rubbing the back of his neck, Lorinna grimaced. "I don't carry a lot of money on me. But if you can give me a few more details on this big guy, I promise I'll come back and give you more cash."

They laughed together, and the tallest said, "There's a dispenser just down there." He pointed with a long arm. "We'll escort you to it."

"Never mind," Lorinna snapped at them. "I think I know who you are talking about."

—✳︎—

Sitting in his car, Barton held his mobile in his hand and knew he had no other choice but to destroy it. But how were his parents going to get in touch? From the position he had parked at the end of the lane, he could observe their back door. His hopes were that whoever this abductor was, he would return with his parents.

With the heater on at full blast, he could still feel the cold creeping in and decided that, after an hour, this guy and his parents weren't going to arrive. As he was about to drive away, his phone sounded. Quickly turning the ignition off to silence the sound of the heater fan, he snatched the mobile from his pocket. Another strange number appeared, and after a moment of doubtful hesitation, he responded.

"Where are you, Richard?" came the familiar voice that seemed to have an echo, as if the phone was being held away from his father or was on speaker.

This was an old trick. Barton grimaced, knowing, if he disclosed his location, whoever this abductor was would be one jump ahead of him. "I'm on my way," Barton replied. "I was held up in a traffic accident. Be with you in ten." This gave him time to hide his car and get into the house and lie in wait somewhere inside and jump this guy. His first reaction was to lock the back door when entering, making sure they wouldn't come in that way. He pulled the table tight against the door. knowing this would make a scraping noise. His next move was to switch his mobile off, another lesson he had learned when you're not sure if the person you're searching for is in the building. Normally, the best way to locate them would be to give them a call.

In his parents' upstairs front bedroom, Barton could observe the street from one end to the other. If this guy turned up in a car, he would spot him, knowing he wouldn't park close to his door, and he would have to walk. And a stranger approaching would create attention from the neighbours; curtains and blinds would be flicking. Remembering how silently this guy had originally entered the house and escorted his parent out, with nobody giving him a hint they had noticed, Barton knew he had to be alert. He'd left all the internal doors open. This way, he could hear the slightest movement.

It's strange when you're in a house you have lived in for many years and you're on high alert; you hear sounds that, in the past, you took for granted and paid no attention to. Now, Barton was jumping at every creek and crack. One crack he knew would have to be caused, and that was the loose floorboard in the passageway, and he knew his father would deliberately step on it. That made him wonder why he'd never heard it when they had first been taken away. He suddenly realised he had been wrong thinking that the abductor had left by the front door, this being the reason he'd never heard that floorboard. They had left the way he had entered. And if they entered the back way again, he was confident he would hear the kitchen table scrape across the kitchen floor.

The street below was poorly illuminated, and it was beginning to rain, making it difficult to distinguish the features of the few people who walked on the narrow pavement below. A car's headlights appeared, giving Barton's nerves a jolt. It was travelling much too slowly and, at one point, made a stop. *This has to be them*, he decided and crept downstairs, heading for the living room.

Absentmindedly, he stepped on the loose floorboard. And at the same moment, he heard a key being pushed into the lock of the front door. Barton froze, as did the sound of the key. He watched as the door slowly opened, letting the dim light from the street cast a beam close to his feet. Standing framed in the doorway was the silhouette of a small figure. Like the release of an overstretched elastic band, Barton dived at the figure, knocking it backwards out onto the wet pavement. A high-pitched scream came from the person as Barton grabbed a handful of greasy hair and pulled him inside the door. With the intruder jammed against the nearest wall, held there by the throat, Barton managed to reach the light switch and was shocked to recognise the young thief Andy Milton. With his free hand, Barton landed a hard slap to the youngster's jaw. "What are you up to now? And how did you get the key to this door?" he asked, watching the blood flow from the young man's mouth.

"Let me go, you mad bastard," Andy shouted, his arms swinging wildly, trying to strike back.

Tightening his grip, Barton hissed at him through gritted teeth, "What are you doing here?" He noticed the youngster's eyes begin to bulge and his tongue hanging out. He relaxed his grip and let young Andy slide to the floor. Using the side of his foot, Barton closed the door, and he dragged Andy by the back of his jacket into the living room, listening to him coughing and choking.

On the sofa, Andy lay in the foetal position. Barton stood over the youngster, giving him time to recover his voice and his breathing. "Well, are you going to tell me what you are doing here?" Barton shouted down at him.

Not quite recovered, Andy made a few indecipherable words, enough for Barton to understand he was here because he knew the house was empty.

"How did you know my parents weren't here?" Barton said, leaning over close to his ear.

"I have a mate who lives here. He told me he saw you parents being bundled into the back of a van."

"Did this mate see the person who was bundling them into that van?" Barton shouted, "And who is this mate? Where does he live?"

"That's none of your fucking business. Now, let me get out of here," the youngster yelled and attempted to get up.

Barton pushed him back down, holding him by the shoulders. "My parents were abducted from here early this morning, I know it couldn't have been you. You were with the cops. So tell me, where I can get a hold of your mate?"

Struggling and fighting against the weight of the bigger man, Andy shouted, "He's where you won't be able to get hold of him. He's in the nick."

"You're a liar. I saw you with your mates earlier. You jumped onto the circular bus."

"Let me up, you bastard. I tell you I've only just been let out half an hour ago."

Releasing the pressure on the youth's shoulder, Barton then gripped the collar of his jacket and lifted him up and threw him out the living room, pushing him from behind to the front door. When Andy scrambled for the handle, the door burst in on him. Barton's reactions were much quicker than the youth's, and he managed to about turn and run for the back door when a group of uniformed police officers charged in.

Dragging the kitchen table from the door, Barton just managed to get it clear when two policemen rushed in on him. With a kick from his left foot, he sent the table crashing into the officers, knocking one of them backward. The other attempted to jump over it but misjudged and fell at Barton's feet, smashing his head on the edge of the door. Knowing that his colleague would help the injured man, Barton didn't hesitate to get clear of the house. The race was now on for him to get to his car before the other officers came charging down the street to get to the rear of the building. Running at full pelt, he soon felt the lactic acid stinging in the muscles of his legs; his lungs felt as though they were made of leather. A few yards from the end of the lane, he heard the siren, and soon, police cars came screaming into the street. His only means of escape was to jump over the brick wall that ran down the left side of the lane. This led to an area where he had spent many hours playing as a boy and was familiar with the terrain. He remembered the steep embankment, at the foot of which he would have to wade through sludgy water.

With his suit trousers soaked up to his knees, he ducked into the culvert that drained the water beneath the street and came out at the side of a small stream. To get to his car, he had to wade upstream until he came to a small footbridge. This landmark was also familiar, and he knew that, when he climbed onto the footpath, he would have to chance edging his way along the quiet dimly lit public park.

Cursing himself for not parking his car in a more secluded place, he was, at the same time, glad he had approached from behind some overgrown shrubs. The two police officers were standing a few metres away from it, and it was obvious to Barton what their intent was. Ducking behind a laurel bush, he watched them standing under a lamp standard lighting up a smoke. Deciding he may have to settle here for a while, he lay flat out and was glad he had done so when the hand touched his shoulder. Had he been crouched, he would have jumped and given himself away. He swung around, expecting to find a police officer towering over him. The sensation was one of surprize and relief when he looked into the darkened face of young Andy. "How the fuck did you get here?" was Barton's immediate response.

"When you threw that table at the coppers, that gave me a chance to jump over them and get out the back door."

"Why did you chase after me?" Barton asked as the youngster lay next to him.

"I didn't. I ran to the end of that back lane and down the street. When I nearly bumped into those two"—Andy nodded at the constables—"I dived in here out of sight. I didn't expect to find you here. Or I would have chanced my luck with them."

"I think those two are here for the night," Barton said, getting up onto his knees. "I'm getting out of here." With Andy crawling at the rear, Barton soon found himself at the side of a busy road. Grabbing the youngster by his jacket collar, he pinned him down, preventing him from getting up. "Stay down until we're sure it's safe to cross the road. They could have a squad out searching for us, and this road will be their main point of focus."

"Who are they searching for?"

"You, for breaking into our house."

"Come on, man. You're a bigger crook than me. You're the man with the gun that everybody's searching for."

"It doesn't matter who they're searching for. If we get caught, we're both in the shit."

"They've had me in and out of that station for the past two days," Andy complained, "something about a girl being shot—"

"We need to talk about that," Barton interrupted and got onto his feet and darted across the road. The only place he could see that offered concealment was to rush up the driveway of the closest house. Here, he crouched between the building and the garage—the only place that offered some shadow. After a few moments of standing against the wall of the house, he realised the youngster hadn't followed. Looking back the way he had ran, he noticed a large vehicle had stopped where he and the youngster had crouched. In the car headlights that passed, he saw young Andy being dragged to the rear of the vehicle by two dark figures.

CHAPTER 10

From the shopping bag, Lorinna got the black hooded jacket and beard out. Checking no one was about, he slipped them on. It took longer than he had anticipated to walk to the street where the Bartons lived. Always having operated from the back door, he wasn't sure which house they occupied. All the houses and doors looked the same on terraced buildings. From where he stood, he could observe the length of the street and every door. Quite a few dwellings were lit, making it more difficult to decide which house belonged to Barton's parents.

Where the little dark figure appeared from confused Lorinna. For the past five minutes, the street had been void of pedestrians; it just seemed to have popped up out of nowhere. Standing at one of the doors, the figure seemed to be having trouble unlocking the one he was attempting to enter. Then, like a flush of cold water, it struck him this was no occupier; this was someone breaking in, and now it dawned on him who that figure was. This time, it had to be the pickpocket, the low-down dirty little thief who he'd paid to plant the gun and who still had his money. As fast as his legs could carry him, he charged up the street. But by the time he got to there, the little figure was inside, and the door got slammed on his face.

He decided it wasn't a good idea to charge in and possibly come face to face with the guy who Guppy had hired to kidnap the old couple, should they still be inside. Lorinna retreated to his hiding place at the end of the street to wait to see if the youngster reappeared and was glad that he had done. He jumped back into the shadows when the police cars came screaming in on both ends of the street, the blue flashing lights like blinding strobes reflecting from the darkened windows the length of the street. A few yards from where he hid, a couple of officers in body armour jumped out one of the vehicles that stopped. He guessed to block off that end, they ran to where Lorinna estimated to be the way to the rear of the tenement row of houses, while the remainder of the cars came to a grinding halt at the door in question. From those cars jumped a squad of officers, who barged in through the closed door.

Making a discreet exit and keeping to the darkest side of the road, Lorinna headed for his bed-sit flat at a fast walk. At the busy road, it took him a while to get across. The traffic seemed relentless. When a gap came, he darted over. That was when he noticed the black Range Rover, parked with its hazard lights flashing. The shock came when he noticed two large black figures fighting a smaller man into the rear of the vehicle. Lorinna knew in an instant who that smaller figure was, visible in the constant lights from passing cars. There was no mistaking that pale countenance, the shoulder-length greasy hair, and the spindly limbs that were fighting against the odds.

With his head bent and hood up, covering most of his face, he dug his hands into his pockets and slunk his way along the road, letting the huge black vehicle pass. He took a mental note of the registration. This was déjà vu, taking him back to the shooting of that schoolgirl. That registration number struck a chord; he knew it was familiar but, at that moment, couldn't place it. So preoccupied with getting clear of that tussle with the two figures and the youngster was he that he suddenly realised he had lost his bearings and had to stop and look around, taking in his surroundings. This was a middle-class residential area with private houses along his nearside, all with wide driveways and double garages with roll-up steel doors. Although the area wasn't very well lit, he felt out of place and noticed he was the only person walking the pavement. In his disguise, it would only take one of the residents to spot him looking so suspicious. In the shadow of the nearest bush, he discarded the beard and the jacket into the plastic shopping bag.

Walking back the way he had come, thinking this was the quickest way back to his flat, he only got a few paces when a big figure stepped out in front of him, holding what he could make out to be a handgun. When the figure closed in on him, he dropped the bag and could feel his knees wabble.

"Just the very man I'm looking for," Barton said and rammed the pistol into Lorinna's chest.

The barrel of the weapon punched into his chest so severely it sent Lorinna reeling backwards. "You again," he managed to gasp.

"Yes, me again, your worst nightmare. And if you don't tell me what I want to know, you'll have no more nightmares."

"Somebody's going to glance out their window and see you holding that gun on me and call the cops," Lorinna said making a display of holding up his arms.

"That's fine," Barton replied with a grin. "Then when the police arrive, all they'll find is your dead body. So get your hands back into your pocket and walk."

Lorinna grimaced. "You wouldn't dare fire that thing. The noise will alert these people."

Shaking his head, Barton turned him around and pushed him along the pavement. "With the noise of the traffic and the fact all these houses will have double or treble glazing, I doubt they'll hear it."

"Where are we going?" Lorinna asked, picking up his plastic bag as he staggered forward.

"To get your car."

"I don't have a car."

Jumping towards Lorinna, Barton grabbed the bag out of his hand and tossed it into the nearest garden. "You're a bloody liar. What happened to the green VW?"

"I had to sell it."

"Why?"

"It's a long story."

"Well, you're going to have to tell me it when we get out of this neighbourhood."

The traffic lights were at green when they reached a crossroads. "Which way?" Lorinna asked without turning.

"Just keep going straight on." Barton gave him a reminder by jabbing the weapon into his spine.

Although the traffic was still busy, they arrived at a spot where there were no houses, and Barton ordered him to stop. "Now tell me the story about you having to sell your car."

Lorinna felt himself being pushed into a deep ditch, landing on his rump. "What can I tell you?" he shouted up at the towering black shadow.

"You can tell me what you did with the money you got for the sale."

"So, this is a robbery?"

The flash from the muzzle blinded Lorinna for a fleeting moment. The explosion sent a deafening silence from his ears penetrating into his brain. In shock, he instinctively rolled over, his face sinking into the soft sludge at the bottom of the ditch. In a panic, he scrambled onto his knees, attempting to get out and onto solid ground. Then he felt the sole of a shoe on his forehead pushing him back into the mud. There he lay, subdued. Now, he realised he had been beaten, and he was panicking, aware this could be his last moment in life.

"Are you going to tell me what you did with the money? Otherwise, the next shot will be through your head."

He realised that, if he told this big man what he had done with the money, the next shot would be to his head. "I paid it into my account," he replied, coughing and spitting mud from his mouth.

Stepping back from the edge of the ditch, with the weapon still trained on Lorinna's head, Barton shouted, "Get your arse out of there and lead the way to the nearest cash dispenser."

Resisting a grin on seeing he was being offered a chance, Lorinna scrambled his way out of the sludge, and on hands and knees, he gazed up at the towering figure. "I've no idea where the nearest one is."

Jabbing the nozzle of the pistol against Lorinna's forehead. "Get on your feet and start looking for one."

Struggling to his feet, Lorinna gazed at the muddy state his suit was in. "I can't go trailing around the streets looking like this; people are going to take notice."

For a long moment, their eyes met. Lorinna could see the big man was mulling over what he had just said. When the click of the safety catch sounded, without haste, he turned, his hands in the air, and headed back the way he had come.

"Keep your hands down at your side," Barton shouted, grinning at the way Lorinna was walking, thinking he looked as though he had just shit himself.

Leading the way through the car park where he had parked the old Fiat, Lorinna was shocked to see that the fire crew was still working on it. He lowered his head and took a quick detour around the scene.

Barton, who had been walking a few paces behind, caught up and asked, "What's all that about?"

"That's another long story."

"Well, when we get to a quiet place, you can tell me all about that as well."

Remembering his last experience, Lorinna smartly replied, "It's nothing, I was just keeping my head down in case the police were still hanging around."

"If you're pissing me about, the police will be the least of your worries."

The only signs of life inside the mall were small groups of youths passing through, possibly on their way to a pub. Lorinna led the way to the bank and to the cash dispenser at the side of the shuttered doors. He could feel Barton's breath on the back of his neck. "Do you mind?" He turned. "This is private. I don't want everybody to know my pin number." This got him a sharp jag in the ribs with the muzzle of Barton's gun. He quickly entered his card and punched in his pin. The information that came up from the dispenser informed them that there was zero cash in the account. Cursing he retried and got the same result. "There has to be a mistake," he cried.

It happened so quickly. One moment, he was swearing at the ATM. The next, he felt the big hand grab the back of his collar, and he was getting pulled with his heels dragging on the tiled surface. The swinging toilet door thumped the side of his leg. He thought the skin had been stripped from it. The next cause of pain was when his head collided with the toilet seat. Two strong arms twisted him around. Now he was facedown looking into the bowl. The hand that held him fast felt like a vice crushing into the back of his neck.

Lorinna screamed. He thought he was about to drown when the water flushed onto the back of his head. "Help!" he yelled. "Someone help me." That was when he felt himself being lifted up by the heels.

"I'm going to hold you like this all night until you tell me what you did with the money from the sale of your car," Barton shouted at him. "How many times do you think this toilet will flush? In that time, I might have to have a piss."

Between gulps and coughs, Lorinna continued to cry for help. "I ... told you ... I—"

"You're a lying fucker," Barton growled at him and flushed the toilet again.

What followed was a long moment of silence and no more movement from his victim.

Barton let his legs go and watched him slither onto the floor. "Are you going to tell me what I want to know? Or would you like drown in that shithole?"

CHAPTER 11

Boris Mannering, aka Boss Man, ran a few lucrative pornographic studios, and his staff was struggling to keep up with the demand. Orders were coming in from all the media outlets they dealt with and from phone calls and, in a few cases, by post. But this was only a part of Mannering's organisation. He ran three high-class brothels near the city centre, and the drugs were flying in and out like sugar in a supermarket. He was also a member of a syndicate that specialised in money laundering. Boss Man was a very rich person, but in his view, he was not rich enough. He wasn't one for flaunting his wealth and lived in a modest bungalow and ran a cheap production car. The three Range Rovers he owned he allocated to his most loyal goons and seldom travelled in them. He was known by his goons as a tight-arsed bastard, although this was never mentioned around his closest friends in case he got wind of it

Sitting in his usual seat at the end of the long table, he glared at the bald Guppy sitting with his head in his hands. "What the fuck's going on between you and Lorinna?"

Without lifting his head from his hands, Guppy replied, "As I told you, Boss Man, he wanted money to hire a pro. To get hold of Barton's parents. The plan was for Lorinna to bring them here."

"Well, that didn't happen," Boss Man shouted. "So where are they?"

Guppy shook his head. "I've no idea."

Jumping out of his chair, which did nothing to increase his height, Boss Man strutted down to the bottom of the table and slapped his hands down on it in front of Guppy. "You'd better find them before this day is out, or it won't be just the carwash you'll be getting as punishment."

Looking into the cold grey eyes of Boss Man for the first time, Guppy replied nervously. "I need more time, Boss Man. Please."

"You don't have any more time. Find Lorinna, and if you're lucky, you might live to the end of this day."

Guppy lifted his bulk from the chair. "I hope you don't mind me asking, but what's it with this old couple? Why do you want them so badly." He looked down at the smaller man and watched as he returned to his seat at the other end of the table. Guppy knew this conversation was over. He headed for the door. He was about to open it when the rough voice echoed.

"When you find Lorinna, kill him and dump the body in the Barton's backyard. Then bring the old couple here yourself."

Guppy was no stranger to the killing game. The schoolgirl was a mistake. He didn't feel it was his fault and didn't have any regrets about it. He felt he was just doing what he had been told. He had got the instructions second-hand from one of the goons. Somehow, the instructions had been twisted, and he had taken it to be he had to shoot the person who belonged to the mobile Boss Man's technicians had put a trace on. Guppy, being on the front line, got all the blame, and he was sent to work at the carwash with no pay, this being one of the Boss Man's money-laundering operations. Disgruntled as he was, he still knew it was the best of two reprisals—the other being a bullet in the head. Now, the latter looked as though it was on its way. He knew who had the Barton couple, but he didn't know where. The abductor was demanding more money, and Guppy had given this guy all he'd gotten from Lorinna and the sale of his car. He was left with two options. One was to find Lorinna and get more cash out of him before killing him. The second was to contact this guy and get Barton's parents and somehow abduct the couple himself and take them to the Boss Man.

Pulling up the collar of his padded jacket against the driving rain, Guppy headed for the mall car park, hoping to find a vehicle that would be easy to nick. For normal jobs, he would ask Boss Man what car he could use. Not this time. He was on his own and would get no help to achieve what he had been ordered to do. What inspired him was the impending killing of Lorinna; it was this smartly dressed skunk who had landed him in this situation. A bullet in the head would be too good for the creep—too quick and possibly painless.

Abruptly, Guppy stopped in his tracks at the sight that confronted him. The old clapped-out Fiat he had given to Lorinna was being hoisted onto a loader. Had it not been for the registration, he wouldn't have recognised it; this was the only part of the vehicle that was unburnt. A crowd had gathered to spectate the difficulty the truck driver was having getting it lifted off the ground. It seemed that, when the overhead grabbers gripped it, the roof came apart and was dangling precariously over the cabin of the truck.

Deciding he had seen enough, Guppy edged his way past the crowd and pushed himself through the revolving glass doors into the mall. Again, he stopped suddenly at another shocking sight and darted into a shop doorway. Lorinna staggered towards him, being pushed from behind by a huge guy Guppy put down to being a pro. Boxer or something like that. Lorinna's hair was flattened as though he had been dipped into water. Both shocked and surprised, he guessed the big guy behind was Barton. Now he had two fish with the one hook, which was more than he had wished for. But this created another problem. He knew, if he had to get more money from Lorinna, he would have to separate the pair. And if he was to dump Lorinna's body in the Bartons' backyard, he would have to find a way of distracting the big man.

It was, he had been advised by his doctor, a nervous affliction, and until he could control this, there were no cure. When Guppy got excited, he became overwhelmed by constant sneezing. This was what caught Lorinna's attention when they passed the shop doorway. He noticed Lorinna fake a stumble in the hopes the big guy would be distracted from the disturbance he was making from his affliction. It didn't work, for with a quick glance, he saw Barton glance in his direction as well. Unperturbed, the big man followed up behind. Could this be to his advantage, he pondered as he watched them arrive at the revolving glass doors.

She stood chatting to a group of youths, a beautiful girl, well dressed, with a good figure. The idea struck Guppy. He fumbled in his pocket and dug out his mobile. "Hi, Charlie," he said into it. "I need a favour."

Charlie was the manager of one of the brothel's Boss Man owned. "I need one of your girls for a few hours, the best-looking one if that's possible."

—〰—

With a grip on Lorinna's jacket collar, Barton pushed him backwards through the revolving door. He had covered the pistol with a large tissue and was holding it an inch from Lorinna's nose. "Don't be a smart arse, if you want to live another minute," Barton whispered hoarsely into his face. "Who was that guy sneezing in that shop doorway? You seemed to have recognised him judging by that look you gave him."

Torrential rain hit them when they got through the door. Barton released his grip and pushed him forward.

"I don't know. Never seen him before. It was the noise he was making that drew my attention," Lorinna replied, hunching his shoulders and tilting his head against the wind-driven rain.

Barton quickened his pace and pushed him against the nearest wall. Holding him firmly by the shoulders, he dug the butt of his pistol into Lorinna's shoulder and, with his face a few inches away, shouted. "My parents have been abducted, and I know that you are involved. That's why you sold your car—to get the cash to pay for a pro. To do the job for you."

Shaking his head and flickering his eyelids to ward off the rain, Lorinna replied, "Dream on, you stupid bastard. You've been watching too many movies."

That comment got him a knee in the groin. Barton's temper flared at that moment and he couldn't control the outburst. If he hadn't been holding him, Lorinna would have bent over in pain; instead, he screamed. In case pedestrians were close enough to hear, Barton glanced around and was relieved to discover they were alone in that area. It was a mistake, and Lorinna took advantage of the distraction and managed to drop below Barton's grip.

The round smacked into the wall at the exact place where Lorinna's head had been. The stone shrapnel hit Barton's hands, and he was forced to drop the weapon. Being an ex-soldier, his natural reaction was drop to the ground, where he managed to retrieve the weapon and noticed Lorinna scrambling along the dark narrow lane.

Crawling on all fours, Barton managed to reach the end of the wall and take cover. That was when the second shot sounded, like an echoing clap of thunder. Again, he ducked lower and soon realised the shot hadn't been fired in his direction. From where he was lying, he couldn't locate which direction the shots were coming from. He could only guess it was somewhere close to the mall doors. That being the case, surely, this would have attracted attention from the few youths hanging around in there and patrons heading for the clubs. Wherever it was it had to have been close for the shooter to have taken a bead on his target through this wind-driven rain, as visibility was only a few yards.

Realising he had to make himself scarce and hoping Lorinna hadn't been shot and wasn't too far away, Barton slowly got onto his feet. He kept to the shadows with his head down against the wind and rain and made his way in the direction Lorinna had taken.

No other shots had been fired by the time he had reached the end of the lane, which could mean two things. One, Lorinna had been shot. Two, the shooter had lost him as well. Barton hoped for the latter. He needed to know where his parents were, and this was the only person he knew who could help.

The sound of someone breathing heavily from behind made Barton crouch down on one knee once more. His hopes were that this was Lorinna. But the figure that appeared from out of the rain was of a heavily built man with a shaven head, his wet baldness reflecting a distant light at his back. In this poor visibility, the only thing that would give you away would be movement. In times like this, Barton appreciated his military training. As the figure passed, Barton could have reached out and touched him. He resisted and let the man pass before jumping at him, swinging an armlock around his neck and forcing him to the ground.

The strength of the man shocked Barton, and he had to hit him with the butt of his pistol before the man lay still but conscious.

"What do you want?" the prone figure said.

"For a start, your gun," Barton shouted.

"I don't have a gun."

"You're a bloody liar, you just fired two shots at me." Barton stood up and to the side of him, his weapon trained on the man's head. "I'll count to three. If you don't hand it over, you're a memory."

Trying to supress the sneezing and, at the same time, pulling the gun from his hip pocket, Guppy cried, "You're that crazy son Boss Man was talking about."

Barton kicked the gun out of his hand. "Who's paying you?"

"Nobody's paying me."

"Don't give me that shit. Somebody must be paying you for you to risk firing off shots in a public area."

Failing to supress the sneezing, Guppy fell into a fit and rolled over, burying his face in his hands. This continued for a lot longer than normal. The more he sneezed, the more he panicked. It was the hard kick to his ribs that brought him to a sudden recovery. He rolled over to his original position and looked up at the big man holding both the guns on him. "Honest, man, I'm not being paid."

"You're a lying shit," Barton shouted. "Who's this Boss Mann you're talking about?"

"I don't know his real name. He's the man in charge and high ranking in the local mob."

"How do I get to him?"

"You don't want to know."

Another kick landed, this time to his shoulder. "I do want to know. I'm sure he's responsible for the abduction of my parents, and you and that other sleazebag are working for him."

Attempting to get up, Guppy said, "I don't know of any other sleazebag's involvement. But I can assure you, as far as abducting your parents, I'm ignorant." He had successfully managed to get onto his hands and knees when he felt the kick on his rump that sent him back down on his face. His reactions were slow when he attempted to get up again. That was when he the muzzle of the gun jabbed into the back of his skull.

"If you were a cat," Barton snarled at him, "your number nine life would have just been called in." He was about to hit Guppy with the butt of his own pistol when a mobile sounded. "It looks like you are an exception and have a number ten." Barton frisked in his own pocket and discovered that it wasn't his mobile but the one the bald man on the ground had in his jacket. "Pull it out nice and slowly," Barton warned, giving the gun another jab, "and put it on speaker."

The voice sounded loud and clear from the mobile, saying the arrangements had been sorted. "When and where, let me know," the voice concluded.

"I have to take this," Guppy said. "it's a funeral arrangement for a close relative." This was a lie Guppy had used many times, and he had it perfected down to the sad expression.

"OK," Barton said and took a step back but let him know the gun was still trained on him.

Guppy, with his mobile at his ear, gazed at the guns pointed at him and said into his phone, "I'll call you back later."

It took all Barton's willpower not to pull both the triggers. Instead, he landed another kick into Guppy's groin. "I warned you not to piss about with me." Barton watched as the bald man crouched over in pain, holding himself between his legs and howling in agony. And at the same time, the sneezing started again. "Normally I would advise you to get the sneezing fits seen to," Barton continued. "But if I don't get honest answers out of you, you won't live long enough to suffer it much longer."

Holding his face and groin, Guppy tried to crawl away. But Barton soon kicked him over onto his back. "Give me more info on the guy you called Boss Man."

"Honest, man, I've told you all I know about him." Guppy gasped between sneezes and throbs of pain.

"Who's that guy you tried to shoot? What's he called?"

"Lorinna," Guppy hastily replied, remembering he had been ordered to kill the creep. *So, what's the difference if someone else kills him?*

"As you seem to know his name, I must assume you both work for this Boss Man?"

"You've got it wrong, man. I don't work for anyone. And I don't know who Lorinna's working for."

Barton's earlier concerns came to light. Someone had reported gunshots, and now the police cars came screaming down the wet windy street. Consideration for this bald goon was the last thing on his mind as he pelted up the dark narrow lane. A six-foot brick wall faced Barton. He knew he could scale it quick enough. What was on the other side might be a problem. Having no time to worry about it, he scrambled over.

CHAPTER 12

Guppy wasn't so lucky; he couldn't get his legs to move fast enough because of the injury to his groin and didn't bother to resist when the constables dived on him. The sneezing fit began to such an extent that his nose began to bleed. "Thank you very much," Guppy shouted at the officers. "That man was about to mug me; he punched and kicked me." He held out his bloodied hand and sneezed in the face of one of the officers.

"You'll have to come with us, sir," one of the constables said. "We will take you to a hospital and get you looked at. And if you're fit enough, you'll have to accompany us to the station and make out a statement."

"Is that really necessary? He didn't get anything, thanks to your rapid response."

"I'm afraid it is, sir. Gunshots have been reported in this area a short while ago."

Putting on his shocked expression and shaking his head, followed by a few sneezes, he replied, "I never heard anything. Do you think it could have been that mugger?"

"We're not at liberty to say, sir," replied an officer as Guppy sneezed on. "So, if you'll come with us, sir, we'll soon get it all sorted out."

Bundled into the back of the police van, Guppy was taken to the nearest hospital and later released with a bottle of painkillers. In a cell in the police station, he was strip-searched and interrogated. After two hours of intensive repeated questions, he was released and had to give the police his address, should they want to question him further. After collecting his belongings, he stood outside on the steps of the station and phoned Charlie at the brothel about the girl.

Everything was beginning to fall into place. Guppy picked up the girl at the arranged meeting place, and she was now walking by his side, heading for his house. She was, in his opinion, a very attractive woman. Now, all he had to do was somehow get her and that big guy with the tied-back ponytail together. He was certain Barton would be as taken in by her as he was. In the meantime, he was planning to spend some good hours with her at his house.

71

His plans with the woman weren't going the way he expected. She wanted paying to service him and paying for the man he was trying to set up with her. Guppy had to pay the last of the cash he had screwed from the sale of Lorinna's car. She was complaining that Boss Man wanted recompense for the lack of earnings she would have brought in at his brothel. The words *Boss Man* brought on a few sneezes, and Guppy had no other choice but to hand her what cash he had—which she complained wasn't enough. He assured her he would sort it out with Boss Man.

He was awakened by the sound of the shower in the next room. When he turned, she was gone. He quickly jumped out of bed and dashed into the bathroom, stripped off, and got in beside her. He soon jumped back away from the spraying water. "That's as cold as ice," he complained.

"I love a cold shower first thing in the morning. Gives me an appetite for breakfast," she replied with a giggle.

"What's your name?" he asked after they had dried off, and he was sitting on his sofa in the living room dressed only in a towel.

"Just call me Mandy. That's all you need to know," she said unwrapping the towel from her body and drying her hair with it.

Guppy couldn't resist reaching out for her, but he wasn't quick enough, and she stepped away, saying, "You've had your money's worth. Now, tell me about this guy I'm to entertain?"

He described Barton as a tall good-looking muscle-bound guy with jet black hair tied in a ponytail. "You'll like him, but you mustn't mention me or any connection with Boss Man's organisation. All I want from you is to distract him long enough for me to do another job. And for fuck's sake, don't tell him you're a whore."

"When and how do I meet this guy?"

Looking confused and holding up a finger at her, he replied, "When, I'm not sure. But you must act like it was all by chance. Try and let him make a move on you first. If that doesn't work, you can use your tarty charm on him."

She slapped him with the towel. "For that nasty remark, you can make or buy me breakfast."

"I don't cook. And you have all my cash, so you'll have to treat me."

She stood up, turned, and trotted to the bedroom, shouting, "Get dressed. Let's go find a burger bar."

Guppy was glad she was paying. She downed three burgers and two cappuccinos. He could hardly finish one burger. "When you're finished, we need to go out and find this guy."

She almost choked on the last dregs of her cappuccino and nearly toppled the sugar bowl. "Are you telling me you don't know where this guy is?"

Standing up, Guppy jabbed his thumb at the girl at the till. "Pay the bill and let's get started."

Mandy remained seated. "If you think I'm traipsing around in all that rain, you can think again." Her blue eyes stared daggers into his.

From a neighbouring table, Guppy lifted a steak knife, darted around the table, grabbed her arm, and held the knife to her neck. "Fucking move your arse."

"I could scream," she cried.

"Try and I'll slit your throat."

Following her out, Guppy replaced the knife and held onto the arm of her leather jacket, steering her towards the mall.

"Do you even know where this guy lives?" she said, trying to free herself from his grip.

"It wouldn't make any difference if I did. The house he lives in is crawling with coppers. He's not going there."

"That's fucking great. You want me to entertain a criminal?"

"You work for a criminal," Guppy snapped. "And most of the men you fuck are in the same league."

"I hope you have a car," she moaned. "I can't walk far in these high heels."

"I have. It's at the other end of the mall in the car park." Her heels were very high. They made her look inches taller than him. "Why didn't you bring more sensible footwear?" Guppy got no reply from her as he pushed her through the revolving glass doors. "I've described to you what this guy looks like, so keep an eye open for him. He could be in here somewhere."

Mandy stopped and glared at him, waving her arms around. "The fucking place is crawling with people. How are we going to spot him in here?"

Taking another grip on her arm, Guppy swung her around, pushing her on. "Just keep your eyes open. We might get lucky."

"Yes, and we might win the lottery," she said, stumbling forward.

"And you might survive, if you don't shut up."

"What's to stop me from shouting for those two security officers?" Mandy said over her shoulders.

Guppy chortled. "You do that and you're in for a shock. They work for Boss Man."

"You could ask them to keep an eye open for this big guy."

"They already are. But we can't ask them. They don't know we work for the same organisation, and it would be too risky to let them know."

Shaking her head, Mandy stumbled through the shoppers when she felt a vice-like grip on her arm, felt herself being pulled into the doorway of the gent's toilet. "What's going on now?" she cried.

"Shut your mouth," Guppy snarled. He nodded his head at a shop a short distance away at the other side from where they stood. "That's him standing over there."

Mandy followed his directions. He was a big guy, a good head taller than most of the pedestrians around him. Satisfied with his looks, she brushed her fingers through her hair, pulled a small mirror from her pocket, and corrected her make-up.

"You need to keep him occupied for the next twelve hours. I'll phone you when I've done the job."

"Don't bother," she replied. "I'll not be in a hurry to get away from that big, gorgeous brute."

Admiring her as she strutted towards Barton, he wondered how she was going to approach him. Guppy was surprised when she pulled out her mobile, holding it towards Barton. He guessed she was saying she had lost the signal. And could she borrow his to make an urgent call? Clever girl, he decided. But then, she was a whore. She'd have rehearsed that move many times.

<h1 style="text-align:center"><u>CHAPTER 13</u></h1>

Barton wasn't sure whether he was searching for a living Lorinna or his dead body. He remembered that last shot must have been aimed at the guy. Barton had checked the bald man's weapon and found only three rounds in the magazine and one up the spout, in a magazine that was designed to hold ten rounds. It seems that bald head had been busy. Barton had been searching the area for hours and couldn't find any trace of Lorinna. Finally, he gave up and decided he needed sleep and would resume the search in daylight. Discomfort had been a part of his past life in the special forces, so sleeping rough wasn't a problem.

He was wrong. Sleeping on a park bench resulted in stiff limbs and spine. *Must be getting soft in my old age.* He grumbled as he walked about trying to get some life into his leg muscles and arching his back. Soon, the hunger pangs began, and he started searching for an early-morning café. The only place that could accommodate him was in the mall. In his wrinkled wet clothing, he was reluctant to go there—could attract attention he didn't need. He would just have to take a chance at going to his parents' house. There, he could get something to eat and fresh clothes. *Maybe after all this time, the police will have left*, he reasoned.

Knowledge of his local area played a vital part, as he arrived a few streets away from his childhood home. Two streets away from it, Barton walked along until he arrived at the narrow lane, now used by residents for pulling their wheelie bins out to the front door. The lane continued to the next street all running parallel with each other. At the end of the final opening, he could observe his front door. Although he was expecting as much, it still came as a shock to see a police car parked there. As he was about to backtrack, a familiar face appeared from around the corner, almost colliding with him. Barton instantly got on the defensive, knowing that old Josh from two doors away from his parents' house and a lifelong friend of his father would get inquisitive, wanting to know what was going on with his old mate. Barton got the first words in. "Why are the police still parked at our house?"

With his index finger, Josh pushed his flat cap back on his head. "I think it's for security. The door are unlocked. They won't want anybody getting in on their watch." The oldster glanced around at the patrol car and then back into Barton's dark brown eyes. "What's been happening? Rumour has it that Tom and Jean are away, and a burglar tried to get in when the house was empty."

Shrugging his shoulders, Barton replied, "Well, you know what rumours are like." For a long moment, he gazed into Josh's old blue eyes and finally said, "Do you think if I gave you the keys, they would lock the house up. Tell them they're your keys, and you would want them back, as your friends who live in the house trusted you with them when they are away. If they agree, get them back to me. I'll hang around here." Barton dug the keys out of his pocket and held them over.

The oldster shrunk back, "I don't really want to get involved, Richard. But as a good friend of your dad's, I'll do it."

From his position of concealment, Barton watched the old man talking to one of the policemen through the driver's window, noticed the keys being handed over. A minute later, the officer in the passenger's seat got out, entered the house, and stayed inside for what seem like hours. When he returned, he locked the front door and gave Josh the keys.

Following a hot bath, clean clothes, and a quick sandwich, Barton was heading back to the mall in search of both Lorinna and the bald man. The wind and rain had passed over, and in spite of his concerns, he quite enjoyed the walk. Shoppers were out and about, some rushing, others mingling at the shop windows. He decided to mingle and was standing at a jeweller's. This window offered a good reflection, as the background had been dressed in a black curtain, and he didn't need to turn to see what was going on behind him. A blond woman dressed in black leather jacket and trousers with a white blouse headed in his direction. Nothing out the ordinary in this place; it was the way she caught his eye through the reflection and headed straight towards him, holding his gaze. At first he resisted turning, until she spoke directly at his reflection in the window.

"I wonder, could you please help me?" she said holding out her mobile. "I think my battery has died on me, and I need to make an urgent call."

Looking into her wide-set blue eyes, he also took in the perfect profile of her face, made up to a professional standard. In her long fingers, she held her phone. Barton couldn't resist taking in the sheer beauty of her body inside the clinging leather suit. He couldn't hold back the grin that dawned across his face and instantly rummaged for his mobile, handing it over to her.

Her fingers lingered when they touched his as she took hold of his mobile. She returned his grin, exposing a set of pure white teeth. "I could murder for a cup of coffee," she said.

Barton took a step closer. "Funny you should say that. I was just feeling the same way." He took a quick glance around him. He was getting the feeling this could be a set-up, but he could see no accomplices or pimps hanging around. In the end, he resigned himself to thinking that prostitutes seldom operated this early in the day. "There's a nice coffee shop just along the way if you don't mind accompanying me," he said and watched as she fumbled with his phone. As they headed for the coffee shop, he gave her some instructions on how to make her call on his device.

It was one of those common self-service establishments often found in shopping malls. She selected a seat as Barton carried the coffee cups, placing one in front of her. "So, what's your name?" he asked, settling on the chair opposite her.

"Mandy," she replied, taking a sip from her cup with one hand and, with the other, sliding his mobile across the table towards him.

Looking into her blue eyes and admiring her beauty, Barton couldn't help but surmise what her next move would be. "Are you a local lass?" He was thinking that, within the next few minutes, she would get up and excuse herself, saying she had to go to the ladies. There she would phone her pimp or accomplice. *All guesswork from experience.*

"No. I live in the city," she replied, smiling. "I was staying with a friend last night, and she had to go to work, so I have all day to kill."

"How do you plan to do that?"

"Just do a bit of exploring—some window-shopping, you know, looking for places of interest. I've never been in this town before."

Barton couldn't hold back the grin that dawned across his face, thinking, *She's good. Must have had some acting experience in her past.* "I've a few spare hours today. Maybe I could be your tour guide.

She returned his smile. "That's very kind of you, but I wouldn't want to impose," she said, drinking the last from her cup.

"You wouldn't be imposing. I was wondering, like you, how I was going to pass in the hours." This wasn't panning out the way he had anticipated. Maybe he had judged her wrong.

She stood up, looking down at him.

"You seem keen to get started," he said, getting up and joining her.

"Why waste time? There must be a lot to explore."

She hooked her arm around his as they walked through the mall. "Where do you live?" she asked.

"I was brought up here, but I moved away," Barton said. "I'm here visiting relatives. I will have to book into a hotel." *Why play hard to get?* he ruminated with a wide grin he made no effort to hide from her.

And she made no effort to act ignorant of his intentions, pulling his arm in closer.

She stopped, pulled him back by his arm, and looked up into his brown eyes and asked, "Where have you parked your car?"

Taken by surprise by her unexpected question, Barton averted his eyes, saying the first thing he could think of, "It's in getting repaired had a bit of a fender-bender this morning."

She frowned, her grin faded, and she carried on walking, pulling him along with her. "Do we need to get a taxi to the hotel you were thinking of booking into?"

"I'll book into the Grand Hotel on Market Street," Barton said, pulling his mobile from his pocket and thumbing in the number. "It's only a short walk from here." She reasserted her arm around his, edging her body closer as they walked out the doors of the mall. It entered his thoughts to ask her how much she was about to charge for the night in the hotel, but he held back, giving her the benefit of the doubt. He couldn't shrug the thought that this was somehow a set-up. The puzzling part of it was, what was there to gain from it and by whom? Could it be in some way connected with the abduction of his parents?

The girl at the reception desk of the hotel gawked at the way Barton paid for the room; she was so used to being handed a credit card. He could feel Mandy's eyes on the bundle of notes as he peeled off the amount the receptionist asked for. He imagined Mandy's brain churning like a calculator, working out how much she could charge.

"Is your luggage out in your car?" the receptionist asked.

He shook his head and took the key from the girl. "It's OK. We'll collect it ourselves later," he assured her, taking hold of Mandy's arm and leading her to the stairway.

The receptionist grinned, watching them climb the stairs and thinking, *Yes. I know what she'll be collecting later*. She giggled and returned to her computer.

Mandy darted into the toilet the moment he opened the door. Barton creeped close to listen if she was making a call, but all he heard was the toilet flushing. A moment later, the door opened, and she flung herself onto the king-size bed, kicking off her high-heeled shoes. Barton gingerly strolled around the bed to the large bay windows. Being careful not to stand too close, he glanced down to the street below. Cars and buses passed. Pedestrians were dressed in heavy clothing against the gusting wind and rain, heads bent forward, some fighting with umbrellas. He couldn't understand what made him look towards the corner of the red brick building at the other side of the street and a few yards down from where he stood.

For a fleeting moment, their eyes met. And simultaneously they took a step back, not wanting to be spotted. But Barton knew he was too late and guessed that the figure in the grey jacket felt the same.

It came as a relief to discover that Lorinna hadn't been killed, and at the same instant, his temper flared, thinking this was the creep behind this set-up with this woman. He turned to see Mandy sat up on the edge of the bed looking at him. Barton jumped at her, at the same time pulling his Glock pistol from his inside pocket. Jamming her down on the bed with one hand on her throat and the other holding the weapon against her forehead, he shouted, "How much are you being paid?"

"I don't know what you are talking about," she yelped. "Nobody's paying me. I just wanted to spend some time with you. I liked the look of you and fancied my chances with you."

"Give me your mobile," Barton demanded, releasing his hold on her throat and stepping back but still holding the weapon on her.

Reluctantly she pulled it from her hip pocket and handed it over.

After a brief inspection and trying it out, he tossed it back at her. "There's fuck-all wrong with the battery. So, who's the guy behind this set-up?"

"I've tried to explain," she said, flicking her blond hair away from her face with a long finger, "I'm here with you only because I fancy you."

Grabbing her by the arm and dragging her off the bed, Barton pushed her towards the window. "That guy in the grey jacket standing at the corner of that building." Barton pointed a big hand in Lorinna's direction. "Is he the guy paying you?"

After a quick glance at the man looking up at her, she turned and shook her head. "I've never seen him before."

"Lying bitch," Barton growled at her and threw her back onto the bed. "Stay there till I get back."

He took a last-minute look at her to convince himself she would stay before he darted out the door.

"Is there a back way out?" he asked the girl at the reception desk.

She jabbed her thumb towards the door behind her desk. Barton slid past her, finding himself in a short corridor and a fire exit at the end. This led him to a small car park. A quick jog past the vehicles, and he was out on the back alleyway that led him to the main street. He was lucky enough to come out opposite to where Lorinna stood. Assuring himself, he dug his hand into his pocket, feeling the Glock. To his advantage, the traffic had slackened off, and mostly buses past. He dodged his way across a short way up the street from his objective. Following behind a man with a large umbrella and keeping his head behind it for cover, he finally reached the corner. But Lorinna wasn't there.

There were two places he could have gone. One, he might have headed into the hotel. Or, two, he could have fled up the narrow street. Chances were he could have spotted Barton. Deciding on the latter, Barton quickly pranced in that direction; two youths led by a big dog sidestepped out of his way. He slowed down and asked them if they had noticed the guy, giving them a quick description. The one holding onto the dog's lead nodded his head towards the end of the street. Waving his thanks, Barton continued his run.

The lane ended at a T-junction. Barton stopped, looked in both directions, and saw no signs of life. It was now down to the flick of a coin as to which way to go. He had turned to his left, hoping he had made the right decision, when a dull thud sounded from behind. He dropped to his knees, knowing what that sound meant—had heard it many times—a handgun shot. It didn't sound too far away. But because of the poor visibility and the wind direction, he couldn't make a judgement as to the distance and only a guess as to where it came from. On hands and knees, he crawled to the nearest wall. Slowly standing and keeping his back tightly against it, he edged his way to where he thought the shot had come from. He held the Glock pistol ready to fire at arm's-length.

It hit his eyes like ice-cold water, blinding him for a short moment. He instantly knew it couldn't be a car headlight; the lane was too narrow. Barton sank to his knees again, watching the powerful beam dancing towards him in the grey evening light. In his military past, his first reaction would be to knock that light out, and he almost did just that. But at the last moment, he resisted, realising this was a different situation. He didn't know who was behind that beam of light. It could be some innocent guy out searching for his cat or dog. The beam stopped and was aimed at something lying on the ground close to the high brick wall that ran all the way down the lane. Barton could now discern the figure behind the torch and also a group walking up behind. It looked as though the full local police force was cramming into the narrow lane.

From the time he had heard the shot, Barton was shocked at the quick reaction of the police—unless for some reason they were already at the scene. Whatever it was lying on the ground, it seemed to be taking up all the attention from the circle of uniformed officers. Taking advantage of this distraction, Barton crawled back the way he had come, knowing it would only be a matter of minutes before the police started searching the length of the lane. The last thing he needed was. to get caught and searched carrying two handguns.

Getting back onto his feet when he reached the main road, he glanced back, expecting a few of the officers to be heading his way. This wasn't happening. It then struck Barton that the item they were flashing the torchlight at could have been a body. Thinking that it could be Lorinna, Barton soon legged it back to the hotel.

He entered again by the back door and was relieved to discover the receptionist wasn't at her desk. Maybe she'd gone to the toilet or for a break. He silently climbed the stairs and entered the room, expecting to see Mandy sitting on the bed or lying sleeping.

She was neither on the bed nor was she sleeping on it. Her body lay on the floor at the side with her legs still up on the duvet. The carpet where her head lay was a mass of blood; her wide-set blue eyes stared lifelessly at him. His first thought was to get out of here and fast. But first, he needed to get rid of any evidence of himself being here. While searching the room, another troubling thought struck him. The girl at the reception would be able to identify him and give a good description.

CHAPTER 14

"What the fuck has happened to you?" Boss Man shouted at Guppy. "Did you manage to waste Lorinna?"

Shaking his head, Guppy replied, "I took a shot at him. He was with that big guy, Barton. I missed because the big guy pushed him out of the way at the last minute."

"So where is Lorinna now?" Boss Man demanded, banging his fist on the large table and making the glass that sat in front of him jump.

"I took another shot at him, but I don't know if it hit him."

"I hope it didn't hit Barton; I want to see that bastard suffer before I put an end to him."

"The man I hired to grab his parents still has them. I don't know where, and he won't disclose that information, as he says, for security reasons. I can tell by Barton's actions that he's searching for them."

"According to the info I've been getting about Barton, he'll find them. And if that happens before I've finished with him, you're a memory."

Guppy knew this was no idle threat. He had been with this strange little man for many years and knew that he himself was walking on a wobbly board. He had made up his mind that, if he was at risk, he wanted to know why. What had this man Barton done to Boss Man for him to go to all this trouble and expense? Easing himself onto the nearest chair, Guppy cleared his throat. He could feel his nerves building to the edge and hoped the sneezing wouldn't start. "If you don't mind me asking," he said and almost regretted saying it, "why go to all this trouble for a big bum like Barton?" A long silence followed; Guppy couldn't hold back the sneeze.

This was nothing new to Boss Man. He had been expecting it, and he waited until Guppy got settled. "It's a long story. I'll tell it to you when I finally deal with Barton. Your priority now is to kill Lorinna and bring Barton's parents here to me." He stood up and slid one of the vehicle keys down the table. "Don't be getting stopped for speeding or bumping another car."

Guppy, in his nervous state, was too late to catch the keys and had to pick them up off the floor. His eyes followed the little man as he left through his private entrance at the far side of the room. Guppy edged his bulk through the main door, leaving it open as per normal instructions. Outside the rain and wind seemed relentless, and he was glad to get into the big black four-by-four Range Rover, letting his condition get back to normal. Mandy the prostitute had secretly sent him a text informing him where she and Barton were. He knew the hotel well, had in the past had an affair with one of the staff. In that time, he had visited his lover on several occasions. She was now drifting somewhere in the river in a strong plastic bag with heavy rocks to keep her company. Guppy remembered the layout of the rooms and how to get in the back entrance and where it led.

The woman at the reception desk had her back to him focused on the computer monitor. Guppy withdrew his handgun from its handmade holster, smashing the butt down on the back of her head. He was surprised that no blood splatters sprayed back at him or the surrounding area. Her head had slumped forward onto the screen. Gripping her underarms, he dragged her into the nearest toilet, shutting her into a cubicle. His next problem was the prostitute hadn't given him the room number. His luck was on his side. The first two rooms were vacant. On his next attempt, Mandy lay on the large bed.

She jumped up and threw her legs over the side of the bed, her wide-set blue eyes gazing at him. "What are you doing here?" she cried with a nervous grin.

"Just checking on my investment. Where is he?"

"He rushed out after he spotted a man down in the street. I think he went down after him. He thought he was connected to our arrangement."

"How did Barton get to know about our arrangement?"

She shrugged her shoulders. "I don't know. I think he guessed it was a honeytrap or something."

"This man down in the street, did you get a look at him?"

Standing up, Mandy shook her head. "Not really. He was in the shadows across the street. All I could see from here was the grey jacket."

Striding towards the bay window, Guppy stared out at the street below. After a while, he turned back on her. "Show me where this man was standing."

She joined him, pointing to the corner of the building. "Down there,"

Barton must have identified the man in the grey jacket as Lorinna; that would be the reason for him to rush out. The spot the prostitute had identified was just over a street width away. And if he'd failed to catch

Lorinna, Barton could return at any moment. The thought suddenly struck him. He knew a good way to get back on the good side of Boss Man and, at the same time, land Barton in the shit, resulting on the big ape getting a long stretch in the nick. He could smell Mandy's perfume, stirring up the old emotions he hated. This was when he lost control. A sideward glance at her shapely body clicked the switch. And before he realised it, he was on top of her on the bed, ripping at her underwear.

Mandy fought him all the way through the session. And at the end, he stood over her feeling disgusted both at himself and her. Guppy quickly pulled up his trousers, reached for his jacket, and pulled out the handgun. And from three inches away from her beautiful face, he pulled the trigger. He pulled her partly out of the bed so her blood would run onto the carpet. Before he left, he cleaned his prints from the door handle and the weapon and planted it under the bedside carpet beneath her body.

Now came the tricky part—getting out of the hotel without bumping into Barton, should he return. He descended the stairs, cursing at himself for not planning this out beforehand, this being the reason he always got into trouble with Boss Man, his always acting on impulse.

Approaching the rear door, Guppy froze. The brass handle twisted. Luckily, he was level with the ladies room, where he had dumped the receptionist, and was inside with the door closed when he heard footsteps on the laminate floor enter and slowly walk past. He didn't need to glance out to know this was Barton. Here he stayed, holding his breath, trying not to sneeze until he heard the big guy enter the reception, before he slowly crept out.

Guppy drove the Range Rover for a few miles before stopping and dialling 999, informing the operator that there had been a break-in at the Grand Hotel. He went on to inform her that he had heard what he thought could have been a gunshot. Pulling away and grinning, he knew his timing was spot-on. The coppers would arrive just after Barton made his escape, not giving him time to clear away any traces of him having been in that room.

Now that Barton had been sorted out, all Guppy had to do was find Lorinna, in the hopes that Barton hadn't found him first. He guessed the big guy wouldn't kill Lorinna, thinking he wanted more information from the man in the grey jacket.

Parking the big four-by-four in the mall car park, Guppy decided to walk back to the hotel and to the area where the whore had pointed out was the last place she'd spotted Lorinna. He had taken the same route that Barton had previously and came out across the street from the place Mandy had pointed at. He didn't need to cross the street to see it had been cordoned off with police tape, and he noticed a female officer standing behind it. His feelings at this scene were mixed. Had he underestimated Barton, thinking he didn't want to kill Lorinna? Maybe it was accidental, leaving his body lying up that narrow road. If that was the case, then it would save him the trouble of dealing with Lorinna. On the other hand, what if Lorinna had killed Barton? If that was what had happened, then Boss Man wouldn't be happy, and Guppy knew his days would be numbered.

—〽—

Lorinna was alive and sneaking his way to the hotel. He had seen Barton crossing the street and heading his way, and without hesitation, he ran up the dark narrow road. Cautiously, he passed a group of youths, one holding a large dog. They were attacking another youth, all of them wielding knives. The man on the ground couldn't put up much of a fight.

When he reached the main street, he had to dart into a shop door when a convoy of police cars came charging up to the end of the narrow road. There were four cars in all and a van. A squad of armed officer debussed and ran towards the area of the assault.

In case someone had noticed him coming out of the road, he certainly wasn't going to hang about for a pedestrian to point a finger at him. The front entrance to the hotel was facing him across the other side of the street, and he soon found himself climbing the few steps to the glass double doors. The reception desk was facing him, and he was glad no one was behind the desk. As he looked around, he was equally pleased no other guests were occupying the area. At the top of the stairs, he noticed that one of the room doors was slightly ajar. Again, he scrutinised his surroundings before heading for that obvious room that he guessed would be occupied by Barton and the woman.

With the toe of his shoe, he pushed the door open. The lights were still on. The room seemed undisturbed—until his eyes fell on the bed and the girl lying half-naked on the floor with only her legs on the bed on top of the duvet. The carpet where her head lay was covered in blood and what he thought could be part of her brain. Lorinna cautiously backed his way out the room and was downstairs and on the street and just managed to get a safe distance when another convoy of police cars pulled up in front of the hotel doors.

Taking all his willpower to dampen the urge to run, Lorinna thought it would be wiser just to mix in with the spectators that had suddenly appeared. They all watched as armed officers in body armour charged up the steps and barged through the glass doors. The excited pedestrians around him started talking. A man behind him said he thought he'd heard a gunshot. That was no surprise. Lorinna remembered having heard it himself but, at the time, thinking it was a long way off.

Wedging his way through the crowd, Lorinna decided the safest place to be at this time was his bed-sit. It could have been paranoia setting in when he decided to take the long way back, in case he was being followed. He had followed Barton and the girl and had stood outside the coffee shop, waiting for them to appear. When they had, he'd tailed them to the hotel. What hit him as being strange was that feeling he got after he had shadowed someone—the burning at the back of his neck, making him think he himself was now the prey. Every few steps he took, he stopped and glanced over his shoulder. When possible, he would dart into a darkened doorway and wait to see if his pursuer would pass.

At the sight of the doorway leading to his bed-sit, the tension drained from his body. He could feel his shoulders relax and drop. At the door, he chanced one more search of the street. All seemed clear. Nobody was in sight. As he climbed the stairs a figure appeared standing at the top looking down at him. Lorinna froze midstride, with one foot in midair preparing for the next step when the small figure jumped down on him.

Although the youth was a lot lighter than Lorinna, the momentum of his body landing on Lorinna sent them both careering down the steps. Luckily, when they landed at the bottom, the bigger man was on top. The blade in young Andy's hand flashed in the dim bare-bulb light above. His knife hand was free, and he stabbed it into the nearest flesh point on the bigger man's shoulder. For a short moment, it didn't seem to have an effect, and Lorinna managed to land a solid head butt on the youngster's nose.

Soon, the effort brought excruciating burning pain, forcing Lorinna to roll off the youngster. His hand went naturally to where the pain was coming from, and he felt the knife was still imbedded in his shoulder.

Holding his nose with his blood flowing though his fingers, Andy scrambled to his feet, snatched the knife out of Lorinna's shoulder, landed a kick to the bigger man's ribs, and shouted, "You got me into a lot of trouble, you bastard. I should slit your throat. If I had held onto that mobile, I would be dead." The youngster jumped back at the sound of the older man's painful howl. It reminded him of a film about wolves he had recently watched on television. Certain that someone must have heard, Andy jumped down the rest of the stairs and scrambled out the door.

Like squirts of water from a child's water pistol, Lorinna's blood sprayed the stair carpet and the surrounding walls as he staggered to his feet. Pressing his hand tightly onto the wound, he lumbered his way to his room using his uninjured shoulder against the wall for support. The key slipped from his blood-soaked fingers a few times before he finally got inside. His eyes were slightly out of focus, and the furniture started to spin around. His mind was still intact, and he realised that, if he didn't do something to stanch the blood, soon he would slip into unconsciousness and possibly never waken.

Three blood-soaked bath towels lay at his feet as he sat on the bowl in the toilet. The only person he could think of who might help was Guppy. The screen and the finger pad on his mobile were covered with his blood, and it took him a long, frustrating, and painful time to finally operate it successfully. But Guppy wasn't answering.

Voices from a long way off sounded with an echo. At first, he couldn't comprehend what was being talked about. After a few painful manoeuvres of his body, he became fully aware. It was a woman's voice, saying, "I heard an awful cry and saw the yob rush out the door. I ran over. The door was open when I entered. I noticed the blood on the walls and carpet. When I got in here after following the trail of blood, I found this man unconscious on the floor. I called an ambulance."

If the female got any response from whomever she was talking to, Lorinna never heard it. The next thing he realised was bright lights shining down at him, sending searing pain into his eye.

"Are you awake?" came a softer younger female voice.

Fighting to get up against restraining hands, Lorinna cried, "Where am I?"

"You must lie still. You've lost a lot of blood," another voice came, this time from a male.

Lorinna couldn't make out the features of the faces looking down at him for the bright lights above them. "How long have I been here?"

"Not long," the same man's voice said. "You were brought in a few hours ago. We had to give you a blood transfusion. You were lucky we got to you in time. Now you have to lie still for it to be successful."

"When you feel up to it, the police would like to interview you," the female said.

A burst of panic rushed though Lorinna's entire body at the mention of the police, and once again, he tried to get up. As with the previous attempt, he was held down. "I don't want to involve the police. It was a domestic squabble that accidently went wrong."

"You have to explain that to them," the female voice said, sounding sympathetic.

"I'll inform them you are well enough to talk to them." The man's voice came from a distance.

"Can I have half an hour to get my head clear, so I can give them a more accurate account of what went down."

"I'll see what I can do," the man replied.

Closing the room door behind them, the man and woman in green hospital uniform left, Lorinna's eyes following them until they disappeared from the window on the door. With his uninjured arm, he lifted the bed covers to see he was only wearing a white gown. The room was small and sparsely furnished, with only a single chair and a small bedside cabinet. Judging by the size of the cabinet, his clothes wouldn't fit inside it. Hoping that the male nurse was successful at getting him time to get out, he first had to find clothing. Not much chance of clearing the hospital grounds wearing only this gown.

Expecting shooting pain to attack his shoulder when he sat upright, he was surprised to feel nothing. It was when he felt a jagging sensation from his injured arm that he discovered he still had a drip attached. This, he decided, could be the reason for the lack of pain, and it had to go. Better the pain than face the police.

He found it painful removing the drip from his arm—to the point where he almost passed out. Aware that time was running out, he rolled off the bed onto his feet. At his first attempt to stand, his legs wabbled, and he fell back, sitting on the bed. The room began to spin. Closing his eyes and supporting his head on his good arm, he sat there unable to move. He could feel himself slipping into unconsciousness.

From somewhere at the back of his mind a flash appeared, jolting him out of his delirium, and he made another attempt to stand. This time, his legs held his weight, although a slight spinning was present when he made to move. In three stumbling steps, he came against the door. His injured shoulder bumped against the wooden frame. Stifling a scream, he felt his eyes flood with tears. He was fumbling for the handle when it opened before he could get a grip.

Standing in front of him framed in the door were two suited men, both wearing a grin that didn't reach their eyes. Lorinna knew he had played right up their street by trying to escape, giving them the excuse to hand out the rough treatment. A hand shot out, sending him stumbling backwards onto the bed. This time, he didn't attempt to stifle his scream when he fell on his injured shoulder.

In an instant, footsteps could be heard trotting along the corridor. He heard the two men hastily close the door from the outside. Through tear-filled eyes, Lorinna looked up at the nurses, seeing them shake their heads. "Those two clowns dived in here and drew me out of bed," Lorinna cried, before they had a chance to enquire if he was OK.

Having been settled back into bed and the drip reconnected, he listened to the argument that was taking place outside the room. Lorinna guessed it was between the nurses and the two suited men who he guessed were detectives. Pain shot from his shoulder as he risked a glance through the window to a grey overcast morning; well, he hoped it was morning. He lay naked in the hospital gown and had no inclination of what time or even what day it was.

<h1 style="text-align:center"><u>CHAPTER 15</u></h1>

Relieved to see that the girl at the reception desk hadn't returned, Barton made a hasty exit through the main doors. Standing at the same place where Lorinna had stood, he glanced up at the bay windows of the hotel and noticed the lights had been turned off. He couldn't remember doing that, and he quickly he darted into the shadows of the high brick wall. The hotel front door was directly beneath the window, or he wouldn't have noticed the bald stalky man jump down the steps and rush up the street in the direction of the mall. It didn't take Barton long to recognise who this character was and decide to follow.

Adding the situation up as he chased behind the bald man, he remembered the shot he'd heard earlier and having thought it had come from somewhere at the end of the narrow lane. Could that have been the shot that killed the woman calling herself Mandy? Barton held back when he noticed bald head enter the mall. It struck him then that this guy must have been in that hotel at the same time as he was. Could he have been hiding in another room?

Waiting behind a crowd entering the mall, Barton, like the rest, turned when the sound of police sirens blasted up the street, and the vehicles flew past. "What now?" a man behind asked. Barton could have answered but didn't and carried on in through the revolving glass doors.

It felt good to be inside, away from the wind-driven drizzly rain. Barton stopped to wipe the water from his eyes and face. Bald head was nowhere in sight among the pedestrians drifting in and out of the shops. Barton gambled; bald head would have continued all the way through to the exit at the other end and would be in a rush when he heard the sound of the sirens.

Darting out the automatic electric doors at the end of the mall, Barton paced across the slabbed area that led to the busy street. He remembered there was a large car park a few yards to his right and headed in that direction, thinking this would be the obvious choice for someone trying to get away from a crime scene.

The police were having the same thoughts as Barton, a group of uniformed officers were patrolling the car park. Barton reconned the bald man would have noticed this and about-turned. But where would he be heading? was the question. Behind, car brakes screamed from the street, and in a natural reaction, he turned to see the bald man run across, narrowly avoiding being hit by a taxi.

Guessing bald head must have his vehicle parked here, Barton decided to loiter about and wait for him to pick it up. The officers were looking rather bored, and one was smoking profusely, tossing his cigarette ends into the bushes that surrounded the periphery of the parking area. Fortunately, Barton happened to be looking in the right area, or he would have missed the slightly built youth stroll through the entrance. Even at that distance, there was no mistaking Andy Milton, the thief the hoodie had paid to plant the pistol. At that same moment, one of the constables identified him as well and shouted to his fellow officers, and they charged. It struck Barton as being strange, for the last time he had seen the youth, he was being thrown into a vehicle by two dark figures. The other confusing thing was why the youngster didn't run—didn't seem to react or try to fight back when the policemen grabbed him.

For a while, things went quiet after the youngster was escorted back the way he had come. Barton scoured the car park from his concealed place behind a bush and could see no law officers, only a few families carrying bags to their cars. Again, he struck it lucky by looking in the right direction at the precise moment. From behind a family car, the bald head appeared. He charged at the woman driver as she was loading her groceries into the boot of her car and pushed her to the ground, scattering vegetables and tins on the tarmac. The woman screamed, picking herself up and pointing to her car that was now racing out the entrance. Bald head must have gotten her keys to have got that car started in such short time. This confused Barton— *unless*, he wondered, *the engine was already running.*

In a minute or two, this woman would be on her mobile, and the police would return. She would report to them what had happened. This might cause some excitement with the officers, and Barton decided to make himself scarce. Keeping his head down, he made his way through the shrubs and was soon on the solid footpath, making his way back to the mall. The drizzle had now become wind-driven heavy rain. He quickly darted through the automatic electric doors to get out of it. Wiping his wet face and jacket with his hands, he noticed the two security officers heading towards him. Barton caught their eyes and put on a grin. *Tweedledee and Tweedledum,* he mused.

"Excuse me, sir," the tallest of the two said. "You can't get out of the exit at the other end. The police have it cordoned off."

"Why? What's happened?"

"An incident of some sort," he replied.

Although Barton knew what the incident was, he still asked, "What kind of incident?"

The shortest of the two stepped closer, exposing a toothless grin and replied, "Did you not hear that gunshot?"

"I thought that was a car backfiring," Barton replied over his shoulder, walking away and mingling with other shoppers—in case they began to remember him from their last encounter. It soon became obvious that they did remember when he noticed them following behind him through the reflection of a shop window. Barton stopped, turned, and faced them. "What?" he asked, spreading his arms out in front of them. He could sense people staring and stepped into a shop doorway.

The officers followed in beside him.

"What is it now?" Barton shouted at them.

The short toothless one's eyes were looking in all directions. And finally he said, "We thought you might want to know something that might interest you."

"What might that be?"

They hesitated and looked around again. Then the tallest officer held out a hand, rubbing his fingers against the tip of his thumb.

Barton got the message and flicked out a twenty-pound note. "What's this important subject you have that I need to know?"

The finger rubbing began again. The tall officer shook his head. "Not enough."

This time, Barton handed them two more notes. "This better be good," he warned.

His companion grinned again and said, "Two plain-clothes coppers asked us if we had seen you. They had a photo of you on their mobiles. So, you can cough up some more of those notes—if you want us to act ignorant."

Barton put on a wide grin. "We lost radio contact. They're my colleagues. We were ordered not to use our mobiles for security reasons."

Toothless grinned again. "That's shit, man. You bribed us. That's not the way coppers work. That has to be unethical and downright illegal."

"Let me see your ID," his companion interrupted.

"I don't carry ID. I'm undercover. So, you two can think yourself lucky for trying to blackmail a law officer. That could land you with a few years inside. So, if you want *me* to act ignorant, you can hand me my money back. And after this operation, I might even forget about this little incident." Barton could see they were unconvinced and shouldered his way through them out of the shop doorway. "OK," he said over his shoulder, "if that's the way you want it. When this is over, I'll come looking for you two."

Not wanting to go near the police cordon, Barton headed for the door he had come in. As he waited with other pedestrians for the automatic doors to open, he felt a hand clasp his shoulder. He glanced at the big hand and restrained himself from grabbing it and twisting it under and around its owner's back and then landing a good hard punch to the back of the neck. He half turned instead and came face to face with a long-forgotten fellow soldier.

"I wasn't sure if it was you," Ex-Sergeant Marvell said. "I noticed you walking from that shop and had to make sure." With a wide grin, he held out his hand. "Good to see you again, Richard. Maybe we could get together for a drink."

Returning his grin, Barton noticed a change to his features but, at that moment, couldn't work out what it was. Feeling his strong grip on his hand, he replied, "That would be good, but don't talk about our time in the regiment."

"It was the long hair tied up in a ponytail that made me doubt whether it was you or not."

"I wanted to change everything that reminded me of the horrors I witnessed and took part in when they threw me out of the regiment. I let my hair grow, let the stubble take away that military look, wore leathers, and rode big bikes for a while."

"It didn't work though, did it?" Marvell replied with a grin. "And it never will."

Releasing his hand, Barton looked closer into Marvell's eyes and noticed the change. Although it was a good likeness, there was no mistake his left eye was false. The only way to tell was, when he moved his other eye, the fake one didn't follow. Not wanting to offend by staring at it, Barton quickly changed the subject. "What have you been doing with yourself?"

"Not long after they chucked you out, I got medically discharged." He pointed a finger at his eye. "Shrapnel. Civvy street did me no favours. I couldn't find any decent work, just labouring on building sites or cleaning out shit houses for the council, sometimes working in hotel kitchens—anything to stay alive. How about yourself? What have you been up to?"

Taking a step back Barton, smiled and said, "Give me your number. I'll give you a call, and we can arrange to meet for a drink. I need to get going —have a meeting shortly." He held out his hand, and after a shake, they exchanged mobile numbers and parted ways, walking off in different directions.

He felt quite hurt for leaving his friend in such a manner, but Barton had decided there and then this was for the best. He didn't want Danny Marvell finding out about his criminal involvement. He couldn't resist a last-minute glance back at his old friend entering the automatic doors. Maybe it was his paranoia kicking in at the shock of seeing Marvell talking to the two security officers. The body language they displayed made Barton think they were familiar. The moment all three of them turned and looked at him, he knew he was the topic of their conversation. Putting his paranoia aside, Barton began to wonder if Danny was some kind of supervisor over them. He certainly looked the part with his pinstriped suit, white shirt and tie, with highly polished black shoes.

The scent of Danny's aftershave still lingered in Barton's nostrils as he pushed his way through the wind-driven rain. Crossing the road to where he had parked his car, he hid behind the same shrubs as before. The place where his vehicle should have been was now occupied by another car. It was difficult to tell if the police were still patrolling the car park. Torrential rain made visibility almost imposable from his position. All that was left for him to do was to creep around the periphery keeping behind the bushes, so as to be certain the constables had gone and taken his car to the compound.

They stood under a tree at the gate with their high-vis, rainproof jackets fastened up to the neck. Had Barton taken another few steps, he would have stumbled into their field of vision. He dropped to the wet ground, and on hands and knees, crawled back the way he had come. But he'd only gotten a few metres when the shot rang out. He froze, lying still and listening for a reaction. It came from the direction of the car park gate, a loud scream. Barton raised his head to see one of the constables staggering against his companion and then falling at his feet. Another two shots blasted in quick succession, and the other constable fell on top of his mate. Carrying two weapons, the last thing Barton needed was to be caught there at the scene of the shooting of two policemen. Barton hastily made his way through the shrubs and out onto the road.

Panic was a sensation Barton had been trained to control, and he was glad of that as he calmly walked along the road. At a time like this, the weather played to his advantage. Very few people were walking about, and motorists would be concentrating on looking ahead, peering through windscreen wiper blades that would be franticly fighting to keep the windows clear. As he reached the mall, doors the sound of the emergency vehicle rushing to the scene stopped the few shoppers as they gasped at the sound.

At the other side of the glass doors stood the two security officers Barton had nicknamed Tweedledee and Tweedledum. Not wanting to be spotted by them, Barton stepped into the nearest bus shelter. From here, he knew he could observe them without their knowledge. The idea hit him—if he could somehow separate them and with a little roughening up, he might get to know the connection between them and Danny Marvell. He noticed an elderly couple approach them. The woman was pointing in the direction of a shop across from where they stood. And after a brief conversation, they all headed for the shop. This scenario gave birth to an idea. All Barton had to do was hang about until the problem at or in that shop was rectified.

The minutes passed slowly before the two officers reappeared at their usual post just inside the doors. Barton's plan may cost him a few of the twenty-pound notes. But what the hell? They weren't his in the first place. He needed two girls to pull it off, and this took a further ten minutes before he decided on this duo; they would have to be together. Finally, he made his choice, not that there was much to choose from in this weather. The giggly teenagers agreed readily when he showed them the money. He briefed them on what they had to do and promised, if all went well, he would give them more cash.

Timing was the essence of the plot. He eyed the first girl's approach of the two guards. A moment later, the other girl came on the scene. Perfect. Barton smiled to himself as one officer rushed off to the toilet, and the other came barging out the doors heading towards him.

Barton let this one run past, before he rushed through the glass doors and headed straight for the toilets, where he bumped into the other officer coming out. A two-handed push to the chest landed the man on his arse. Barton dived at him before he could recover, lifting him up by the collar of his uniform jacket and pushing him into the nearest cubicle. The officer screamed, but a good hard punch to his groin soon shut him up. Barton grabbed him again and sat him on the toilet seat. He drew his pistol from the back of his belt and pushed it against the officer's nose. "I'm going to ask you a question that I already know the answer to. I want confirmation from you. If what you say differs from that, then it's goodbye planet Earth.

He gazed up at Barton through tear-filled eyes. "What is it you want, man? I don't know if I can answer any questions. I just work here for a shit pay. I know nothing," he replied, raising his arms.

Pushing the barrel harder into the man's nose, Barton forced the guard's head against the cistern. "What's the relationship between your company and Danny Marvell?"

"No relationship that I know of."

"Bloody liar," Barton shouted, clicking off the safety catch.

"Honest, man. I don't know," the officer cried, whimpering like a wounded dog.

He prided himself for his superfast reactions. And yet, it all happened so unexpectedly that it shocked Barton, to the point where all he could do was lie there doubting what his own eyes were taking in. The cubicle door had burst open. The figure in all combat clothing had jumped over Barton, pushing him between the bowl and the wall. The flashing of the blade caught his eye. Barton held up his gun-holding hand as protection, fearing he was about to become the victim when the knife slashed at the guard's neck twice in both directions.

Before Barton could react, the figure was out the door and could be heard running along the corridor. With a last look at the guard to see if he could do anything for him, Barton realised the man was choking on his own blood. He had seen this before and knew the man had only a few seconds left. The last thing he wanted was to be discovered by the other officer or a member of the public. He hastily made to chase after the figure when he kicked something against the guard's foot. With the shock of seeing the bloodstained knife, Barton could feel the hairs on the back of his neck rising.

Charging out the cubicle door, Barton almost collided with a woman pushing a man in a wheelchair. Her eyes widened with shock, she was and on the point of screaming. Realising he was still holding the gun, he pointed it at the woman. This made her gulp back her scream and buckle at the knees, where she fell down behind the wheelchair. He left her there and charged on, hearing the man in the chair shouting abuse at him.

At the end of the corridor, he made a quick left turn and crashed into the other security guard, who seemed to be rushing to find his colleague. Barton pushed him to the side with a swipe of his arm and received a barrage of curses as he ran towards the entrance. He had a bit of luck when he approached; the door was open, giving him time to get away before the woman with the wheelchair and the other guard sounded the alarm.

In his hasty escape, he hadn't noticed the group of policemen standing talking close to the bus shelter he had previously occupied. They were in conversation with a couple of suited guys Barton guessed were detectives. This confirmed his suspicions that now the search was on, and he was the fugitive.

In a sudden burst of speed, the constables and the suits rushed through the glass doors and barged past him, shouldering their way through the pedestrians that surrounded Barton. This was confirmation that the other security officer and the woman had discovered the murdered guard.

CHAPTER 16

The room door opened, and wearing a smile, the young nurse entered carrying a shiny steel tray. Placing the tray on the bedside cabinet, she said, "I have to change your dressing." And with a set of small scissors, she set about cutting at the bandages. After a few whimpers from him she concluded, "You should be able to get discharged today after the doctor has a look at your wound."

"Can I get my clothes?" Lorinna asked as he watched her dress his wound.

"You were brought in during the late shift. As far as I know, the police have them."

Although he could make a good guess at why the police withheld his clothing, he still asked. "Why?"

She shrugged her shoulders on her way out the door. "Who knows, maybe to find traces of whoever it was who attacked you." Without waiting for his response, she smiled and closed the door.

Taking deep breaths and trying to control a panic attack, Lorinna directed his mind's eyes to focus. When it showed him the detectives surfing through the details on his mobile and also finding no wallet or means of identification, he knew this was the reason for the rough treatment the previous evening. He remembered his last call had been to Guppy. Although he'd gotten no reply, he was sure they would be able to put a trace on it. It wasn't that he was concerned about the bald-headed ratbag being caught. Rather, it was what Guppy might reveal to them about his involvement in hiring a pro to kidnap that old couple that had him on edge.

A sharp pain shot through his shoulder when he turned at the sound of the door handle being operated. Three suited men entered. The leader, Lorinna guessed, was the doctor. He was wrong. The leader held up and ID card with a wide grin that showed an obvious set of false teeth.

"How are you feeling this morning?" the detective asked. "They tell me you should be getting discharged today?"

Gently shaking his head, Lorinna replied, "I don't know."

"Well, when the doctor says so, we will pick you up and take you to a nice comfortable interview room," one of the detectives said from behind the leader.

Lorinna closed his eyes. "Get the doctor. I think I'm about to pass out again," he said with a whimper.

"Piss off," the leader said, and all three surrounded the bed. "Now get on your feet. Or will we carry you?"

With a deafening scream, Lorinna swung his legs over the side of the bed, knocking one of the police off balance. The tubes in his arms ripped free as he dived for the door, but he only got a few feet along the corridor when his legs buckled under him. Within a second, the three men were on top of him, holding him down on the floor.

"What's going on here?" an angry male voice shouted from somewhere down the corridor.

Feeling the weight lifting from his body, Lorinna attempted to get up, but he was pushed back down.

"This is a very dangerous man," one of the detectives shouted.

"Nevertheless, he is one of my patients," the angry voice shouted, this time sounding closer.

Feeling hands gripping his good arm, Lorinna felt himself being lifted onto his feet. Next, he was being carried back into the room and placed back in the bed.

"He's not fit to be discharged yet," came the angry voice.

"Well, you'll have to put up with us until he is. Our orders are to retain him at all costs." This voice sounded from the door.

Glancing in that direction, Lorinna saw yet another suited man standing there.

"And who might you be?" asked the angry voice.

Sounds of agreement came from the detectives. "That doesn't concern you, Doctor. I'm here to make sure these officers retain this man and never at any time let him out of their sight. Only because of his injury is he not in cuffs," the figure at the door concluded.

A moment later, he slipped out the door and was gone. The officers led the way out, followed by the doctor, making it obvious that some kind of agreement had been made.

Left on his own when the doctor and the detectives were having a heated conversation outside, Lorinna decided he had to get out at all costs. He began to work out a plan, knowing it could be a thousand to one that it would work. But what else was there? Through the glass door, he noticed the doctor walk away. And to his surprise, uniformed officers were replacing the suits. Could this be to his advantage, he pondered, when and if his plan materialised?

He found it difficult to control his excitement when the young nurse walked in carrying fresh dressings for his wound. "Are the police still outside the door?" he asked as calmly as he could, trying to sound indifferent as he watched her change the dressing.

She nodded. "Getting in the way. Sitting down at the nurses' station. Drinking tea."

This was where it became tricky. He needed to know where the nurses' station was in relation to the room he was in. *Would he have to pass it to get to the door out of the ward?* How to ask her without arousing suspicion. "Now," he said, "that's a good idea. Could I have a cup of tea please? I feel very thirsty."

She stood up after finishing the dressings. "I'll get you that tea as soon as I've finished with another patient."

This wasn't working out to his satisfaction. He needed her to walk to the nurses' station so he could time her return. He also worried that the constables could have finished their drink and returned to stand outside his door before she came back with his tea.

He needn't have worried, for she was entering his room a few minutes later, saying they were having a break, and the tea was being poured out. This didn't give him much time to prepare to put his plan in motion. Stupidly, when she said she had another patient to deal with he'd relaxed, thinking he had time in hand. Now this had to be done the instant she placed the cup on the bedside cabinet. All he could hope for was that he had enough power in his left arm to knock her out with a single blow. If not, she would scream, and that would be the end of it.

With a tightly balled fist and all the strength he could muster, he struck her on the back of her neck. She fell forward onto the cabinet, the cup and saucer crashing to the floor. All Lorinna could hope for was that the sound of the crashing crockery couldn't be heard.

He sat still for a moment and could hear no reaction from outside in the corridor and set about stripping off her uniform. With the drip still attached to his arm, this made the job almost impossible with one hand. As he was about to pull down her trousers, she moaned and tried to scream, but he managed to land another blow to her head. This put her out again.

The job of dressing in her clothing became more difficult than stripping her. He had to rip the drip off his arm. Finding her size slightly smaller than his, donning her clothing proved to be an arduous task with one hand. He couldn't fit her jacket over his injured shoulder, and he had to strip off the dressing. This he used to tie her wrists and gag her mouth. She lay moaning and kicking on top of the bed when he left the room.

He stood in the doorway scanning the corridor for signs of life. He decided he had picked a lucky moment when all the staff must be busy or having a meal break. Voices could be heard from a room three doors away, and he guessed that was where some of the medical team might be. But he was concerned about where the uniformed constables were. An illuminated sign at the end of the corridor indicated that the fire escape door was around the corner and about ten paces away. Without a moment's thought, he rushed towards it and discovered it had been left open. Lorinna stepped out and found himself standing on a small metal balcony. At his side, a set of stairs led him down to the rear of the building and close to a private car park reserved for staff members only, according to the sign he passed. By the time he had reached the first car on a line of about twenty, he was drenched with the wind-driven rain. The thin material of the nurse's uniform did little to keep his body dry, this being the reason he didn't feel the blood seep down his arm and stain the trousers.

He would have loved to be able to break into one of the cars, but this was one criminal activity he had never learned. As he reached the end of the line of vehicles, he could feel his legs wabble at the knees and had to support himself against the bonnet of the last car. An out-of-focus face appeared at the windscreen. Although the glass was drenched and running with rain, he could make out the vehicle's occupant to be a blonde-haired woman. She turned her head. He heard the door open. She stepped out and disappeared from his vision. Next, she was at his side, helping him off the vehicle. Her voice sounded distant with an echo, and he heard her say something about a staff member collapsing. Could she get help?

The dark figure appeared like a dust devil; only it wasn't sand that formed the twisting shape but, rather, wind-driven rain. Lorinna's only thought was to get away, and he struggled against the woman's grip. But she held him firm until the strong hands of the ghostlike figure dragged him to the ground. "I'll handle this one," he heard the deep voice say. Next, he was being lifted and dragged by his underarms, causing excruciating pain from his injured shoulder. Across the tarmac surface he went, his bare feet painfully trailing behind.

Through his agony, Lorinna realised that the man dragging him wasn't alone, and he could make out dark figures following, forcing the blonde woman in the same direction he was being dragged. After what seemed like a half a mile, everything stopped, and he was dropped to the wet ground. Another burst of pain attacked him when the woman was thrown on top of him.

A welcoming relief came when she rolled off him, but that was short-lived when he felt himself being lifted by his underarms and feet. The metallic sound of a van door opened, and the next thing he felt was his head and body landing on the steel surface of the interior of the vehicle. Shortly after and fighting with all her strength, the woman was thrown in beside him. She was accompanied by two men who sat on the floor next the rear door that soon got slammed. Within a few minutes, the van was in motion. And by the way he and the woman were being tossed about, it was clear the driver wasn't wasting any time.

The trip didn't last long before they were being pulled out by the two men who had been posted at the doors. The woman fell face down on the rough surface of what looked like the site of derelict houses. Lorinna couldn't prevent himself from landing on top of her. She screamed and punched at him, using language that would have embarrassed building site labourers. Painfully, he rolled off her and found himself lying in a pool of water. He felt himself being pulled by the collar of the flimsy uniform jacket onto his feet, and with the woman by his side, they were being pushed from behind, heading toward an open steel-shuttered door of one of the derelict houses.

Inside, they were forced into a windowless box room with only a bare bulb for light hanging from a long flex. Two smelly armchairs faced them, which they got pushed onto, the woman facing him. The two men who had been in the van were standing at the door. Each had an assault rifle resting across his arms. Another man came from behind with a ski mask over his head and walked towards them carrying lengths of white nylon rope. Lorinna screamed, knowing this was going to be a painful experience, as the man looped the rope over his head and pulled it tight, jamming his arms against his ribs. Satisfied that Lorinna was secured, the masked man did the same with the woman, who yelled, kicked, and cursed, forcing one of the gunmen to grab her hair and pull her head back over the padded chairback.

The two men stood just outside the open door. They were smoking and deep in conversation, and soon they were joined by the hooded person.

Lorinna shouted, "Who are you what do you want? This woman has nothing to do with whatever it is."

The woman, her voice hoarse from screaming, said, "It's me they want. It's unfortunate that you were there to witness this."

—⟋⟍—

The first stroke of luck happened as Barton had crossed to the other side of the street. The youth had been walking as if he was being pursued. After every few quick paces, he'd stopped, leaned against the nearest wall, and looked around. Keeping a good distance away and still keeping him in sight, Barton had followed. Young Andy led him to a run-down street with a few houses that were still occupied. He watched the youngster fiddling with the lock on the door of one of the buildings. After a few minutes, he entered. Barton was wondering if the young thief had decided to try burglary and decided to hang about to see the results and nab him on his way out the house.

Fifteen minutes later, almost at the point of giving up, he'd noticed another man entering the house. This had made Barton's heart skip a few beats. It only took an instant for him to recognise that slim jaunty figure opening the door, this time with the proper key. Barton remained in the shadow of an empty house as Lorinna, in the grey jacket, entered. From time to time, he had to step out to make sure whoever came out of that door first didn't dart around the gable and out of sight.

It was at a moment when Barton had taken a step out that the sound like a wounded animal's howl had come from the just inside the door. And soon after, the youngster had barged out and run in his direction. Taking a quick backwards jump into the shadows, he'd watched the youth run at full pelt down the street and soon disappear out of sight in the misty wind-driven rain. Turning his attention back to the house, Barton saw a woman walk in through the open door. He knew it wouldn't be a wise move, but the urge to investigate was strong and made him start to walk towards that house. He had stopped dead in his tracks when the woman rushed out holding her mobile to her ear. He heard her yell into it, "Police and ambulance." Barton had soon retreated back into his cover.

The first to arrive had been the medical team, followed by the police. And finally after a short time, the ambulance had come screaming into the street, like the other emergency vehicle, its blue lights flashing. Deciding it was time to get the hell out of this place, he'd used the old building as cover and crept in the same direction young Andy had taken. Not being able to resist a look back before getting out of sight, he'd seen the medical team carrying a stretcher with someone on it. *Could that be Lorinna?* he had wondered as he rushed towards the town centre. It occurred to him, if that was Lorinna on that stretcher, he must still be alive. He guessed the police wouldn't let the body be moved from the crime scene.

"The nearest E & A hospital," Barton had instructed the taxi driver as he climbed into the rear seat.

All he got in response from the long-haired man behind the wheel was a nod. Five minutes later, he'd climbed out at the main entrance; he'd paid the driver, and by the time the vehicle pulled away, the entrance door had swung open, and a group of police officers had rushed out. Barton took a quick step back out of their way, lowering his head.

The uniformed officers had grouped for a few minutes before they'd split up into pairs. Barton had decided they must be on the hunt for something or someone. As it was too risky to go inside, in case more policemen were in there, he had strolled across the car park and found a bus shelter. From there, he'd observed what was happening at the front doors and most of the surrounding area without looking too suspicious, as other people were standing in there as well, maybe waiting for a bus or just sheltering out of the rain. A heavily built woman had chortled and said, "The pigs are busy tonight." Barton, like the rest, had joined in her laughter but had been more concerned than amused.

A bus crawled into the car park and pulled up at the shelter. Barton stood back to let all the occupants squeeze past. Now, he was going to stand out being there on his own—a likely suspect for an ambitious rooky. At the last moment as the vehicle started to move and the doors began to close, he jumped in. After paying the driver, he only got halfway along the passage before the bus stopped, the doors opened, and two constables entered. Barton took a vacant seat at the rear and, like the rest of the passengers, watched as the policemen walked along eyeing all the occupants, making it obvious they were searching for someone. Barton kept his head low but tried not to look suspicious. The oldest-looking constable glanced at him, held his attention. Barton's blood started to flow like ice water, and he was tempted to look away but knew that would be a big mistake. Finally, the constable shook his head and followed his companion out the doors.

The bus continued and soon stopped again. Barton jumped up and stepped out before the other passengers attempted to. It was the look that constable had given him that was now worrying him, like there had been a hint of recognition. He was taking no chances, lest the policeman were to pass on his suspicions to his superiors and that bus were to be stopped again by them soon.

Across the street where he had found himself after getting off the bus, he noticed a van parked on an open site that was surrounded by condemned houses. *Strange*, he thought, *a well-looked-after almost new van parked in a place like this.* It was the sound of a man's cry that caught his full attention. Barton had heard that sound before in his regiment days; that was the scream of a man being tortured. He began cautiously walking towards the van and had to dart into the shadows when a group of men appeared, struggling to pull a person dressed in hospital clothing from the rear doors. Following that group, another two men pulled a woman out. Then all headed towards a steel-shuttered door of one of the old houses.

That all-too-familiar metallic click rang close to his ear. Barton froze when he felt the barrel of a weapon tight against the back of his head. Holding up his arms his palms outstretched, he said, "I've no money and nothing of value."

"Just keep your hands up and follow the rest into that building," a female voice snarled from behind.

"I just got off that bus and came in here for a leak," Barton pleaded as he was being pushed towards the old house with the open steel doors.

Inside under the dim light from a bare bulb, a figure wearing a ski mask turned to the woman and demanded, "Who's this?"

"I found him hanging about at that high wall near the entrance."

"Do you think he saw anything?"

"I'm not sure," the woman replied, "but he seemed to be interested in this place."

The blue eyes peered through the small round holes on the ski mask, staring into Barton's. "What's your game, mate?" At the same instant, he brought both his hands up, holding a pistol pointed at Barton's face.

Raising his hands farther, Barton replied, "As I told this woman, I got off the bus and stepped into the yard for a leak."

"He wasn't taking a leak when I jumped him," the woman snapped, butting in. "He was standing against that wall looking as if he was taking an interest in what was going on."

Waving his gun to the side, the ski mask ordered, "Lock him in that room with the others."

Feeling the barrel of the weapon stabbing into his back, Barton was pushed along a corridor, at the end of which he saw two men standing at either side of a door. One of the men reached over and opened it. The other gripped his arm. And between him and the woman behind, Barton was pushed inside. He stumbled over a woman's feet. He heard her moan and saw she was tied to the old padded chair she sat on. Although the room was dimly lit, he could make out her features. Even with a broad strip of black duct tape over her mouth, he could tell she was an attractive and mature intelligent woman, the professional type, like a lawyer, a doctor, or an MP. Picking himself up, he saw another chair. And to his surprise, he recognised Lorinna, now in hospital attire, also tied and gagged.

"Search him and tie the bastard up," the woman demanded, the gun in her hand still trained on him.

The two men jumped on him, knocking Barton off balance, and he felt himself being pinned down on the bare floorboards. He struggled and managed to get them off, but the woman stepped over, pushing her pistol into the back of his head. He heard the mechanism being operated and had no choice but to submit.

"A bloody one-man army," the woman exclaimed when the men showed her the weapons they had found on Barton. She reached over him, testing his bindings before slapping a length of duct tape over his mouth. Satisfied, she stepped back. "Who are you? What are you?" she demanded.

Stepping closer to her, one of the men said, "He could be one of her bodyguards."

"Well, he looks big enough. And if I hadn't stepped in, he would have made short work of you two." She dropped her weapon and the two Barton had into her black leather shoulder bag and left, the two goons following.

Propped against the wall with his hands secured behind his back and his legs stretched out, Barton decided he was dealing with amateurs. In a matter of minutes, he was on his feet, using the wall to hoist himself up. Hopping over to the woman, he pushed her out of the chair, using his shoulder. She fell forward, and he placed his face close to her hands. She got the message and managed to peel the tape from his mouth. Using his teeth, he released the knot on her hands. This took time, and he was worried the goons might return before he had succeeded. She quickly got to work on his bindings, and after, that they repeated the same job on Lorinna.

Looking down at Lorinna, Barton decided he was in no condition for fight or flight and said so quietly to the woman, who agreed with a nod. Putting his ear against the door, he could hear the creaking of the old floorboards and knew this meant the two goons were standing at both sides of it the way they had been when he'd been forced to enter. With a few basic hand signals, she nodded and moved close to his side. Barton took a deep breath and heard her do likewise. His only hope was that this door was as old as the rest of the interior. With a quick flick of his hand, they both charged.

The sound of the door being blasted open was like a shotgun going off in the close confines. Luck was on their side. One of the goons had been standing in front of it and took the whole impact of them both kicking at the door simultaneously. She dived at him. And Barton, taking advantage of the surprise, soon knocked the other goon out with a good punch to his chin.

She grabbed the collar of his jacket when Barton turned to help the man in the hospital uniform. "What are you doing?" she whispered. "We need to get out of here. He'll only hold us back."

"I need to get information out of this guy," he replied.

Leaning over, she took hold of his arm; Barton took the other, and they half carried, half dragged him out of the box room. The goon who had been hit with the door had recovered. She, being closest to him, landed a kick to his groin. He doubled over and fell. This impressed Barton, and he tried to catch her blue eyes to let her know. But she was so preoccupied with getting this guy in the hospital uniform out that she didn't notice.

Dragging him along the sparsely lit corridor, they noticed a light under a door. They stopped and let Lorinna slip to the floor. Barton crept over and held his ear to it and could hear muffled voices from inside. Looking at her, he held his finger to his lips and then silently returned and took up his position on the man's arm. She lifted his other arm. At the steel door, Barton supported the man while she carefully turned the bar handle. He cringed, hoping this door had been well oiled, and the hinges wouldn't make a noise.

After only a few inches, the blood-chilling squeak of metal rubbing on metal gave them away. The door from down the corridor burst open, and a group of men rushed out. All Barton and the woman could do was drop Lorinna and run.

They soon discovered how difficult it was trying to run across what looked like a courtyard littered with debris from the derelict houses in the dark. He knew that, at any moment, shots would be fired at them the moment the goons sighted them. Gripping her upper arm, Barton pulled her into one of the buildings and steered her through to the back door and outside, where he dropped to the ground behind the remnants of a garden shed and pulled her down next to him.

"We should have kept on running," she whispered breathlessly.

"That is what they would have expected us to do." He pushed her head farther down when a sudden beam of light flashed from inside the building they had just passed through. "They must think we're hiding in one of those old houses."

She lifted her head and shook it, wiping her face. "It looks and smells like someone or a dog has had a shit here, right where you pushed my face," she hoarsely protested.

He shushed her and pushed her head back down as the beam of light danced close to where they were concealed.

After a few whispered curses, she said, "They're not going to give up until they find us."

He leaned over to her ear, "What makes you say that? They have who they were after."

"No, they haven't. It's me they were after."

Barton almost gave their position away. Amazed at what he had just heard, he unconsciously raised his head to gaze at her. "You!" he exclaimed. "Why do they want you?"

"It's a long story. You don't want to know."

"Yes, I do want to know. Thugs are out there searching for us, and they're heavily armed with intent to shoot at us on sight."

"This is not the time or place to talk about it."

"When do you intend to talk about it? We could be dead in the next couple of minutes. So, start by telling me your name and who you are."

Placing her hand across his mouth to quieten him, she pointed a finger at the torch beam approaching. They ducked down, listening to the sound of footsteps getting closer. Barton's hand fell on a short length of wood. Hastily, he picked it up and lobbed it towards the nearest building. The footsteps stopped; the beam of light shot towards the area where the wood had fallen. Barton chanced a glance and saw the shadow of a tall person heading in the direction where the noise had come from.

Jabbing his finger into her shoulder, Barton indicated they should move. She read his intent, and keeping as low as possible, they crawled from shadow to shadow. After a few near encounters with their pursuers, they found themselves on a tarred footpath. She was about to stand, but he pulled her back down. They continued on hands and knees until they came to the parked van he'd seen earlier in the courtyard of the old houses.

"That's the vehicle we got thrown into," she whispered.

"Stay here," he said, clasping his hand on her shoulder and returning her whisper. "When you hear that thing starting up, run like fuck and get in the passenger's side."

Although he'd decided his pursuers weren't up to the job, he knew they wouldn't be amateur enough to leave their van unguarded. His guess was spot-on. The woman who had crept up on him, ramming a pistol into the back of his head, sat in the driver's seat, the light from her cigarette exposing her features as she took a pull at it. A quick glance told him this was a tough woman, and he realised he would have to put all his skills into subduing her. He also realised, at the moment she thought something untoward was happening, she would immediately start that van up, and he hoped the woman he had left behind would run towards it.

Picking up a handful of small stone, Barton tossed them at the side of the van. The engine instantly fired. The distraction worked. The female driver stubbed out her smoke, and at that moment, her attention turned to the woman running in her direction. This gave Barton time to yank open the door and pull her out. A few well-placed punches, and she lay unconscious beside the front wheel. After a quick frisk, he located her weapon and jumped in beside the woman.

Through his side mirror, he saw the flashing of the torches. The goons holding them charged out into the courtyard. With the scream and smell of burning tyres, Barton made the van jump into life and was out on the busy road, heading in a direction that led he had no idea where.

The Transit van had been well looked after and serviced, possible fine-tuned, and Barton began to enjoy handling it out into the countryside. After the milometer registered five miles, he pulled into the start of a driveway. He turned on the cabin light and turned to her, looking intently into her blue eyes. "What's your name? And why are those thugs after you?"

"Jackie," she replied. "I'm a witness to a shooting—supposedly a mob shooting, according to the police."

Hoping his shock didn't reflect on his features, he had sudden a flashback of the scene—the group of girls screaming after the shot was fired, the black four-by-four rushing down the street and hitting young Andy. Barton suddenly became aware she was staring at him. Turning his head away from her quickly, he said, "What makes them think it was a mob shooting?"

"They didn't say it outright but strongly hinted, saying I should be under their protection."

"Why would the mob shoot someone in front of a witness?" He returned his attention back to her blue eyes.

Shaking her head and shrugging her shoulders, she said, "I don't know. Maybe they didn't see me sitting in my car; the lights in the multistorey car park had been turned off."

Grinning, Barton pointed his finger at her forehead. "You still have some of that shit on your face."

Using the sleeve of her brown jacket, she wiped it off. But it didn't come away cleanly, and she sniffed at it. "I need a shower," she complained. "I smell like shit and feel like it."

"I wouldn't advise you to go home. If that lot are, in fact, the mob that I know, they'll be watching your house."

She cringed back against the door. "You sound as if you are a part of a mob; I heard that woman saying something about you being like a one-man army."

His mind shot back to a few mob shootings. They always made sure there were no witnesses around. Had some goon ignored this precaution? That being the case, why had the mob just picked out this woman? *There has to be more to her story*, he decided. Putting the vehicle into gear and getting it on the move, he said, "Do you have another place where you can stay?"

"Only my parents. They live just outside Liverpool. But I don't want them involved in this. Do you have a place?

"Yes, but there's no furniture in it. I was living with my parents until such times."

"Would they mind if I stayed there just for tonight?"

Shaking his head, he glanced at her. He could only see her long blonde hair covering the side of her face and flowing over her slender shoulders. "My parents' house is also under surveillance."

She was now looking out her side window at the passing houses. "Who has *them* under surveillance?"

Choosing to ignore her question he said, "We'll have to find a bed and breakfast for the night."

"That's a bit presumptuous," she complained.

Remembering the brief frisking the thugs had done on him, Barton and was surprised they hadn't found the bundle of notes he was carrying. "I was thinking of getting separate rooms."

She turned away from the window, saying, "So was I, but those thugs took my bag with my cards and my mobile in it."

"No worries. I have some cash. Those idiots didn't go to too much trouble searching me."

"At this time of the year, I don't think there will be too many places open for business."

Completing a turn on a sharp bend, Barton had to jump on the brakes and only managed to stop a few feet from a que of vehicles.

"Now what?" he shouted.

Jumping out and prancing to the front of the van and to the other side of the road, Jackie, along with the other rubbernecks, craned their necks to see what the hold-up was. She soon darted back into her seat beside him. "It seems to be a police cordon. That man I talked to says they might be looking for someone."

In his mirror, Barton noticed all the cars behind turning around, and he followed suit. A huge road sign informed him that a roundabout was up ahead. He took the turn for Sheffield, hoping to find a place to sleep for the night.

She spotted the sign at the last moment, and Barton had to reverse to get into the small driveway. A dim light shone above the door, and another, in an upstairs front room. Barton rang the bell a few times before he got a reaction from an elderly man with a long white beard and supported by a walking stick. Before the man had a chance to speak, Jackie butted in, asking for two rooms for one night. The oldster stood aside and indicated for them to enter.

"We don't have two rooms vacant," the woman who had joined the old man in the hallway said.

Jackie nodded, "That will have to do. It's only for one night."

At the top of a narrow steep set of stairs, the woman—who, if she was the oldster's wife, must stand a good head taller than her husband (thus, giving Barton a few moments of secret humour)—had to duck her head, like him, to get in the small doorway. When she turned on the lights, he was surprised at how spacious the room was. The furniture was sixty's style with a lumpy double bed.

"Do you not have any luggage?" the woman asked.

Shaking his head and handing her some of the twenty-pound notes, Barton said, "Our van is about to give up on us. Knew we would never make it home."

CHAPTER 17

Sitting in the four-by-four playing games on his mobile, Guppy happened to look up in time to see the youngster prance past. Although he had never met the youth Lorinna described, something told him this was him. He got out of the vehicle and followed. He found this young man on the cautious side, possibly due to his way of living, always looking over his shoulder. Guppy had to stay quite a way behind, almost losing him a few times. He wanted to jump this youth in a dark and isolated area in case Lorinna's description was inaccurate. He didn't want any witnesses or to maybe bump into some of youth's mates in the area where he could be heading.

The chance came. The conditions were perfect. The youth turned into a dark passageway leading to the rear of what Guppy put down to being an abandoned warehouse. He watched the youngster enter through an open door, and without giving it a second thought, he charged into the darkness of the interior. He didn't notice the mattress on the floor and tripped and fell, ramming into the young man as he stood, trying to turn on the light on his mobile.

They lay grappling on the floor until the younger man had no more fight left. "What do you want?" he gasped from beneath the heavy body.

Getting back on his feet, Guppy grabbed the youngster's arm and lifted him up, pulling him so close his face was only a few inches away. "Where's the guy who paid you to hide that gun in the Bartons' garden?"

Smelling Guppy's breath, Andy turned his head away. "I don't know what you're talking about, man."

"You are a lying little shit," Guppy shouted, grabbing his chin and forcing him to make eye contact and ramming his head against the wall. I saw you talking to him. He was wearing a black coat with the hood up." Although this was a wild guess, he could see he had created a reaction by the look on the youngster's face. "Tell me where he is, or you're dead meat."

Andy decided this bald man was a psychopath and could feel his urine run down his legs. He knew from experience the only way to save himself would be to humour him. "OK, pal," he replied in a trembling voice, "I admit I know the man you're talking about. I found out where he lived, and I saw him being carried away in an ambulance."

"What hospital did they take him to?"

"I don't know, man. I didn't hang about. The police were involved, dozens of them."

Releasing his grip, Guppy watched the youth fall at his feet. Pulling out his gun, he pointed it at his young features. "If you're lying, you little shit, I'll find you again, and you know what will happen to you." He took a few steps back and landed a thumping kick to the youngster's ribs before turning around and walking away, enjoying hearing his youthful howls.

If Lorinna was now in hospital, any money he would have had on him would be kept in the hospital safe, along with any other valuable items, most importantly his mobile. Guppy began to think Lorinna must have been a victim of an attack for the police to be involved. He stopped at the door and looked back at the youngster curled up on the mattress. Surely, that skinny little shit wouldn't be fit enough to bring Lorinna down—unless he had crept up behind him with some kind of weapon. That being the case, then this little shit would have robbed him and could still have Lorinna's phone. He quickly dashed back in and grabbed the mattress, jerked it up, and grinned as the youngster rolled off it.

Trying to get onto his feet and at the same time screaming, Andy felt the big hands on the back of his neck pushing his face down on the dusty floor. "What do you want now? I've told you all I know."

By the neck, Guppy lifted him onto his feet like a rag doll. "No, you haven't. I think you somehow broke into that man's home and beat him up while he was asleep and robbed him." He pushed the young man towards the door. He dived forward to follow him and, again, tripped over the mattress.

Andy took advantage of this moment's delay and rushed out the door. His next advantage was his familiarity with the area, and he soon found a hiding place he'd had to use in the past to escape from his victims.

Cursing and shouting threats at the youngster, Guppy struggled to his feet and gave chase. But by the time he reached the door, his victim was gone, disappeared into the darkness of the surrounding buildings. "You little bastard," he roared. "I know you're here somewhere; I'll find you and tear your guts out."

After a brief search around the outbuildings of the warehouse, Guppy abandoned the search, deciding there were too many places for the little shit to hide. He thought it better to find out what hospital they had taken Lorinna to."

As he pressed the remote to unlock the vehicle, his mobile rang out its melodic tune. Guppy swore. He kept meaning to get that tune changed but never got round to it. He jumped in behind the steering wheel and pressed the reply, although he didn't want to hear the Boss Man's rasping, gruff voice.

"Yes, Boss Man." He said the words he'd repeated over and over again to the little man's instructions.

Knowing that it was against his instruction—only in an emergency was he to call the man he had hired to abduct Barton's parents—he did so anyway. On the third attempt, he finally made contact. "Beat up the old lady," he instructed, "not too seriously, enough for Barton to start panicking. And drop her off at her home. Keep the old man, get him to phone his son saying he has to go home and see if his mother is all right."

That sorted, Guppy started up the four-by-four and headed for the nearest hospital, which only took him a few minutes to locate. As he looked at the front entrance through the rain-soaked windshield, a big problem came to mind. Lorinna wouldn't have given his real name to the reception desk, and given the enormity of the buildings, it could take hours to locate what ward he was in. While he searched, he was sure he would be stopped by the security, and this could involve the police. And if he didn't have the name of the person he was visiting, well, he didn't want to think of the consequences.

An ambulance arrived. And an idea struck home as he watched the team wheeling a patient in through the A & E. doors. He had seen this happen before when a relative of the patient followed behind the team. All he had to do was wait until the injured person was taken to a ward, and he guessed that the ward Lorinna was in wouldn't be far from it.

After informing the receptionist he was a relative of the person who had just been brought in, he was told to take a seat in the waiting area. On the clock above the reception desk, Guppy recorded every minute and was beginning to get concerned that he was running out of time to set up the trap for Barton when he arrived at his parents' house.

The two suited men who approached the reception desk caught Guppy's attention. His instincts told him these men were police officers. Lowering his head and gazing at them through his eyebrows, he could tell a heated conversation was going on between them and the man behind the desk, although he couldn't hear what was being talked about. This scene behind the glass front of the desk went on until two uniformed constables appeared at the side door. After a few words, the suited men and the uniformed police rushed out towards the main exit.

Drawing the conclusion that only Lorinna could cause so much concern, he decided to follow. He stepped out the main exit door. It seemed luck was on his side when he noticed the police officers were having a discussion with the uniformed men standing at the door of an unmarked car. Guppy soon got into the big Range Rover and waited until they made a move. A problem emerged when the unmarked car got on the move, leaving the uniformed men making their way in the opposite direction on foot. Who to follow was his concern. Guppy knew he had little time to decide and settled on the unmarked vehicle.

Slamming on his brakes when the unmarked vehicle turned into the run-down area where he knew Lorinna lived, Guppy jumped out of the vehicle at the end of the cul-de-sac. He walked the short distance to get into a position where he could see what was going on. The street lighting was sparse, and with the drizzly rain, he had to get closer and ducked into an open doorway. For a long moment, he stood observing the movements of the two officers sitting in the car with the interior light on. A creaking sound from behind made him turn.

From the total darkness, a figure appeared. And in less than a heartbeat, he felt the crushing blow on his forehead that sent a bolt of lightning through his vision.

—␋␍—

"I'm going to dive into that bath," Jackie said, "and see if I can soak the smell of that shit off me." She picked up the few towels that had been placed on top of the bed and slipped out the door.

Getting himself settled down on the leather padded armchair, Barton nodded at her and picked up the remote for the old-style box television. The picture was grainy, and the volume was low. After a few attempts, he got onto the news channel. The schoolgirl who had been shot was still big news. The reporter was saying it was a gang-related shooting that went wrong. The police were appealing for witnesses. They were also wanting witnesses to the wounding by gunshots of two police constables in the town centre car park.

"Not much chance of them getting any," Jackie interrupted as she entered the room, wearing only a towel around her torso and carrying her clothes. "Look what's happened to me."

Surprised at her sudden entrance, Barton almost dropped the remote. "That was a quick bath," he commented with a grin, at the same time admiring her tanned body and sumptuous breasts, the white towel reaching an inch below her crotch.

She returned his grin, wrapping another towel around her dyed-blonde hair. "The bloody water was stone cold," she replied, padding over the pile worn carpet on bare feet and sitting on the bed.

"I don't mind the cold water." Barton grinned and rose from the chair, leaving the remote on the bed beside her. He stepped back, gazing into her blue eyes. "Have you used all the towels?" He reached to grab the one she had wrapped around her body, but she must have anticipated and swung her legs out the other side of the bad and out of his reach.

Standing at the other side of the bed, she giggled and said, "You'll just have to drip dry yourself."

"No way," he shouted, at the same time jumping over the bed. Managing to get hold of the towel that was wrapped around her body, he tugged. She clamped her arms around it, and they grappled until they both ended up lying on the bed with her on top. She put up a feeble fight against his grip when his arms encircled her shoulders. Looking deeply into his dark brown eyes, she knew the fight was over; her resistance was gone.

—m—

A slight knuckle knock on the door made Barton jump. She had been lying with her head on his chest and almost fell out of the bed. "Breakfast is being served," the female voice said.

Jackie pulled the duvet and wrapped it around herself but wasn't quick enough to get out of Barton's reach and he soon pulled it back onto himself. She stood naked, and the next thing his hands gripped was her arm. "Let's skip breakfast." He grinned, pulling her on top of himself.

"No," she said and rolled off him, lifting her clothing off the floor and bundling it in her arms. She skipped out the door into the toilet, saying she was starving after all that action.

Barton was up and dressed when she appeared, also dressed. "Maybe we *should* get something to eat," he said. "This could be a long day."

Not realising how hungry he was, Barton soon wolfed the food and noticed Jackie didn't try to hide her appetite. After a few cups of tea, she suggested they get on their way. To where, he had no idea. "Where do you want to go?" he asked as she stood up.

She was out the door first and quickly turned on him. "Did you get up during the night and move that van?"

Edging past her and shaking his head, he directed his attention to where he had parked the vehicle, only to see the parking space empty. Rummaging through the pockets of his leather jacket and jeans, he finally found the keys. "I think it's been nicked," he said, holding the keys in his hand. "And whoever it was must have a spare set, or the alarm would have gone off. And as we were in the front room, we would have heard it."

Nodding, she said, "I'll go inside and ask to use their phone and get a taxi."

"Whoever these guys are must have followed us here. And getting a taxi might be what they expect us to do." Barton walked out the driveway onto the road and stood there until she caught up. He pointed at a bus stop opposite them. "I wonder when the next bus will be along." He set out towards the bus stop.

"We could stand here all day," she said breathlessly after trotting behind him. Finding it difficult to spot vehicles heading toward them, Barton had to step out onto the road to see past the high conifer trees that over hung the roadside. Sometimes, he had to jump back when cars approached at speed. It was at one of those moments when the white van swerved into the bus stop layby.

Barton was quicker than the two men who got out the passenger's side, and he jumped into the shrubs, dragging her by the arm. She yelled and lost her footing, firing words of abuse at him, as he pushed her, facedown, into the long grass. But to survive what he decided would be a shootout, and he hadn't a weapon to defend himself, he had no other choice but to leave her lying there.

After struggling for a while through the thick undergrowth, he stopped to listen and couldn't hear any pursuers behind. Thoughts of leaving Jackie lying among the undergrowth pricked at his conscience. *Shit,* he cursed at himself, thinking back to his military life and how he'd sworn never to leave a fellow soldier behind. And never take the same track back to where you came from. Always use another route. That way, you wouldn't run into your pursuers if they'd decided to follow your trail. This was a motto he'd had drilled into him, and he'd lived by it.

Taking a different direction back to where he could hear the traffic, he found himself on a muddied track that seemed to be heading for the road. Although his footing was sluggish, he soon found himself at the roadside. From a short way off, her heard the sound of a heavy diesel engine revving up, and a moment later, a bus passed him. He had judged his sense of direction perfectly and knew he was only a short way from the bus stop. Walking along the grass verge, a sudden thought made him stop. If that bus had pulled out from the layby, then that white van couldn't have been parked there. Had Jackie been found and picked up and, as before, bundled into the back of it? Or had they killed her and left her body lying where they had discovered her? The latter being the case, when her remains were discovered, the old couple from the bed and breakfast could give the police a good description of him.

As the traffic sped past him in both directions, he slowly continued towards the bus stop. Because of overgrown shrubs and overhanging conifers, he stumbled onto it unexpectedly. Not wanting to be seen loitering there, he stepped back into the bushes and was about to duck down when the white van swerved into the layby. The driver's door swung open, and Jackie jumped out and waved to him. She quickly jumped in, this time on the passenger's side. In two large strides and a jump, Barton was behind the wheel, ramming the vehicle into gear and tearing off down the road, causing other road users to swerve and brake. His first glance at her shocked him. Her blonde hair was matted in blood. "Are you all right?" he asked. "What happened to your head?"

Without looking at him, she shook her head. "Those two clowns thought they were going to have a good time with me when they found me hiding behind a bush. Luckily, I had found a length of metal scaffolding pipe when I fell. When they tried to grab me, I smashed the first one on the head. He fell at my feet. The other tried to run, but he tripped over the same hole in the ground that I did, and I let him have it as well." She touched her head and saw the blood on her fingers. "That must have happened when I tripped; it's nothing serious."

"You seem to have lost quite a lot of blood." He made a last-minute turn into a narrow farm track and shut off the engine. Leaning over, he moved a few strands of her hair to the side with a finger. "That looks quite a deep cut, it might need attention."

"I'll be OK," she insisted. "Find a filling station, and I'll go into the toilet and clean up."

"What I don't understand," Barton said with a puzzled look in his eyes and drumming his fingers on the steering wheel, "is there must have been other of witnesses to that shooting. Why pick on you?"

She turned and stared into his brown eyes and, after a moment's hesitation, said, "Because I was the only witness who stepped forward with a statement." The look she saw in his eyes told her he wasn't convinced.

"I get the feeling there's more to this than you're telling me," he replied and started up the engine.

Turning her head and staring out her side window, she felt the vehicle reverse out onto the main road. She muttered, "What I'm telling you is all there is to it."

In silence, he drove, passing through numerous villages and failing to come across a petrol station. Finally, he said, "The first café we come to, I'll pull in. You can get cleaned up in the toilet while I order coffee."

"Then what?" she asked.

"I need to get back to my parents' house to see what's happening."

"I thought you said it could be under surveillance?"

"I've thought of that, and I've come up with an idea."

He pulled off the busy road at the sight of a small restaurant a few yards ahead of them and parked the van in an out-of-use driveway that led to an old church.

She struggled to keep up to his walking pace as they headed for the restaurant. "I'm going to attract attention walking into this place with blood all over my head."

"Cover your head with something," he said over his shoulder.

"Like what?"

"Like a tissue or something."

Shadowing Barton into the restaurant, she pulled the collar of her jacket up, and ducking her head, she slipped into the toilet. Luckily, it was close to the entrance, and she got inside unnoticed, while he got seated and attracted the waitress.

He smiled as she got settled on the seat opposite him, still trying to dry her hair with tissues. "I've ordered tea and sandwiches."

"I'm not all that hungry," she said, gazing round at the rest of the sated customers, with the feeling she was the centre of attraction, wiping her wet hair with a length of toilet paper.

"We couldn't just walk in and use their toilet and walk back out again."

Finishing the job on her hair, she rolled the tissues into a ball and placed it on the table. She was about to talk when the waitress approached and placed their tea and sandwiches in front of them. She thanked the girl for lifting away the rolled-up tissues and waited until it was safe to talk. "What's this idea you've come up with concerning your parents' house?"

"I want you to do a walk past. See if you can spot or hear any movement inside or near the house. I'll be concealed in a position where I can see you and spot any suspicious characters there waiting for me to turn up."

Picking up her cup and taking a sip, she looked at him over the rim. "This is getting rather complicated. Why are they watching your parents' house?"

"Waiting for me to turn up," Barton repeated.

"Why?"

"It's a long story."

"If you're expecting me to get involved, I think I've right to hear the story. And if it is the same mob that's involved, what's to stop them from jumping on me again?"

"It's obvious that the gang who grabbed you were just thugs hired by the mob. The people they have watching my parents' house are pros."

Picking up a sandwich and nibbling at it, she said, "You must have upset someone badly for them to go to all this trouble to get you?"

Nodding, Barton took a sip of his tea. "I must have. But I don't know who I've upset or what I've done."

"I think the best thing for you to do is find out the answer to both of those questions."

"My first job is to get my parents back and safe. Then I'll soon discover what it is and who it is." He placed his cup on the saucer, leaned over the table, and whispered. "Then all hell will break loose. And if you want to testify on that murder, you had better stay close to me."

"So now you *are* my bodyguard," she replied with a wide grin, remembering the words from the woman with the gun.

CHAPTER 18

Trying to appear not to be paying too much attention to the cigar-smoking overdressed man pacing the room, Boss Man sighed. "I don't know what makes you think I'm skimming some of the profits from the last five consignments. All I'm taking is my percentage."

The man stopped and leaned over the table, his chestnut-coloured skin glistening with perspiration. His deep brown eyes glaring, he slapped a wad of papers down in front of the little man. "How do you account for the six million that has somehow disappeared?" He straightened up and resumed pacing. "Creative accounting. Is that what they call it?"

Slapping his hand on the table, Boss Man stood up. "The last five consignments haven't had the same quantity as the ones before. I've contacted your bosses and complained. The word I got back was they were investigating."

The tall figure stopped and pointed at the papers. "The figures show that the consignments were complete."

Reseating himself, Boss Man grimaced. "Well, start investigating the smugglers."

"Most of them didn't know they were carrying."

"So, investigate the ones who did know."

"That's been done."

"And?"

"They've been dealt with after the second shipment showed that some of the merchandise hasn't been accounted for. I'm also informed that couriers have gone missing, and the big guns suspect they had been intercepted before they delivered, and an imposter had made the drop."

"That would account for the missing goods," Boss Man said picking up the bundle of A4 papers and scanning over the figures printed on them. He glanced up in time to see the man drop his cigar butt on the floor and grind it into the polished boards. "You ever do that again," Boss Man shouted, pointing at the smouldering ash, "and you won't get out that door."

The man grinned. "You're lucky. I usually piss on it to put it out." Before stepping out the door he turned and said, "I know you're involved in this. And when I find out how, you won't have a building left for me to piss my smoke out on." He slammed the door, the bang sounding like an explosion reverberating through the building.

In a frenzy, the Boss Man jumped up and rushed to get the door open, hating that feeling of being closed in. Getting seated again, he could feel his heart pounding inside his ribs and struggled to get his oxygen mask on. Only getting time for a short gasp, he had to take it off and hide it under the table when Guppy stuck his head in. "What the hell happened to you?" he said, pointing to the huge plaster on the big man's head and, at the same time, trying to control his breathing and breaking into a fit of coughing.

This was no shock to Guppy; he had seen Boss Man suffer like this many times and knew not to hang around. He instantly about-turned, saying," I'll come back in a few minutes."

The few minutes turned out to be nearer half an hour when Guppy walked in and found Boss Man on his feet, prancing around the long table, from time to time stopping to adjust the chairs. Guppy knew the signs. He knew big trouble was afoot and decided to stay by the door and be silent until Boss Man calmed down.

As if by the click of a switch, the little figure stopped, pivoted around and faced him. "According to those records"—his voice quivered and sounded an octave higher than normal—"nearly half of the last five shipments of cocaine has gone amiss, which is bullshit." He strode to the far end of the table and picked up the papers and tossed them at Guppy. "Find out what's going on and who the fucking informant is."

Getting down on one knee, Guppy collected the papers and placed them back on the table. "Boss Man, I thought you wanted me to get Barton's family and bring them back here?"

Aiming a small sharp finger at the bigger man's chest, he snarled. "Get them, and we'll soon get Barton. Once we've killed him, we can point the finger, saying he was the interceptor of the couriers.

Feeling a sneezing fit develop, Guppy quickly asked, "Do you think Barton is involved?"

"Of course he's not involved."

"I've set it up for him to go back to his parents' house. His mother is there now. The father's been instructed to phone him, telling him where she is."

Returning to his seat, Boss Man spread his arms on the table and said, "When Barton shows, just blow him away. The next shipment is due. Get everybody out there and make sure they're well hidden. I don't want that big bastard getting away."

Admittedly even to himself, Guppy wasn't the brightest of the bunch, but he was confused about how the Boss Man's accusation of Barton's involvement in the missing drugs would go down with the mob bosses. They would have interrogated all the couriers and would soon discover he wasn't one of them. He knew the mob's method of getting the truth, and when Barton denied any knowledge of them, a lot of blood would spill. He could see now why the little man had changed his mind. To Guppy, it was the little man himself who was the culprit. He had been ordered many times to intercept and confiscate a number of the bags and deliver them to different locations, where agents would be waiting to buy them. Prancing down the steps of the building, he shrugged his shoulders and repeated the little man's maxim to himself. *Just do and don't ask why.*

Sitting in the vehicle, drumming his big fingers on the steering wheel, he wondered why Boss Man was so obsessed with Barton. He could understand that, by eliminating Barton, he could put the blame of the missing drugs onto him. To his knowledge, it was only recently that the cartel had discovered that the shipments were being tampered with. Shaking his head in confusion, he started up the engine, intending to head for the street where the Bartons lived. After getting to know the area, he'd phone Nicholas Cartonnier, aka Knuckle Duster Nick, and arrange for a gang of thugs to meet here.

He wondered if the guys who dropped off the mother would still be with her. Guppy didn't have the intellect to know what fear meant, but this guy he had hired to abduct the couple scared the shit out of him. He had parked the vehicle up a narrow lane and confidently walked the length of the street, looking for likely directions Barton could approach from. His plan was to trap Barton inside the house, making it easier to block off any escape routes. The problem he faced now was, if that abductor was still there, how was he going to get Knuckle Duster's thugs in? The guy was a pro and would eliminate the lot of them.

As he passed by the window of the Barton house, his mobile sounded, drawing the attention of a few passers-by. He cursed at it and quickly grabbed it out of his pocket. Knuckle Duster Nick's name came up, and he reported he couldn't get a response from Barton's mobile. "We tried with all our phones and got nothing."

After an outburst of curses that only got the attention of other people using the street, making them stop and stare at him, Guppy could feel a fit of sneezes coming on, and he quickened his pace back to where he had parked the car. "Where are you all?" he shouted. "Get the fuck here pronto." Barton could be on his way here now. His next call was to the man inside the house, but he got no response.

—m—

Jumping out of a large white van wasn't a good idea in the area around where Barton's parents lived. Most of the residents would assume it was a delivery and would rubberneck to see who was getting it. Deciding to abandon the van and walk the last half mile wasn't to Jackie's approval. She complained she'd had done enough walking in the past two days. "My car is still parked at the hospital." She pointed at the large white building at the end of the road. "That should save us a bit of time."

With raised eyebrows and a grin, Barton put his hand on her shoulder. He looked into her blue eyes and noticed a hint of pain in them. "That's going to make thing easier if we need to make a quick getaway." He dropped his hand and took hold of hers, and together they started walking towards the hospital.

Sitting in the passenger's seat as she drove, following his directions, he said, "The goons who are watching the house won't recognise this car, so we can park beside the rest of the vehicles at the side of the street in a place where we should be able to see the house. After a while, if we see no movement, I'll get out and head around the back. Give me about five minutes, and then you get out and take a walk past the door, and listen for signs of life on your way past."

Walking up the back lane to his parents' house, Barton had to stoop below the level of the wooden fencing. There, he stalled for a while to listen for movement before climbing over. A quick dash up the slabbed path, and he ducked to the side of the door that led into the kitchen. With his back pressed against the wall, he sidestepped his way to the nearest window. A sharp glance through the glass proved the small dining room was clear of human life. It was when he made his way back to the door that he heard what sounded like a female sobbing inside. He stopped and hunched down and crawled his way past it until he reached the kitchen window.

Slowly raising himself a few inches above the window ledge, he almost fell backward from the shock at what he saw. She was leaning across the kitchen table her arms outstretched, her long blond hair swept over her head. The man standing behind her had a hand on the back of her neck, holding her head down on the table, and the way she struggled gave Barton the impression Jackie was being raped.

It took all Barton's willpower not to grab the pistol he had taken from the woman in the van and blast the man away through the window. Behind him, the sound of someone climbing over the fence made him drop flat on the ground. Normally, his father would have cut back the rosebushes at this time of the year. He was glad that this hadn't happened, as they gave him the cover he needed. Although there was no foliage on the bushes, they were high enough to cast dark shadows that concealed him. The idiotic head that appeared climbing over the fence wore a white baseball cap, a perfect target even in this wet misty morning.

He resisted taking the shot, knowing it would alert any other goons lurking about. Barton lay still and was glad he had done so. The white-capped figure stumbled past, followed by two others, He watched as they steadily walked towards the back door, three of them, one following the behind the other. When the leader reached the door, he gave it a gentle knock. When it opened, two entered, and one stayed outside. Barton could see this character was holding a pistol, pointing it towards the fence.

The row of rosebushes stopped short of where the man was standing by about five metres—enough open ground for the gunman to take a shot. Groping around the fallen rose leaves for something to create a distraction, Barton found a garden trowel. This he lobbed to the far side of where the man was standing, hoping he wasn't the nervous type that would shoot at anything that moved or made a sound. The trowel must have hit something metallic, and the noise made the man dart inside the door. This wasn't what Barton wanted. He was already on his feet about to charge and had to duck back down, should the others inside come out to investigate.

He couldn't afford to think of what could be happening to Jackie, knowing that it would arouse his temper, and he would most likely make mistakes. He almost did just that when he glanced towards the fence and saw two men forcibly escorting the old neighbour who was friendly with his parents. Walking them between them, they pushed him in through the door. It didn't take Barton long to guess that this oldster must have intervened, wanting to know what was going on. Halfway to the door and stepping out quickly, Barton just managed to get down far enough to be out of sight.

Two minutes of silence elapsed, giving Barton time to think of his next move. The conclusion never materialised when a scream from a female shattered his thoughts. He jumped up, the gun in his hand, and was about to rush in through the door and blast at anything that looked hostile when two of the men rushed out and began searching the garden. Lying back in his cover, he watched the searchers combing the opposite side of where he was, knowing that, within a few minutes, they would stumble onto him.

Lying in wait with the gun, he prepared to shoot his way out of this situation and maybe rush into the house, catching the goons by surprise when they were still recovering from the shock of hearing the gunshots. Realising this would need to happen in a matter of a few heartbeats, like a carnivore, he tensed his muscles set to pounce.

It came at him like a nightmare. All he could do was duck back down and try to make sense of what his eyesight was telling him. The door burst open. Jackie rushed out. Half of her clothing had been ripped off. She had only made it halfway along the slabbed path when the shots rang out. Her legs carried her for a few more steps before they gave way under her, and she fell facedown on the slabs.

CHAPTER 19

Finding himself back on the padded chair, only this time with no restricting ties or duct tape around his mouth, Lorinna could remember being dragged out by the shoulders by a woman and Barton. He guessed they had been forced to abandon him when the thugs gave chase. That was as far as his memory took him. Above his head, the bare bulb hanging from a long brown cable gave little light, but it was enough for him to take in his surroundings. The inch crack at the foot of the door illuminated the concrete floor, and he could make out a trail of blood spots. This brought on thoughts of his injury, giving rebirth to the pains from his shoulder. A glance made him cringe at the sight of the crusted blood all the way down the left side of the hospital jacket.

Loud heated voices came from a short distance. Lorinna guessed there must be another room along the corridor where the thugs must have gathered, probably blaming each other for the escape of Barton and the woman. He realised it would only be a few minutes before they entered this box room, torturing him, wanting to know where Barton and the woman would have gone. The answer to that was beyond him, but would they believe him? Somehow, he needed to get out of this place before that happened. The strong smell of urine and faeces offended his nostrils. He looked down at his crotch to see the green trousers were soaked all the way down both his inner legs. He gagged but realised this could be the reason the thugs were not coming near him. Maybe they were arguing over who was to approach him.

Easing himself up off the padded armchair proved to be painful. He could only use his right arm, and when he finally got to his feet, his legs buckled under his weight. Luckily, he managed to support himself against one of the padded sides, letting his weakened limbs get used to the burden of carrying him. This seemed to take for ever, and he was sure that at least one of the thugs would come into the room.

Slowly, he eased himself away from the support of the chair. And although his legs were still wabbly, he risked taking a gentle step. Holding his breath, he grinned, feeling his legs get stronger. He stumbled towards the door, letting his upper body fall against it. The door hadn't been repaired since Barton and the woman had kicked it in, and he felt himself falling and landing with a painful crash on top of it on the stone steps outside. As he lay there trying to suppress the yell that threatened to come out of him, all he could do was watch the door along the passageway burst open and a bunch of thugs charge towards him.

A barrage of kicks and punches came at him. This time, he couldn't suppress his yelling. Lorinna was sure they were going to kill him, and a voice inside his head told him to give in—that there was no more fight left in him, and there was nothing to fight for. A high-pitched voice sounded from a long way off, echoing along the corridor. He was almost at the point of passing out when the beating stopped.

Through a hazy double vision, a woman appeared. As the thugs stepped back; she shouted words that were inaudible, and he felt himself being lifted by many hands.

The sudden jarring of pain woke him, and he found himself back on the padded armchair. The double vision had cleared, but the haze remained. Blurred faces appeared close to him. The slap although with a soft hand, made him jerk back, sending a shock of pain that convinced him it must have given him whiplash.

"Are you with us?" a female voice asked.

His mouth felt dry. His lips were like wood. He pronounced the words but wasn't sure if they had come out.

"Who are you?" she demanded. "Why were you trying to get into that woman's car?"

He felt something cold being pressed against his mouth, and then the cold welcoming water flowed in. At first, he couldn't swallow and had to cough it out. But on the second attempt, he managed. "I don't know what you are talking about? What woman's car?"

She took away the glass. "Let me remind you," she said, handing the glass to one of the thugs. "Look at the clothes you're wearing. You're one of the hospital staff. Why would you want to get into that woman's car, unless you're her husband or a relative? And how did you receive that injury to your shoulder?"

The vision of the youth diving at him from the stairs to his bed-sit flat entered his head, and he gave her a vague outline of the event. Someone must have found me when I lay in the toilet, a woman I think it was." He went on. "The next I knew, I was lying in hospital bed."

She turned and waved the thugs out the room. Standing at the door, she said, "A very convincing story, but I find it hard to believe. I'll give you five minutes to come up with the truth. If, by then, you don't, then I'll turn my back and let the boys work on you until you do."

Realising this was his only chance of surviving, he shouted at her as she was about to turn her back and leave. "OK … OK! I'm with an organisation that deals in many illegal activities."

For a while, he thought she hadn't heard. Then after a few steps, she stopped, turned, and slowly swaggered over to him. The grin on her face frightened him. It give him the impression she had known this all along.

"What kind of activities?" she asked, towering over him, her legs between his.

"Drugs, protection, money laundering, prostitution, people smuggling—you name it, and they're into it." Drawing his legs in, he stared into her brown eyes. "Why do you want to know all this?"

Taking a step back, she held his gaze and smiled. Without another word, she turned on her heels and was gone in a few rushed steps out the door.

Worrying if he had said enough to save his life from the thugs, Lorinna decided the only thing left to do was to sit there and await his fate. Time seemed to stall, and his eyelids became heavy. He could feel himself drift into a deep sleep, and to keep this from happening, he gave his injured shoulder a twist. It worked. He let out a howl, and at that same moment, the metallic scraping of the entrance door sounded. Was this more thugs coming in? Or was it the ones who'd are already been there leaving? He wished for the latter and sat listening for the slightest sound. All he could hear was his tinnitus ringing in his head.

Guessing he must have sat there listening for an hour, and nothing in the building stirred, Lorinna decided to try to get away. On top of the injury to his shoulder, he also had to cope with the bruising on his legs and body from the beating he'd gotten from the thugs. Numerous attempts to stand ended in him falling back on the armchair. In the end, he rolled off and crawled to the flattened door. There he lay, trying to regain his breath and listen for tell-tale signs of movement.

On one hand and knees, he painfully made his way to the steel door at the end of the corridor, losing his balance and falling over numerous times. He stopped to listen close to the room he thought the thugs had occupied—and still no sign on life. Assuming they had abandoned him, he continued towards the metal exit. He came to the next obstacle he had face and cursed himself for not having thought about it. He discovered that the bolt locking mechanism that opened it was out of his reach. Somehow, he had to get onto his feet. The first attempt failed when his right arm buckled under him. Finally, by pressing his back against the wall and, at the same time, stifling his yells of pain from his shoulder, he got onto his feet, aware it was the wall that was his support. Moving away from it, he realised his legs would collapse under his weight. Judging the distance, he edged his way closer, and using his outstretched right hand, he threw himself at it. This time, he couldn't supress his scream. But he was successful at hitting the mechanism, and the door creaked open under his weight.

Lying facedown, Lorinna felt his injured shoulder getting damp and realised he must have opened the wound; he could feel the pinching of torn stitches. How to get back onto his feet faced him as one of his life's biggest problems at that moment. But soon, he discovered it was becoming the least of them, when numerous hands gripped his arms and legs. He realised he was being carried, facedown, back into the building. This time, he got dumped on the floor of the room the thugs had occupied. He knew better than to glance around at the people who had just carried him in here. It could end up being the last thing he ever did. Guttural laughter broke out when he heard one of them complaining about blood all over his hands.

"You're lucky," a deep voice shouted from the area where his feet were. "My hands are full of piss and shit from the bastard."

"We need to call an ambulance," a young female voice cut in.

"And have them bring the coppers to find us out of our box with the smack," another man shot back.

"What are we going to do with him?" the female asked.

"We fuck off, leave the bastard here. That's a hospital uniform he's wearing. If the medics come and find one of their own like this, they'll get the law involved." This came from the man with the deep voice, and Lorinna could hear footsteps rushing out the room. A few minutes later, the steel door was being closed.

"We could phone an ambulance once we're out of here," Lorinna heard the female say when he heard them outside, rushing past the boarded-up window.

Rolling over onto his back wasn't as painful as he had anticipated, and he grinned and noticed the light coming through the spaces between the boards on the window. Was this morning or afternoon? he wondered. A shadow momentarily blocked the light. Someone was still out there. He fretted and tried to shuffle himself into the darkest corner.

The steel door grated noisily open. Only three or four footsteps, he estimated, and whoever it was would be in here. Curling himself up with his good hand protecting his face, he lay there, hoping this person wouldn't enter this room. But how could they not? The door had been left open.

Gazing between his fingers, Lorinna's heart skipped a few beats at the sight of the large figure standing in the doorway. Although most of the light was from the corridor behind, he could see this man was in combat green and wearing a ski mask. Expecting to get further beatings or even shot, he braced himself and tightly closed his eyes, pulling his legs up tighter and cowering into the corner.

Time seemed to drag, and no other sound or movement came from the figure at the door. A quick glance to make sure he was still there gave Lorinna another heart-jumping fright. The figure was still standing there like a statue. "What do you want?" he managed to stammer out, and instantly regretted doing so, panicking that his stupidity could provoke the man into action. Again, he closed his eyes, expecting the worse. But nothing happened. He risked another peek through his fingers. The door frame was empty.

Expecting to hear the rusted hinges of the steel door, Lorinna began to relax. The feeling didn't last long. No sound came from the door. After some panic-induced thoughts, he worked out that the door must have been left open when the man in the combat suit entered, and he hadn't closed it when he left. This time, he didn't allow himself to relax. He just couldn't shrug off the developing feeling that this character could still be in the building.

CHAPTER 20

From his hiding place behind the rosebushes, Barton studied Jackie lying on the path, hoping to see some movement from her. As the minutes ticked by, he could see no signs of life. He wanted to get to her and check if she may just have knocked herself out from the fall. His hopes were that she could have tripped over one of the loose slabs, and the shot missed. What was beginning to trouble him, though, was why the goons inside hadn't come out to investigate her condition or to make sure she had been hit and was out of it.

His eyes darted from Jackie's body to the back door. Neither seeing nor hearing any movement from inside, he made a dash for her. Although the winter daylight was fading, the blood from her head was obvious, seeping onto the slabs and clogging the joints. He didn't need to bend closer to know she was gone.

Knowing the condition of these old terraced house—the thin walls and lack of double glazing, he knew the neighbours would have heard that shot, and the police would be on their way. This explained why the goons had never appeared to check on Jackie's body; they would be long gone by now. He knew he himself couldn't afford to hang around, but he also knew he had to get into the house.

Confident that the goons had fled, Barton barged in the back door, the weapon in his hand ready to let the lead fly if he had been wrong. Nobody confronted him in the kitchen. He met the same results in the dining room and lounge. The bedrooms were likewise deserted. No signs of the goon. As he was about to close the back door, the sound of police sirens made him run for the fence and vault over it. Dashing along the lane, he searched for Jackie's car, hoping to find it parked at the end of the street where it had been when he'd gotten out of it.

The space was now occupied by another vehicle. Maybe she had moved it closer to his parents' house in case she had to make a quick getaway? Deciding not to search further, Barton turned and headed back the way he had come. Luckily, he'd made it around the corner of the last building when the police cars came screaming in at the other end of the street.

Choosing not to run and possibly attract attention, he stopped and peeked around the corner, his shoulders tight against the wall of the last house on the block. The scene was utter chaos. Police in high-vis jackets scrambled all around the building, some running in his direction, others controlling the neighbourhood rubbernecks. Making a tactical retreat and keeping to the shadows as much as possible, he found himself at the footbridge that spanned the small stream where he had spent most of his childhood trying to fish with a long pole and string. Scrambling down the embankment, he waded under the bridge, following the flow of water and knowing he would come to the busy A580. Once there, he knew where he could buy a cheap car from a dodgy back-street dealer going by the name of Jimmy Stitch. A common slogan around the area had it, "If you want stitched up, go to Jimmy Stitch."

Being well into his sixties Jimmy's once red hair was now white and thinning at the temples. Walking with the aid of a stick, he gazed at Barton through thick-lensed glasses and grinned, exposing a toothless mouth. "What do you want?" he asked.

Holding his hand out, Barton said, "Remember me, Jimmy?"

Shaking his head and leaning closer, Jimmy gazed into Barton's brown eyes. "Memory's not as good as it used to be, like the bloody rest of my body. What can I do for you?"

"I need a cheap car."

"Like everybody else who comes here." The grin came on again, and he ushered Barton around the rear of the building. He stopped at the gate and pulled it open, saying, "Take your pick. If the law turns up, you make yourself scarce."

Parked against the back wall of the building, he saw four well-used vehicle. According to their number plates, they were each about fifteen years old. Barton walked around them, checking the tyres and the bodies and opening the doors to check on the cleanliness of the interior. Approaching Jimmy, who's eyes were everywhere, Barton jabbed his thumb over his shoulder. "How much do you want for that blue Ford?"

Jimmy took a step back and craned his neck around the corner of the building and returned with his toothless grin wider than before. "I need to get a grand for that one."

Returning his grin, Barton shook his head. "If the boot was full of cocaine, it still wouldn't be worth that."

After half an hour of haggling, Barton drove the vehicle away, watching Jimmy wave at him through his inside rear-view mirror. Parking this car near the shopping mall could be a problem, he began thinking as he headed in that direction. Remembering the constables who had been shot earlier, he figured the police would be patrolling the car park, with teams of forensic scientist working around the area. If this vehicle had been nicked, and they found it with his fingerprints all over it, they would know he was still in the area. Abandoning it the way he had with his other car was out of the question. His next concern was to get off the A580 and find a way back using the quieter routes. *Less chance of the police being on them*, he told himself.

No such bloody luck. He cursed at himself when he turned onto a B-class road and noticed a patrol car parked in a layby up ahead. It was too late to turn around. They could spot his manoeuvre, decide it was suspicious, and give chase. Checking his speed and avoiding looking at the car, he drove past. After a mile of constantly glancing in the mirrors, he relaxed, content they weren't going to come after him. His period of relaxation didn't last long when he spied a police roadblock at the beginning of a village about half a mile up ahead. In a last-minute glance in the mirror before he swerved off down a private lane, he saw the police car he had just passed come charging up behind, blue lights flashing and siren blaring.

The private road ended, and he was faced with nothing but a dirt track, which didn't do the old car any favours. Slowly, it bucked and bumped. Sometimes, he could hear the sump scrapping off the high centre between the ruts. He rammed on the brakes at the brow of a steep hill. At the bottom a metal farmers gate blocked his way. Jumping out and taking in the surroundings, Barton decided the only way out of this place would be to reverse. The high banking on both sides of the track gave him no room to manoeuvre the old car to turn it around.

He was about to jump back into the car when the sound of sirens wailing from a short way off made the decision for him. He slammed the vehicle door and, at full pelt, ran towards the gate. Jumping over it he was faced with a ploughed field. His progress was going to be slow, but that would also be the case for his pursuers as well. At the far side of the field, he noticed an old shell of a building and headed towards it.

He knew the drill, knew that the next move the police would make was to get a helicopter up. He ran through the open arched doorway of the building and came out in a courtyard. He could hardly believe his luck and wondered if his eyes were deceiving him. Parked a few yards away stood a Land Rover, its engine ticking over. Barton had a quick look around; the owner was nowhere in sight.

Expecting the owner to give chase, Barton soon got the vehicle on the move, bumping along the farm road, his foot flat to the floor. The reason the farmer hadn't given chase earlier was because he was working on the fence. When he saw and heard his vehicle come charging up the road, he jumped out, waving his arms. Without the slightest hesitation, Barton drove the Land Rover straight towards him. The man only got out of the way by a few inches.

The helicopter response was slow, and Barton was well on his way and had joined the A580, before he heard it circling overhead. The top speed of the vehicle, Barton discovered, was just over sixty miles per hour. As he drove along the dual carriageway heading east and following the signs for Manchester, a convoy of police vehicles charged up the western side, sirens blaring, blue lights flashing, and headlights on full beam. Barton counted ten in all. He could see other drivers rubbernecking, wondering what was going on. He didn't need to. His only thoughts were to get out of this area fast.

Knowing it wouldn't take long for the farmer to get on his mobile and report his Land Rover being nicked, Barton abandoned it at the back of a closed-down filling station and walked about half a mile before calling a taxi.

Giving a taxi driver a modest tip was his practice. Not giving them one would linger in their memory, and giving them too big a tip would have the same results. The last thing he needed was for this driver to remember him, knowing that the police got a lot of information from the drivers about their fares. Telling the driver to keep the change from one of the twenty-pound notes was, in Barton's opinion, modest, and he quickly thanked him and walked along the lane that led to the car park next to the mall. The lighting was sparse, and the overgrown laurel bushes offered dark shadows should he required to dart out of sight. Walking towards him was a couple pushing a baby buggy. Barton sidestepped to let them pass. The youth following some paces behind them struck a note of recognition. Barton let him pass and then followed.

It was that youthful strut that assured Barton who this young man was. He remembered it from the day Andy had walked towards that café in search of the hoodie. The last place Barton wanted to be seen was in the shopping mall. He stood back as the youngster ducked in through the revolving glass doors along with other shoppers. Guessing what the young man's occupation was and checking the time on the clock at the entrance, Barton didn't like the idea of waiting for him to return. Could be another two hours, and there was always a chance young Andy could leave by another door.

Deciding to take his chances that the security wouldn't notice him among the crowd, Barton headed for the revolving door, all the while searching through the plateglass to see if they were on duty there. The two officers he saw were strangers to him, and he confidently pushed his way through.

Not wanting to linger near the entrance and maybe get the attention of the guards, he mingled with the rest of the shoppers as they drifted along the tiled flooring. That feeling Barton had developed during his years in the regiment began to manifest. He could feel eyes on him, sending that familiar chilling sensation through his body. Although he knew not to ignore it, on the other hand, he couldn't let the person watching him know he was aware.

Strolling close behind a tall man and a short heavily built woman, he tailed them into one of the shops and stopped behind a clothing rack, where he could observe through the large window, for anyone who looked interested in where he might have gone. A female assistant disturbed him, asking if she could be of assistance. Barton made the mistake of letting himself get distracted and turned towards the young girl. It only lasted a few seconds, but in that time, the tall slim figure walked past the window, confirming he had been following the right man. Before Barton returned to continue his observations, the figure had drifted into the passing crowd.

Thanking and smiling at the girl and with a slight wave of his arm, he strolled out and joined the crowds walking past in all directions. From a distance up ahead, a female voice screamed. And like the other pedestrians, Barton stopped and looked in that direction. Next, he felt himself being transposed from all directions to the place where the scream had come from. Barton didn't resist and went with the crowd. Tall enough to look over the shoulders of most of the people in front of him, he noticed a woman bent over someone lying at her feet. "He tried to steel my bag," she shouted at the gathering. "I hit him with this ornament." She held up a metal Buddha.

Hearing the woman's confession, Barton guessed who she was referring to and was about to nudge his way out of the crowd when a group of security guards barged their way to the front. The woman stepped away, letting them take charge. "It's that thieving little shit," he heard one of them shout. Thinking one of the officers might be the mate of the one who'd gotten his throat cut in the toilet, Barton made a discreet departure through the spectators.

Not being too perturbed by young Andy's misadventure, Barton pushed his way out the door, thinking the little shit had gotten what he deserved, although it put paid to him wanting a few words with the youngster, thinking he may know what had happened to Lorinna. He hoped the youth had survived the smack on the head; it would then just be a case of finding out what hospital he had been taken to.

In a matter of only ten minutes, the paramedics rushed past Barton as he stood inside the bus shelter. It took them another five minutes to carry young Andy out on a stretcher. Barton intercepted them, saying this was his son. "Can I come with you to the hospital?"

"Sorry, sir," the medic in charge apologised. "We're not allowed to carry family in this vehicle. But we will be taking him to the local hospital, just down the road."

CHAPTER 21

This time, Guppy had company in the Boss Man's office. He walked in, followed by Knuckle Duster Nick, who, without invitation, parked himself down on the nearest chair. Guppy cringed, knowing the little man insisted he had to invite his visitors to sit before they attempted to. The sudden slapping of the little man's hands on the long table made both men jump. "Who fired that fucking shot?" he demanded.

Guppy looked down at Nick. "We think it must have been Barton."

Nick nodded in agreement.

Glaring at Knuckle Duster Nick, Boss Man shouted, "Who told you you can park your filthy arse down on my chair?"

Knuckle Duster sprang to his feet, knocking the chair backwards. It crashed on the floor. "Sorry, Boss Man," he said, at the same time picking up the chair with a mocking grin.

"Who the fuck was that woman?" Boss Man shouted, getting onto his feet.

Guppy sneezed a few times and said, when he finally recovered, "I found her listening at the Bartons' front door. Thought she might be one of the family. We nabbed her and dragged her in the front door so the neighbours wouldn't see us."

"And where was Barton while all this was going on?"

Both men shrugged their shoulders at the same time.

Slapping his hand down on the table again, Boss Man roared, "He must have been there if it was him who fired that shot. Why hadn't you nabbed him? You had enough bodies to search and find him."

Knuckle Duster piped in. "You said to nab him inside the house. We were in there waiting for him."

Boss Man pointed a gnarled little finger at Knuckle Duster Nick. "Who the fuck's talking to you, you piece of shit? Speak when your spoken to."

Knuckle Duster Nick's temper burst, and he made to jump up, his wide-set eyes blazing when the big hand from Guppy on his shoulder held him down. With a swipe of his arm, the heavy hand got knocked away, but he remained seated, drooping his shoulders and slumping back on the chair.

The sight of this rough-looking scar-faced hairy man losing his cool sent a bolt of fear through the Boss Man, and he jumped back behind his chair, his hands on the back of it ready to lift and swing it. An icy moment of silence passed as all three men gazed at each other. Finally, when they all seemed to be relaxed, he stepped away from his chair and said, "Where have you taken the old woman?"

For a long moment, Guppy looked at Knuckle Duster Nick and then back at Boss Man. "She wasn't there."

"What do you mean, she wasn't there? You said you had it all arranged."

Lowering his head, Guppy said, "I did. At least I thought I did. But that guy who abducted them didn't turn up."

Slapping his fist on the table and firing threats at them, he shouted, "Get it done today. Get onto that guy, and get that woman to that house." Letting out a deep sigh, Boss Man seemed to relax for a moment and then asked, "Have you eliminated Lorinna?" Reseating himself, he drummed his fingers on the table. He stared at them in turn. Getting no response, he said, "I take that as a no."

While Guppy had the grace to lower his head, Knuckle Duster Nick grinned and shrugged his shoulders. This, to the Boss Man, was total disrespect. He turned to Guppy, and slapping his hand on the table to get the bigger man's attention, he asked, "Do you have a gun on you?"

He grinned when Guppy nodded. He pointed a finger at Knuckle Duster Nick. "Shoot that bastard."

Gawking at the little man, Guppy said, "What? Now ... here in your office?"

Being lighter, younger, and a lot faster, Knuckle Duster Nick was up and out of his chair and running out the open door before Guppy had the chance to drag his gun from his inside jacket pocket. He made to give chase when Boss Man stopped him. "You can add that shit to your list. But first, I want you to get the old woman and put her down; that should bring her son out of his hiding place."

Replacing his gun back in his inside pocket, Guppy avoided the little man's gaze. "I don't think he has a hiding place," he suggested. "He's just one of those lucky bastards who seems to always be one jump head of us." He was about to ask the question that had been biting at him about why Boss Man was so obsessed with getting hold of this man Barton. But at the last minute, he bit his tongue, remembering the response he'd gotten last time he had asked.

"What I don't seem to get to grips with is why that woman was listening at the Bartons' door? Did you take the time to enquire who she was and what she was doing there?"

"The boys gave her a rough time, slapped her about, but she never said a word of why she was there or who she was."

"Obviously not rough enough," Boss Man snapped. "How did she manage to get away? As you say, Barton shot her while she was running up the back garden path."

"I was in the toilet when all this went down," Guppy replied, shaking his head. "I threatened to blow them away for letting her do a runner. They said Knuckle Duster Nick was trying to have a go at her, so they left him to it and went into the other room. The next thing they heard was the shot."

This time it was the side of the little man's fist that banged on the table, "I need to get this guy Barton dead, so I can point the finger at him for intercepting the drug carriers and skimming the cash."

He knew he may be taking his life in his own hands by asking, but the impulse was overwhelming, and Guppy came out with it. "Do you not think the cartel would want him alive so *they* could get the satisfaction out of killing him?"

Rubbing his hand, Boss Man shook his head. "I can't take the chance of maybe one of them believing him when he denies any knowledge of it."

The law will be all over that street where the Bartons live. There's no chance of the son turning up there," Guppy complained.

"As I've told you, get the old woman. That should bring him out in the open. I don't have much time. The cartel is out looking for blood, and in a few days, they'll come here wanting answers. If I don't come up with a believable one, I'm going to have to point the finger elsewhere."

The look in the Boss Man's eyes said enough. Guppy could feel a fit of the sneezes coming on. It took all his willpower not to grab his gun from his pocket and blow the little man away. The consequences of that were obvious. The huge black glass mirror on the wall behind Boss Man's chair was two-way. Guppy had stood at the other side of it in the past and knew that every move was being watched and every word listened to.

Amused at Guppy sneezing and the snot running down his hands, Boss Man knew he had hit a raw nerve. And he knew Guppy had witnessed the local cartel agents' method of making people talk and the slow torturous death of their victims. He lost count of how many times the big man sneezed, and soon, blood began to run from Guppy's nose. This was what he had expected. He knew Guppy's weaknesses and took advantage of them. With a wave of his hand, two goons appeared at the open door, one carrying a towel, which was instantly wrapped around Guppy's face. Boss Man smiled as the goons pushed Guppy out the door with both his big hands covering his face with the towel.

Finding himself standing on the top step of the outside door, Guppy suddenly felt the towel being ripped from his hands. The blood had stopped, and he watched the goons return inside, one holding the door while the other wrapped the towel and placed it into a plastic bag. Confused, all he could do was watch as the door was locked from the inside by one of the goons. Slowly, as he stepped onto the street, he began to put two and two together. The conclusion brought on another fit of the sneezes. He recalled hearing Boss Man saying that the cartel had its own laboratory with all the up-to-date equipment and some of the world's best scientists on the payroll. Now, he fully understood what the Boss Man had really meant when he'd mentioned pointing the finger elsewhere.

As had been the case the last time, Guppy had to make a few attempts to call the abductor of the Barton couple. His instructions were straight to the point. "And get her into her house today," he ordered before cutting the call off.

At the rear end of the four-by-four, a special metal compartment had been welded into place underneath the luggage area. Lifting the carpet and finding the sliding door, he opened it to reveal a special keypad that had been hidden in the console and punched in the code. The steel door glided open silently. Inside, all the weapons had been wrapped in soft cloth and then covered with polyethene sheets. Guppy grinned. "Now," he said aloud to himself, "the war against Barton *really* begins."

—ɷ—

One of the floorboards creaked, convincing Lorinna the man in the combat outfit was still in the building. Lowering his hands from his face, he slowly glanced around the dimly lit room and failed to spot him. Feeling his legs begin to cramp he stretched them out; something stopped him from straightening them fully. He glanced down at his feet and saw a wooden crate, roughly about four-by-two he guessed. What confused him was how this thing had gotten in here without his knowledge. He couldn't remember stumbling into it when he crawled into this corner. Had he somehow blacked out? Using his good arm, he dragged himself around for a closer look. Giving the box a push to try and judge the weight, he found it didn't move. Again, he tried and got the same result. Gingerly using his fingers, he tried to lift the lid, it moved easily, and he slid it over. He reasoned it must be made of thin plywood. Another push, and the lid slipped off the top, falling noisily on the floor. A hand shot up from within the crate, gripping his wrist. In shock, Lorinna fell back, pulling his wrist free and bumping his head on the back of one of the padded chairs. He was attempting to scramble away on his knees and good hand when he felt a grip on his legs restricting him.

With his good hand, Lorinna managed to snatch at the leg of the chair, and the pulling stopped. The grip loosened, and painfully, he managed to turn and face the person behind. At first, all he saw was a flow of white hair that reached down over a head. Suddenly, a small hand with liver spots flicked it back. Lorinna found himself staring at the face of an elderly woman. "Who are you?" he screamed, trying to scramble away from her.

Managing to get onto a seated position, he watched her stiffly get out of the crate, using the side for support. He noticed she wore was a dressing gown. "Who are you?" he asked again and wondered whether she'd heard him as she silently staggered towards the doorway. "Can you please help me?" he shouted, but he still got no response and watched her struggle over the toppled door and disappear along the corridor. In his state of confusion, it took him a few minutes to recall where he had seen this woman before. It finally struck home. He knew he had to somehow get onto his feet and catch her.

Using the padded chair for support, Lorinna got onto jelly legs and staggered towards the open doorway. He didn't make it and didn't need to. She came staggering towards him, having been pushed from behind by the figure in camouflage clothing and ski mask, who quickly followed her, his gloved hand on the back of her neck steering her back towards the crate. The man's other hand hung down by his side. Lorinna squirmed at the sight of what he carried in it—a yellow nail gun.

Propped helplessly against the wall, Lorinna could only watch as the woman was jabbed in her neck with a hypodermic syringe. Almost instantly, her body slumped, and she was bundled back into the crate like a rag doll. Next, the lid was pulled back over the top, and the figure in camo gear got to work reinforcing it with short planks that were lying on the floor. Then came the banging of the nail gun.

After checking his handiwork, the man in camo gear turned towards Lorinna, at the same time pulling a small black plastic case from the magazine pocket down the side of the leg of his trousers that Lorinna thought contained a mobile phone. He was wrong. He watched the gloved hand open the lid and pull out another syringe.

Struggling to the limit of his ability, Lorinna had no more fight. The next thing he felt was a slight prick to his thigh. In the first few seconds, he felt he was floating on air. Then he started to spin, his whole body corkscrewing down into a dark endless abyss.

CHAPTER 22

Barton decided it was too risky to try to get to young Andy. If the woman who'd knocked him out had reported the incident to the police, they would be hanging about wanting a statement. Barton was aware it was only a wild guess that the youngster was somehow connected to his parents' abduction. But even the slightest grain of info could turn out to be helpful. With his options running out, Barton thought his priority was to go back to where he and Jackie had abandoned Lorinna, with the hope the goons hadn't killed him. Jackie being their main objective, maybe they'd have abandoned the derelict estate to search for her.

Remembering it was only one stop from the bus terminal at the mall, Barton thought it best to walk and avoid the CCTV installed in the bus. By that time, darkness would have fallen, giving him better cover. Wind-driven drizzly rain had started, giving him an excuse to pull up his collar and cover his identity from other walkers. He had seen his identikit in one of the local newspapers as being wanted for questioning by the police, warning people not to approach as he could be armed and dangerous.

The walk took Barton a lot longer than he had estimated, and by the time he approached the same building as he had done previously, darkness had fallen, and visibility was down to a few feet. This time, being more careful should the goons be prowling about, he got down on his hands and knees and monkey crawled over the scattered debris until he came in sight of the steel door. To his surprise, it lay open. He began to wonder if he had been spotted, and this was a trap. Or was he being paranoid? One way of finding out. He stood up, expecting to be charged at or even shot. He stood as still as a statue, his eyes peeled and his head tilted forward, listening for signs of movement from within the building. The minutes passed, and nothing stirred. But still, he dared not relax.

As he was about to take a careful step towards the steel door, a figure appeared. The dim light from the corridor exposed the person was in combat clothing with a hood over his head, casting a sudden memory flash of his days in the regiment. Again, Barton dropped to his knees, watching the figure dragging a wooden crate out the door.

With his back to him, the figure headed in Barton's direction, Barton lay flat and rolled over behind a block of concrete. The combat-suited man passed within a few feet, dragging the crate noisily over the rough ground. Barton estimated the crate to be about four feet by two—big enough to cram a man of Lorinna's size into. Hoping he could be wrong, he lay still and let the figure disappear out of the cul-de-sac behind the first building.

This time, he ignored caution and rushed in through the open steel door. His first stop was to search the room on his left that the goons had occupied. Finding it deserted, he rushed for the one where he had been held captive, almost tripping over the fallen door. Stumbling into one of the padded chairs, he noticed a naked body lying behind it. Although he was a few yards away from the body, he could still hear rasping breathing coming from it. The first thing he recognised when he approached was the features of the man. Couldn't mistake that face when he remembered it only inches away from his in his last encounter.

Lorinna lay flat on his back with his hand stretch out, palm upwards. It didn't take Barton long to realise that Lorinna had been heavily sedated and was still out cold. Blood lay beneath both his hands, and it wasn't hard to see why. he had been nailed to the floor. Whoever did this knew what they were doing. A masonry washer had been used so the nail head wouldn't pass through the flesh.

Not knowing how long Lorinna would be out and also realising that, when he finally came to, he would be in a great deal of pain, Barton knew he would get little sense out of him and questioning him would be pointless.

He thought about the character in combat gear. He couldn't have gone far dragging that crate, unless he had a vehicle parked close by to load it into. When Barton had first recced the surroundings, he hadn't seen one. With a last look at the naked man on the floor, Barton sympathetically shook his head, saying aloud, "I'll send help as soon as I can." He rushed out the building in pursuit of the man in the combat outfit. He knew there was no chance of him being able to get the nails out of Lorinna's hands without causing more damage.

The crate had scraped a track through the rubble, and even in the dark, it wasn't hard to follow. At the end of the abandoned buildings, the trail stopped at the solid surface of the pavement. The traffic sped past in both directions. And just when Barton was at the point of giving up, a grey van pulled out of a side street a few yards away, causing oncoming vehicles to brake and swerve, horns blasting. Instinctively, Barton knew this was what the man was using to transport the crate.

A woman being dragged along by a hairy dog not much smaller than a Shetland pony came staggering towards him. Barton held out a hand to steady the animal until he got it to stop and asked the woman if she had her phone. She reluctantly nodded. "There's a man in that building." He pointed out the one with the steel door that was open. "He's in need of urgent medical attention. Could you call it in for me please?"

"I need to know what kind of medical attention," she said, pulling her mobile from the hip pocket of her jeans, "so the paramedics know what they're dealing with."

"An accident with a nail gun."

"Yuck!" the woman exclaimed. "That sounds serious." And quickly, she started fingering the digits on her phone.

He walked away, leaving the woman fighting with her dog. She wanted to stay, but the animal had different intentions. Barton darted behind an out-of-use telephone box. Most of the windows had been smashed, and he soon started gagging at the smell of urine and faeces. He decided to suffer it, hoping the ambulances would turn up soon. From this position, Barton could observe the entrance to the derelict housing estate. He grinned to himself as he watched the woman finally getting her pet seated in front of her. With a sudden turn of its head, the beast jumped up and darted in among the dereliction, dragging her with it.

Rushing out from behind the telephone box, Barton dived through the entrance to find the woman had tripped. She stood wiping her clothing and shouting after the dog. "Where did it go?" he asked.

Pointing at the open steel door, she replied, "In that old house," and made to chase after it.

Catching her by the upper arm, Barton shook his head. "You don't want to go in there."

Wrenching her arm free, she stepped clear of him and shouted, "Gilbert! Come back here."

Gripping her arm again, he urged, "You stay here and wait for the ambulance. Show them where the injured person is, and I'll go in and get Gilbert."

Surprisingly, Gilbert hadn't entered the place where Lorinna lay. He was leaning on both his front legs on a bench scarfing the remnants of a discarded pizza in the room that had been occupied by the goons. Grabbing the collar of the beast, Barton fought him out beside his owner, arriving just as an ambulance, accompanied by a police car, swung into the courtyard. Luckily, the ambulance was in the lead, giving Barton time to jump in through the nearest open doorway.

As expected, caught in the headlights of the vehicles, the police officers entered first. They wore high-vis jackets, as did the medics. The woman stood at the entrance of the courtyard, fighting to keep Gilbert from jumping up on the female officer, who Barton thought had been left behind to question her. Barton's hopes were hanging on the police not doing a thorough search of all the derelict houses as he watched them from the upper floor of the house he and Jackie had previously scrambled through.

A tall gangling medic ran out from the building and opened the rear door of the ambulance. After a moment of rummaging about inside, he ran back in, carrying what Barton though was a breathing apparatus. His attention was drawn back to the woman being questioned by the female officer. Although he was out of hearing distance, he could tell she was talking about him, trying to describe his appearance by raising her hand above her head, indicating his height. Then her hands went to her hair. This was her talking about the way he had his hair back in a tight ponytail.

It was Gilbert who distracted them from the interview when he jumped up at the sight of the medics and the rest of the police officers easing they're way out the door and carrying a stretcher. Barton decided it was time for him to make a hasty retreat, knowing that, when the ambulance left, the female officer would report to her colleagues the information the woman had given her. The next to happen would be a full-scale search.

Managing to get out of the cul-de-sac of derelict houses without being spotted, Barton headed along the pavement with the intent of getting away from the law enforcement activity that would shortly begin. The lighting was much better here, and he decided to walk along the grass verge, among the shadows cast by the trees and bushes of the gardens along the way. Every so often when he found a darkened spot, he would stop and recce what was happening behind him.

At the first sight of it, Barton froze. The huge hairy beast stampeded towards him and jumped on him, knocking him back into a clump of shrubs.

"Gilbert," he heard the female voice cry, "where are you?"

After slobbering all over Barton's face and neck, Gilbert decided to return to his owner. Barton got back onto his feet and was busy wiping his face with his sleeve when she appeared.

"If I was you," she said, "I'd get myself away from here. The police seemed to think you were responsible for what happened to that man."

"Is that what you think?" he asked.

"It's nothing to do with what I think."

"If it was me, why would I ask you to call for an ambulance?"

Before she replied, the sound of the police cars made Barton step back into the shadow. She and Gilbert stepped in beside him.

"You don't need to hide," he said, at the same time taking hold of Gilbert's leash.

"The last thing I want is the police asking me more questions."

"Do you have something you don't want them to discover?"

She shook her head. "No. I just don't want to get involved in what could turn out to be a lengthy court case."

"I told you it was an accident."

"Not according to the policeman who came out of that building. He said it was an assault. He said that man had been nailed to the floor by both his hands and had been sedated. How could that have been an accident?"

"I had a good idea you wouldn't want to get involved. That's why I said it was an accident."

Deciding he wanted to urinate against the bushes, Gilbert tugged her around, so her back was to Barton. But she held the leash firmly. "So, what's your involvement in all this?" she managed to say while playing tug-of-war with her pet.

"I stumbled on him while I was looking for a place to get my head down."

"Even in this darkness, I can see you don't look like a homeless person."

"I'm not. I just find myself with nowhere to stay for tonight."

Deciding he wanted to continue his walk, Gilbert started pulling her. She didn't resist and got dragged away at a trot. Barton caught up and paced out beside them. "I think I will look for a B & B. There might be one along this road.

With Barton's help, they managed to slow the beast down to a walking pace. "I don't think you'll find one in this area." She panted.

As he was about to ask her if she knew where the nearest one was, a patrol car swerved in front of them, its blue lights flashing. Two officers jump out and approached them. Gilbert didn't like the surprise and started barking and growling at them and tugging at his leash to get away.

Acting like a passing pedestrian, Barton smartly walked on, hearing one of the officers say they would like to ask her a few more questions. Could she come to the station in the morning? She must have consented, as the officers got back into their car and drove past him. Barton stopped and turned. She and Gilbert came charging towards him. "Is that you getting an invite from them?" he asked her on her way past him.

Finally, she got her pet under control and walked back towards him. "I wish I hadn't come this way," she complained, breathlessly. "I normally go the other way, which takes me through the town centre." With a few stern words from her, Gilbert reluctantly sat at her feet, his mouth wide open, panting, his huge tongue lolling down the side of his face. "If you're desperate for a place to get your head down, I have a small caravan parked about a five-minute walk from here. I'll take you there, if you're interested."

"That'll be great." Barton grinned. "I'll pay you for the use of it."

CHAPTER 23

Driving along the A580, with his headlights on full beam, Guppy had no idea where Barton could be. He knew his chances of finding him were one in a million. He had tried to phone Lorinna and got no response. Stopping in a bus stop layby, he called the abductor. He had to try a few times and finally got a reply. After a brief conversation, he was none the wiser as to where he could find Barton or why the woman hadn't been delivered to her house and was informed that a gunshot had been heard and he'd had to make a change of plans. His final call—and it was with reluctance—was to the Boss Man. After listening to the scorn and curses, he asked, "Could you get some of the guys to help me find this man Barton?"

"I'll send a team out," came the rough voice. "I'll get them to ask around their taxi driver friends. I want that man dead before this night is over. You meet the guys in the mall car park."

At the sight of the leader of the team, Guppy thought his luck has changed. Or had Boss Man changed his mind about wasting Knuckle Duster Nick? Remaining seated in the vehicle, he watched as the team approached. Knuckle Duster Nick quickly jerked open the door, grinning from ear to ear.

"What's the plan?" he asked as Guppy stepped out beside him.

"How many cars have you guys brought?" he asked, looking at the team and counting how many.

"We have three," Knuckle Duster Nick replied, still wearing the wide grin.

Glancing around the car park, making sure the other users weren't within hearing distance, he drew the group in closer with a wave of his arm. "Two to a car, the rest on foot searching in the mall and surrounding area. The ones in the vehicles drive around the local streets and the suburban areas. Does everyone know what this guy Barton looks like?"

Some of the team nodded. Others shook their heads, and Knuckle Duster Nick broke the silence. "He's a big guy, built like an ape, easy to identify and has his hair tied back in a ponytail. It won't be hard to pick him out in a crowd."

"Check in all the pubs and cafés. Ask the taxi drivers if they've seen him. His identikit picture was in all the local newspapers. Get a hold of one and carry it with you. Show it to all the bums and crooks you know.

"What will we do with him when we get hold of him?" one of the guys asked.

"Bring him to me. Make sure he's well secured, even if you have to carry him. I take it you all have phones and you know each other's numbers?"

This caused a rumbling as they all started fishing out their mobiles. Shaking his head, Guppy got back into the driver's seat of the Range Rover, opened the window, and said, "Nick here will give you my number."

Starting up the engine to clear away the misted-up windscreen, Guppy watched them separate, heading to where they had parked up. He shook his head when he heard them arguing over who was to travel in the vehicle or who was to walk. His confidence in them finding Barton was quickly diminishing.

The consistent pounding of hail on the windscreen and the roof of the vehicle gave Guppy a, and he jumped up, realising he had dozed off. A quick check of the time, and he relaxed again; only a few minutes had passed. Again, he had to jump when his mobile sounded. No name or number came onto the fascia, but he knew who the caller was.

"What's happening?" Boss Man shouted.

"I have the search party out, but so far, nothing."

"Well," came the rasping grunt, "you'd better find that bastard. The cartel goons are going to be here first thing in the morning."

Remembering what he had witnessed in the past, the way the cartel goons dealt with people who crossed them, Guppy began another sneezing fit. He was relieved when the fit stopped to find no blood had come this time. Ramming the vehicle into gear and turning onto the main street, he decided that, if anyone could find Barton, it would be him. In the rear-view mirror, emergency blue lights flashing caught his eye. Like the other road users he pulled over to let the ambulance pass. Had he known that, inside the ambulance lying on a stretcher, was Lorinna, he would have forgotten about finding Barton and chased after it.

After completing a tour of the town centre, he pulled back into the car park. A check at the time, and half an hour had passed without any word from the team—not that he was confident there would be. He phoned Knuckle Duster Nick; the signal buzzed a long time before he got an answer. When he did, he could hear background music, and a woman's voice bellowed close to Nick's phone. "Where are you?" Guppy shouted.

"We're still searching," came the slurred reply. This time, a man's voice could be heard shouting to somebody about getting the drinks in."

"You're a lying bastard. You're in a pub, Guppy shouted. "Get those bastards out searching, or you're dead meat, the fucking lot of you."

"There's no need," Knuckle Duster Nick readily replied. "We know where he is."

"Where is he?" Guppy barked. "Why didn't you call me and let me know?"

"I tried, but your phone was engaged. He's with Donnie's girlfriend in her caravan, and he's not going to go anywhere in a hurry if I know her."

Hearing laughter in the background, Guppy said, "Have you left some guys there to keep an eye on him in case he decides she's not his type?"

"No need. That caravan was rocking like a dingy in a stormy sea."

Guppy had a grin to himself at the picture Nick described. "Get the guys together, come over here, and we can all charge that caravan together."

Whilst waiting for the team to arrive, Guppy risked another call to Boss Man and got the usual grumpy response. That soon changed when Guppy informed him they had Barton trapped. Boss Man sounded pleased. But that mood didn't last long when Guppy had to inform him about not having taken out Lorinna, not knowing where the old woman was, and the fact Knuckle Duster Nick was still alive and helping him.

"You're like an orangutan in the cockpit of a jet fighter," Boss Man shouted. "Get the job done, or you know what will happen. First job is deal with Barton; the rest we'll talk about."

The three assorted cars came into the park. Guppy flashed his lights to get their attention. One behind the other, they passed in front of him. He followed them out, keeping close to the rear of the last vehicle in case he should lose sight of them at a junction. Luck was on their side, as the rush hour was over, and only a few other cars were to be seen on the surprisingly short drive. Discovering Barton was only about a mile away from where he was parked made Guppy shake his head and curse at himself.

The rear car indicated to turn into a small road. Guppy followed and pulled up behind it. He jumped out before the rest had a chance to and gathered them around, asking Nick what the score was.

Looking somewhat proud of himself for being singled out as the leader of the team, Knuckle Duster Nick said, "At the end of this road, there's a small caravan park. It's only a two-minute walk. I thought it best not to drive into it in case the guy we're after hears us and does a runner."

"OK," Guppy said, "we head down there in single file being as quiet as possible. When we get there, we spread out and circle round the caravan, block off any escape route. Nick and I will barge in and, if necessary, blow him away, although I'd rather take him to a quieter place to do it."

"Can we blow that bitch away as well?" the young man at Guppy's elbow said. "I spent a fortune getting her an engagement ring. I could do with getting it back now she's in that caravan fucking that guy."

Guppy had to grin at this and said, "You can do what you want with her after we nab that bastard Barton."

"There's a few other occupied caravans close to the one he's in," Knuckle Duster Nick said. "I don't think it would be a good idea to shoot him, if that's what you've planned."

"If I have to shoot him," Guppy explained, "everybody run like fuck. I need one of you here with the cars to turn them around and keep the engines running." He took one last glance at the team to assure himself they all understood his instructions before he led them down the road.

Six caravans stood lined up inside a high-wire meshed fence. At the open gate, Guppy whispered to Knuckle Duster Nick, "which one is it?"

"The one in the middle." Nick pointed at it.

Cursing, Guppy said,"It had to be. We'll have a hard job surrounding it without being heard by somebody's dog. People who live like this all seem to have dogs."

The words hardly left his mouth when a dog barked, and soon, a chorus of barking began. "Fuck. We can't go in there now with that racket," Knuckle Duster Nick said.

"Everybody get down," Guppy ordered. "When he comes out to see what's going on, I'll plug him."

From their hiding place they watched the occupants of the other caravans come out to see what the dogs were barking at. But nobody appeared from the one in the centre. Guppy began to wonder if anyone was inside it, maybe the idiots had pointed out the wrong one. No lights shone from it, unlike the neighbouring ones. It was as if a single word of command had been ordered when, suddenly, all the dogs were let out. In a stampede, the beasts of all sizes and breeds barked and bounded for the open gate.

Knuckle Duster Nick was the first on his feet running for the vehicles. The rest of the team soon followed, leaving Guppy cocking his pistol and firing at the animals. The rounds must have hit the target. A few of them yelped and fell. But it didn't stop the rest from charging at him. He managed to fire off a few more rounds, this time hitting the leading dog. The pack stopped and retreated back to their owners, whimpering and howling in pain.

Using the cover of the long grass at the side of the narrow lane, Guppy headed back to his vehicle, hoping to find the rest of the team sitting in their cars. He cursed to discover that only his Range Rover was there. He soon got it on the move, knowing the police would have been called. His hopes were to get clear of this narrow road before they came charging in.

Getting a safe distance away, he pulled into the side of the road and phoned Knuckle Duster Nick. It took a long time for Nick to answer. "Where are you?" he roared.

"We're in hospital," Knuckle Duster Nick replied with a nervous tremble in his voice. "The driver of the leading car had to jump on his brakes to avoid hitting a police car. The two behind ploughed into the back of him."

"Are the coppers there with you?"

"Just a couple of young constables. It seems the patrol car was on its way to investigate gunshots at that caravan park."

"Do you think they suspect you lot were involved?"

"All these two coppers seem to be interested in is charging the driver for dangerous driving and having too many passengers in the vehicles."

"Have any of you clowns been hurt badly enough to keep them in overnight?"

"I don't think so. They're just examining the last two guys. The rest of us have been discharged."

"The cars," Guppy shouted. "Are they written off or what?"

"I should think so. The middle one ended up on the roof of the one in front, and the leading car's back bumper finished up on the back seats."

"Have any of you given a statement to those two coppers?"

"They're only interested in who the drivers were, and so far, nobody's admitted to it."

"Where are the copper's now?"

"Waiting to interview the two who are now being attended to."

After a few sneezes, Guppy said, "Are the two coppers in the same room as you lot?"

"Not at the moment, but they could be any time soon."

"Get out now. Leave the two who have to be interviewed. Nick a couple of cars. And meet me at the same place as the last time." Guppy delayed a moment to let the instructions sink in before continuing. "I have a feeling Barton is in that caravan. He must have spotted one of you clowns and kept his head down. He's a tricky bastard. We have to get back there before he does a runner."

"After all this time, he must have done that," Knuckle Duster Nick sharply replied.

"With all those coppers wandering about searching for a shooter, I doubt whether he'll make a move until they've gone—"

Nick interrupted before Guppy had a chance to continue. "The coppers will have searched all those caravans and found him if he's hiding in that one. I don't think he'll have hung around when he heard them arriving with all the sirens blasting out."

"Remember, he still has Donnie's girlfriend with him. He won't have gone far. When the coppers stop searching, she'll want to return to see what damage they might have caused, and he might return with her."

"We heard shots when we reached the cars. What were you firing at?"

"That pack of dogs. I think I hit a few of them," Guppy replied proudly.

"Donnie tells me his girlfriend was looking after his dog. I hope you didn't shoot it. If you did, he'll go mental. That big ugly beast is his baby. He thinks more of it than he does of her."

"Never mind what dogs got shot. Just you lot get out of there and get some vehicles and meet me at the mall car park—by which time I hope the coppers will have left. Then we can get back out there. This time, we'll be more careful not to be heard or spotted."

<h1>CHAPTER 24</h1>

Greeted by a chorus of dog barks, Gilbert cowered down at her feet and whimpered. Barton patted his head in reassurance. Reluctantly the beast got back onto his feet, but stayed behind her as she encouraged him to walk beside her. Side by side they strolled through the open gate, her pulling her pet. Barton counted six caravans lined up close to the rear of the tall mesh fence. She steered him to the smallest and most neglected-looking one in the centre.

"This is it," she said. "Sorry for the state it's in, but I only use it now and again." She handed him the dog's lead and pulled open the door.

"Do you not lock the door?" Barton asked, restraining Gilbert from jumping in behind her when she entered.

"I lost the keys ages ago," she replied from inside.

Gilbert couldn't hold back any longer and dived inside, jerking Barton's arm and forcing him to trip over the step. Regaining his balance and having to lower his head, he sat on the nearest bench seat.

She was busy lighting a battery-powered strip light, which didn't look as though it had much life left in it. Barton was impressed at the condition of the interior. Unlike the outside, this looked as though it had been kept clean and dry—giving him doubts about her claim that it hadn't been used very often. It gave the impression of someone living in here permanently or at least on regular overnight stays. Although the kitchen area was small, it had all the necessary equipment for living in. The bed was a double small size when she unfolded the two seats at the rear end. In his opinion, it looked well used and had that odour of recent occupation about it. From a cupboard above the bed, she pulled out fresh bedding and placed it on a cabinet close to where he was sat.

In the few inches that separated them, he could smell her perfume. She seemed aware, smiled, and said, "You don't need to pay me for the use of it, but you could treat me to a meal and a drink." She reached out and took his hand, edging him to the edge of the bed, and grinned when he didn't resist her gentle tug down towards her.

They had left Gilbert in the caravan. He sniffed at the bed, and smelling his minder, he settled down to a deep sleep. Gently closing the door, she led

Barton out through the open gates, seemingly knowing her way along the side of the high mesh fence and coming out on a busy road. She steered him to the left, and they came to a high arched stone gateway. A short way up the tarred driveway, a well-lit hotel confronted them.

Not being formally dressed for an establishment like this, they received dubious glances from both the staff and the other patrons who were sitting at tables set in an array of stylish silver cutlery and trays. Champagne bottles in ice buckets sat ready to be opened in front of the customers on pure white Egyptian cotton cloths. On the centre of each table, a four-branch silver candelabra sat. A waiter approached and ushered them to a table. Walking at her side, Barton gave her arm a gentle squeeze. "You really know how to treat a gentleman."

Getting settled on the seat and having trouble with the slits on her tight jeans, she grinned at him, "I'm teaching you how to treat a lady."

When they approached the reception desk to pay the bill, the young black man's eye popped at the sight of Barton paying in cash. Confused, he turned and spoke to an elderly bald man, who, in response, shrugged his shoulders and nodded. This was the last thing Barton wanted, knowing it would draw attention. If any of the staff or the other customers waiting to pay recognised him from the identikit picture in the local papers, the police would be called. Although he enjoyed this girl's company and her lovemaking, he was regretting taking her up on her invitation to stay the night in her caravan.

She was standing on the step outside the main door when he gripped her arm and pulled her towards the avenue. "We need to get out of here fast." Ignoring her confused look, he said, "I'll explain later."

Stopping her abruptly at the arched gateway and hushing her with a finger on his lips, he listened for the sound of police cars. But that wasn't the sound that offended his hearing. It came at him like a nightmare, and he was back in a war zone—the constant cracking of gunshots close by. His experience kicked in, telling him the direction the shots were coming from. "We can't go back to your caravan."

She was the one pulling at his arm now, dragging him behind the stone gate pillars and crouching down, shouting, "Was that what I think it was?"

Staring down at her in the shadows, he said, "It came from the direction of the caravan park."

Jumping up and pulling at the collar of his jacket with both hands, she said in a whimper, "We left Gilbert in the caravan. I hope he's all right, or my boyfriend will kill me."

"There's no chance of us going back there to check. Whoever is doing the shooting could be looking for a target. And anyway, those shots will be getting reported. Before long, the police will be crawling all over the place. And if they find you at another incident within a matter of hours and a short distance away … well, your guess is as good as mine." Taking hold of her wrists and pushing them down by her side, Barton then took hold of her shoulder and steered her at a forced pace away from the direction of the park.

At the first junction, they were forced to stop and could hardly believe what they were witnessing. A police car with its warning lights flashing pulled out of the side road, forcing a car on the major road to make an emergency stop. Two more vehicles behind consequently rammed into the back of the first one, and the other one ended up on the roof of the first. She was still suffering from the shock of the gunshots. Now this incident proved to be overwhelming her. She buckled under him. He managed to support her, preventing her from falling at his feet.

Struggling to keep her from falling with one hand, Barton tried to unfasten the catch on the silver chain he always wore around his neck with the other. Failing to manage, he finally pulled it up over his head. At end of the chain, he located the key to the flat he had not yet moved into.

The smell of fresh paint hit him as he carried her inside. In the room he planned to use as his lounge, paint cans littered the bare floorboards. Using a drip sheet and folding it a few times to make a cushion, he sat her down carefully, supporting her against the corner walls. Even in the brief time he had known her, he couldn't dissolve that feeling of familiarity, as though he had known her all his life and knew her every thought and reaction. As though she had somehow read his mind, her eyes opened. She struggled to get up and Barton restrained her, resting his hands on her shoulders. "Sit there a while longer," he advised. "You've had a bit of a shock."

Her wide-set blue eyes scoured her surroundings through strands of dyed blonde hair. "Where is this place?" She fretted, looking into his dark brown eyes.

Gently withdrawing his hands from her shoulders, he said, "It's OK. This is my flat. I haven't moved in yet." Seeing that, she looked unsettled and uncertain. He sat down next to her, putting his arm around her shoulder. "Where do you live?" he asked, pulling her closer to his body.

Looking deeper into his eyes as if trying to predict what his reaction might be, she finally replied, diverting her eyes down at her feet, "I live with my boyfriend."

Catching her small chin with his finger, he turned her head and looked into her eyes. "What's your name? We've been with each other for a few hours, made love in your caravan, and we don't know each other's names."

Twisting her head away slightly, she replied, "Does it matter about our names? After this night is over, we'll never see each other again. I need to get our dog back and get home to Donnie, my boyfriend."

Getting back onto his feet and helping her up, Barton shook his head. "We can't go back to that caravan park tonight."

Standing close to him, her head only reaching the centre of his chest, she looked up at him. "I can. I live there when my man's away on a job. It's not safe at his place for a woman living there on her own."

Grimacing down at her, he replied, "It doesn't seem to be safe living in your caravan, considering we heard gunshots coming from that direction."

She moved away from him and looked around the room, waving her arms. "We can't stay here. The place is empty. There's no sign of furniture, and it's fucking cold." She shivered, wrapping her arms around herself. For a while, they stared silently at each other. Suddenly, she dragged her mobile from her hip pocket. "I'm going to get a taxi and take a chance that my boyfriend is at home, I'll say Gilbert broke away from me to chase a cat or something, and I lost him."

Stepping closer to her and taking the hand she held the phone in, he said, "Don't you think it would be quicker just phoning your boyfriend to see if he is at home?"

She nodded and turned her back on him, walking out of hearing distance. Barton stepped back to give her more privacy, but no sooner had she punched in the number than she was back at his side.

"He threatened to blow my head off if I don't bring his dog back tonight."

"Is he at home now?" Barton asked.

"I'm not sure. It doesn't sound like it by the background noises."

"What kind of background noises?"

"I'm not sure, but I thought I heard a loudspeaker, the kind you hear in a hospital."

"Is that where he works?"

"You've got to be joking, I think he's a crook like you, I once found a gun hidden in his underwear drawer. When I asked him about it, he punched me and told me to mind my own business."

He placed a hand on her shoulders. "He sounds like a very loving boyfriend."

"Like fuck he is. He can be a very violent man and a bully. He says if I ever leave him, he'll find me and blow my head off."

"You don't give me the impression of a battered partner."

"He's clever enough to hit me where the bruises won't show."

Remembering how little light there had been inside the caravan when they stripped off their clothes, he realised he wouldn't have noticed any bruises she had. The strip light had died on them during their lovemaking, and they'd had to grope about to get dressed. "Do you have family you can stay with?" he asked.

"That would be the first place he would come looking for me."

"We could try and make ourselves comfortable here. And in the morning, I'll arrange to get my things delivered."

Stepping back, she looked up into his brown eyes, her expression becoming serious. "Are you asking me to move in with you?"

"Where else can you go if he's going to blow your head off for losing his dog?"

She gazed around the empty room. Her shoulders dropped submissively. And she grinned. "I suppose we can spend an uncomfortably night here. And in the morning, if all is clear, we can look for Gilbert. But you're going to have to keep me warm."

He reached out and folded his arms around her waist. "I'll do my best."

"Well." She grinned and kissed his lips. "If you repeat the way you performed in the caravan, I think I'll burst into flames."

CHAPTER 25

Guppy sat in his car, struggling to stay awake. He was trying to concentrate on the radio when a knock came on his window. He jumped and turned to see the unkempt bush of hair silhouetting a white bearded face. Guppy operated the window, and before it was completely open, Knuckle Duster Nick shouted, "We're all here, but we could only get an old Transit van."

Starting up the engine, Guppy glanced at Knuckle Duster Nick. "Get those clowns loaded into that van and follow me," he ordered.

Before pulling away, he decided to give them a few minutes to get loaded. The time dragged on, and no sign of the van. He drove out of his parking slot and began searching for it. When he finally found it, the team was pushing it in an attempt to get it started. Guppy jumped out in a rage, slamming the door of the Range Rover. "Fucking leave it," he shouted at Nick. "Get some of those clowns into my car."

With Knuckle Duster Nick sitting next to him on the passenger's seat and the team of four crammed in the back, Guppy pulled onto the kerb and shut off the engine. "We can walk from here. Stay off the narrow lane when we get to it and creep along that broken wall. That way, we will be able to spot if the police are still there."

"How about those dogs?" Knuckle Duster Nick said. He glanced at the clock on the dashboard. "It'll soon be daylight."

"If the coppers are away, I've enough weaponry to blow them all away—and the bastards who live there."

With an open mouth and a look of horror, Knuckle Duster Nick grasped Guppy's arm. "You can't kill all those people. That'll create a nationwide hunt for us. It'll be on every TV news bulletin and in all the newspapers. We'll never get away with it. Every copper in the country will be on the search. Every man, woman, and child on the street will have been alerted. The mob will disown us. They might even send a team of shooters after us."

Tearing his arm free from the scrawny dirty little hand, Guppy barked, "That's a chance I'm willing to take." He added in a more subdued tone, "Hopefully it might not come to that if we spot Barton first."

Jumping out of the vehicle without closing the door, Knuckle Duster Nick shouted at the four men crammed in the back. "I'm out of here. I don't want anything to do with this."

The sound of the gunshot inside the vehicle came at the occupants like a bomb exploding. The four men scrambled for the doors. Finding the child lock had been set, they fought to get over to the front seat, but Knuckle Duster Nick's body blocked their way. Three more explosions came, followed by shouts and yells. When the smoke cleared and the rancid smell of cordite had gone, all went silent.

Another body lay jammed between the two front seats. The thug called Donnie lay halfway out the broken rear window. He was still alive and kicking to get free of the body that lay over his legs, trapping him.

Calmly Guppy stepped out with a grin and walked to the rear. Donnie's head was protruding out the broken window, his face covered in blood. Guppy jerked the back door open. Donnie screamed at the painful twisting of his neck and body. The screaming intensified when Guppy lifted Donnie's legs and twisted his body around the door, leaving the head still jammed against the broken window. Sheer silence followed the snap of Donnie's neck.

Exhausted after hauling the bodies out of the Range Rover into the shrubs at the roadside, Guppy sat slouched over the steering wheel trying to get his breathing back to normal. *Too many smokes*. He cursed at himself. An old man riding a disabled scooter shouted and signalled that he wanted past. Disgruntled at being disturbed, Guppy started up the vehicle; pushed it into gear; and, at full throttle, rammed the old man and his scooter into the deep ditch at the opposite side of the road.

The situation now being changed, Guppy decided to go it alone. After parking the vehicle back in its original place, he opened up the secret compartment behind the rear axle and selected a Sterling ArmaLite assault rifle, checked the magazine was full, filled his pocket with spares, and headed for the caravan park.

Following his own instruction, he used the partially demolished wall as cover and crept up to the mesh wire fencing. Although he was half expecting it, it still came as a shock to see so many police cars parked inside the forecourt, so many officers walking about, and so many photographers flashing their cameras at the bodies of the dead dogs. Men in plastic overalls were picking up spent shells from his last position at the gate. He realised Barton wouldn't dare come near this place now.

About to get up and make his way back, he noticed a quick change in the police action. They all seemed to regroup. After instruction from what looked like a senior officer, some of the constables mounted the vehicles and swerved out of the forecourt, chasing up the narrow lane, while others stayed behind. The reason for this manoeuvre didn't take long to dawn on him. All the shots he had fired inside the Range Rover had been reported.

Guppy knew that, within a few minutes, the report from the officers who had driven away would be radioed to the ones left behind—which would lead to a full-scale search of the area. He had no other option but to get away. Heading towards the Range Rover was out of the question. By now, it would have been commandeered, and a tow truck would soon be on its way to pick it up.

Crawling alongside the fence, he finally reached a public footpath. This led him to the road, where, only a few hundred yards away, he had parked the Range Rover. Running in the opposite direction, he noticed a large arched stone gateway with a sign telling him that the narrow road behind led to a hotel. He took a last-minute look around to make sure nobody noticed him walking through the arch.

Having to step off the narrow avenue when a car approached, Guppy reasoned this would be overnight guests leaving and hoped this would be the last of them. Approaching the steps, he cocked the assault rifle and rushed through the doors. The reception desk faced him. Holding the weapon threateningly, he approached the young black man behind the desk. "Give me all the cash you have," he roared.

The young man's eyes widened. He held up his hands nervously, saying, "We don't handle much cash. It's mostly credit card business."

Guppy raised the weapon slightly. "Give me what cash you have," he demanded, holding out his free hand.

Hastily, the young man punched a few icons on a screen in front of him with trembling fingers, and a drawer opened below it. He lifted out the few twenty-pound notes Barton had previously given him. "That is all the cash we have," he explained, placing the notes on the desk.

Horrified, Guppy stared at the notes. "Is that all there is? Surely, a big hotel like this must have a safe?"

"What's going on here?" came a voice from behind.

Guppy swung round, still holding the weapon in the ready position. A tall suited man stepped towards them and stopped at the sight of the weapon trained on him. His narrow-set eyes popped, and he instantly shot his hands up.

Waving the gun in the direction of the desk, Guppy said, "Get in behind there with your colleague and get me some cash out of the safe."

"The safe isn't in there," the tall man said, sidestepping behind the desk, all the while keeping his eyes on the weapon.

"That's shit," Guppy shouted. "Places like this always have a safe in the reception. Now get to it and get it opened. I want all the cash and jewellery that's in it."

"I don't know the combination," the man pleaded.

The single shot shattered a large mirror behind the young man. He screamed and ducked down behind the desk, whimpering like an injured dog. The tall man let out a high-pitched howl and dived down on top of the youngster. "I'll give you three seconds," Guppy roared. "If I don't get what I want, I'll blast this place down about your ears."

The door behind the room the tall man had come out of opened up. Instinctively, Guppy turned and blasted a volley of rounds at it. The girl who entered was busy putting on her jacket and was lifted off her feet by the impact, landing back the way she had come, the swinging door closing on her.

Below the desk, the young black boy was struggling with his mobile, trying to contact the police. Finally, after a few failed attempts, he managed to dial the emergency number. But by that time, Guppy was on top of them. A single shot struck the young man on the back of his head, sending blood splatter all over the floor and desk.

The tall man tried to shout at the mobile and received a smack on the side of his face. He yelled and cowered into the corner under the desk, his hands over his head. He began crying like a baby. "Please don't kill me," he pleaded. "I have a wife and children."

Grabbing the man's collar, Guppy pulled him out and pushed him to the floor. "Get that safe open, and I might save you."

Their eyes met, and Guppy could see tears running through the blood splatter on his face. Struggling to get onto his hands and knees, the man quickly crawled to where the safe was hidden. His trembling fingers weren't obeying his commands, and he had to try numerous times before he finally pulled the heavy metal door open. He fell back, watching this big bald man filling his pockets with cash that didn't amount to much.

Pushing the barrel of the weapon against the man's forehead, Guppy shouted, "Is that all there is? Was it worth the lives of that young man and girl? I take it you're the owner of this place?" He didn't give the man a chance to answer. He squeezed the trigger, only this time feeling justified—feeling that this creep deserved what he got.

He pushed his way through the swinging doors and delayed a moment to look at the girl lying face up on the floor. There were no doubts she was dead. Three distinct wounds on her upper torso confirmed it. That familiar numb sensation at the front of his head started. This was the part when he hated himself. It was as if the front of his brain had turned to ice, and no matter how hard he tried, he couldn't find any remorse. The voices inside his head told him that what he had done was justifiable, and he had to get cash to pay off the abductor of the old couple.

Continuing along the corridor, he felt a fit of the sneezing developing. He rushed past doors on either side until he could go no farther and was faced with a blank wall. To his left was a wide carpeted staircase. Three women stood at the top looking down at him. At the sight of the weapon in his hands, they scrambled out of his sight, yelling and screaming.

Realising these people could identify him, Guppy knew more killing had to be done. It was their fault for sticking their noses in. Fortunately for them, the sneezing fits started, worse this time than he could remember, and he had to buckle over onto his knees, dropping the gun and covering his face with both his hands when blood started to run. The last thing he needed was to leave traces of his DNA at the murder site.

He remembered that one of the doors he had passed was labelled, "public toilet." Picking himself up, he grabbed the weapon and rushed to it. After he'd washed his face in chilly water, the bleeding eased off, and he stuffed his nostril with toilet paper. With the sneezes gone, he changed the magazine on the ArmaLite and headed off in search of the three women.

CHAPTER 26

The night had been uncomfortable but not cold. Barton had turned on the heating to its maximum, and sleep had come fitfully to both of them. Pacing around the room trying to ease the stiffness out of his bones and listening to her moan, he reached down to her outstretched hand to help her up. "If we have to stay here another night," Barton said as she got to her feet, "I'll have to at least get my bed brought here today."

On her rush to the toilet, she called, "We need to see if Gilbert is still alive."

Standing outside the toilet door, Barton said, "The law will still be there. With all that shooting, they will be treating it as a serious incident. They won't leave there for weeks."

The door flew open. "How are we going to get our dog back?" she shouted at him.

After a few moments' thought, he replied, "The only thing I can suggest is that you go there yourself and ask to get into your caravan to check everything is all right. You say you heard there had been some kind of a raid there."

Combing her fingers through her hair and adjusting her T-shirt and jacket, she said, "Don't forget. I'm to go into the police station for more questioning about that guy you say you found in that old house. If they identify me asking about my caravan just a few streets away, that's not going to look too good for me."

Taking her hand, Barton looked into her blue eyes. "You say you live in the caravan, that you left your dog there and went to spend some time with your boyfriend."

Pulling her hand free, she said, "Do you think they're going to swallow that shit?"

"No, but they don't have a choice."

Having walked with her most of the way, Barton watched her turn into the narrow lane leading to the caravan site with reluctance. He wondered how long this would take before she returned and didn't like the idea of loitering about so close to the incident site. Hunger pangs were biting in his gut as he strolled along the road.

After a short distance, he turned in time to see her being driven past in the back of a patrol car. In the brief moment their eyes met, he saw she didn't have that look of being stressed that most people would have after being interviewed by the police. He was shocked by her cool demeanour, giving him the impression this was just another day at the office for her.

Being so involved in these thoughts, Barton hadn't notice he had walked past the entrance to the caravan park and was nearing the stone arch to the hotel. The sirens blasted out behind him, and he froze, thinking they were onto him and that the woman he had spent time with had shopped him.

Deciding it was too late to get out, he stood in preparation for what was about to happen. The first patrol car flew past and swerved in though the archway. This was followed by another two. Barton sighed with relief and was on the verge of laughter when he noticed the familiar form of a barrel-chested, bald-headed man running out of the shrubs and down the road. He resisted chasing after this man, knowing that, in a few minutes, the police would give chase, and he might be caught up in it. He decided, instead, to hunt down the man calling himself Lorinna. He knew, if the big bald man got caught, there would be no chance of him discovering where his parents were.

Not having a vehicle, Barton marvelled at how time seemed to fly past. What he knew should have been a few minutes' drive was now an hour's walk, and he made up his mind to have a good breakfast before heading for the hospital where he thought they would have taken Lorinna.

Realising this was Sunday morning when he reached the town centre and discovered that all the cafés were closed, he carried on towards the nearest hospital, his stomach rumbling all the way. He still didn't know how he was going to discover if Lorinna had been taken to this hospital. If it turned out not to be the case, then he would have to go back to Jimmy Stitch and buy another dodgy car. What troubled Barton about that idea was the cash was running low.

Entering through the large double glass doors, the first sign he noticed was an arrow indicating the direction of the restaurant. Without hesitation, Barton followed it and soon found himself at the rear of the queue of the self-service bar.

He soon sat down to a plate with three eggs, four rashers of bacon, and two slices of fried bread, finished off with three ladles of beans and a large mug of tea. He'd picked up his utensils and was about to get wolfed in when he heard a rather loud male voice from the table behind saying he felt sorry for the guy in the next bed to Tommy.

"Those nails must have been painful getting hammered into both his hands," a female replied.

Barton instantly stopped, his knife and fork about to cut at the bacon pausing in midair. He chanced a secret glance around to see a man and a woman drinking tea or coffee. He decided he must get more info from them. Picking up the bowl with sugar cubes and placing it out of sight on the chair next to him, he turned and caught the woman's eye. "I hope you don't mind me asking. I don't seem to have any sugar at my table. Could I pinch some from your bowl?"

The man looked over the rim of his glasses and grinned, pushing the bowl over. "Knock yourself out."

The woman smiled and said, "Have they not put sugar on your table? Can't get staff nowadays."

Lifting out a few cubes from the bowl, Barton looked over at the man. "Are you from this area?"

They both shook their heads. "No. We're just visiting a relative," the woman replied. "We're from Huddersfield."

"I hope your relative isn't too ill, nothing serious."

"He'll survive," the man replied. "Had an accident on his motorbike."

"I'm visiting a work mate. He had accident with a nail gun. I'm not sure what ward he's in. I'll need to enquire at the reception desk."

"Is that your mate?" the woman eagerly replied. "He's in the next bed to our relative in ward sixteen."

Thanking them, Barton turned and resumed eating his breakfast. As he was about to take a bite of the fried bread, the couple passed. The man, letting the woman walk on, bent over and whispered, "The coppers are keeping a vigil on that guy—two plain-clothes guys. One is wearing a black bomber Jacket and jeans. The other's in a long grey coat wearing a trilby."

Barton nodded his appreciation and watched him join the woman standing waiting at the door.

Looking down at his half-eaten meal and having trouble resisting finishing it, he knew it to be unwise to linger here any longer. A thought occurred to him. *Has that couple identified me from the identikit picture in the local papers? How many others in here could have?*

Keeping his head down, Barton was making his way to the glass exit door when it suddenly opened, and she walked in, accompanied by two uniformed police officers, one a woman, the other a youngster about ten inches taller than his female colleague. In that passing brief moment, their eyes met. Barton failed to read anything in her expression, as she was quickly ushered on. Knowing it was risky for both of them, he decided he couldn't resist following. He had to find out if she was being escorted to ward sixteen, maybe to identify Lorinna.

Even with lots of people walking back and forth, it wasn't difficult to follow them. The young male constable was a good head taller than most of the people crowding along the corridor. Under these circumstances, Barton's own height was a disadvantage, as he also was a head taller. Nevertheless, with his head down, he followed. Up ahead was an information board with numerous finger pointers giving directions to the ward numbers. The tall constable turned left at the junction of the corridors. Must be heading for ward sixteen, Barton decided, and held back a moment. He didn't want to be spotted by the two plain-clothes coppers.

Sure enough, from where he stood, he could see the two constables enter the door to ward sixteen, one behind the other, with her in the middle. Strange how some thoughts come unexpectedly. The vision of Gilbert lying on her bed in that caravan made him wonder if the huge Afghan hound had gotten out when the police entered the caravan.

Ward sixteen seemed to be a busy one, with people entering and leaving, making it difficult for him to concentrate on trying to detect who and where the plain-clothes policemen were, who, according to the man in the restaurant, were keeping a vigil on Lorinna. The deep inbuilt sense of being watched from his regiment days hadn't materialised. Maybe, he thought, they were resting up somewhere. That piece of wishful thinking didn't last long when the officer in the grey coat and the trilby walked past him and took up position a few yards from the ward door. Barton had to grin, thinking, *They change from the uniform but don't seem to be able to change their body language.* Head constantly turning, eyes on everything, neck stretching, tense posture. Probably the result of bad training due the lack of funding.

Had he not been so engrossed in detecting the plain-clothes officer, he wouldn't have missed her walking out the ward without her escort until she walked past him amid other visitors. Barton had no doubts she had seen him. He had noticed that slight nod of her head signalling she was being followed.

A quick glance back told him trilby man was still at his post and didn't look as though he was interested in following her. His partner in the black jacket and jeans could be anywhere. A few guys had walked past dressed the same. Barton began to doubt if he had read her signal correctly. Giving her time to reach the door, he began to follow, all the while scouring his surroundings for signs of someone taking a keen interest in her.

He almost blew it. He was about to push the door open when, through the glass, he saw her get into the rear seat of a car. Two men stood by the side of the vehicle; one had opened the door. The giveaway sign that they were police officers was the way the door opener put his hand on her head as she stooped to get in. Stepping aside to let other people out, Barton watched the car pull away.

The way the car park had been designed, the driver would have to head towards the door and then turn, following the white arrows on the tarmac indicating the way to the exit. It was when the car was at its closest to the door that the shock hit him. The driver was the man he had borrowed the sugar from, and sitting next to him was his female accomplice.

—w—

Even with his eyes closed tightly, the bright light still penetrated through his lids in a blinding scarlet haze. Lorinna's first thought was a search light or a powerful torch, and he was still lying spread-eagle on the floorboards of that old house. All a nightmare ... or was it? No, it wasn't. His eyes flickered open. The white light above his head sent shock waves all the way to the back of his sockets. To avoid the searing light, he tried to move his head to the side. Panic struck home when he discovered he had no control over this movement. An attempt to shield his eye with his arm also failed. In a panic, he tried to get up, only to discover he had been strapped down. His scream brought a welcoming shadow, and he could see a dark shape towering over him.

"Glad you're awake," the deep voice echoed. "We thought we could be here for weeks."

"Where am I?"

"You're in hospital." The deep voice came again, this time the shape moving away, letting the blinding light hit him again.

As before, he tried to protect his eyes by trying to twist his head and bring his arms up. "The light, it's hurting my eyes."

"Try not to move," a female voice said. "I'll put a cover over them to dull the brightness down."

The deep voice came again, close to his ear now. "What's your name?"

Finally, after a long silence, Lorinna said, "I can't remember."

"That's crap," the deep voice said, It sounded as if this person was moving away. "I've been informed that you've had no injury to your head, so you can't have lost your memory."

The sweet smell of perfume entered his nostrils, and the next moment, a tissue was placed softly over his eyes. From the same distance, he heard a soft female voice saying, "He's lost a lot of blood. That could account for a temporary loss of his memory."

"How long before we can interview him?" the deep voice asked.

The female must have shaken her head and walked away, for Lorinna never heard her reply. Trying to remember what had happened and how he'd gotten into hospital, he drew a blank. He decided that the female wasn't far wrong. But there were things that did enter his head, and he knew there was no way he could ever forget that person in the camo suit and ski mask or the gnarled hand that had gripped his wrist when he'd moved the lid off that crate. Thinking of that hand with its liver spots and the force that was applied made him try to wiggle his fingers. The movement was restricted and caused pains to shoot from his hands up his arms.

Still suffering from the shooting pains in both his hands now, he felt the tissue being removed. This time the searing light was more tolerable, and he could make out the features of a woman as she towered over him. This only lasted a few seconds, and she was gone. He heard her say, "Never seen him before."

"Are you sure about that?" the deep voice asked. "You were interviewed at the site, and it was your mobile the call was made from."

"I told you at the site, and I told the interviewing officer at the station, that a man ran out at me, saying someone in that building needed emergency medical treatment."

That was the last words Lorinna heard. For a time, all he could hear was the normal sounds of a hospital ward. He judged there must be about four other patients in here with him. This was comforting to him, knowing the police observation would soon be called off when they learned nothing from him. And with all these witnesses, the man Barton wouldn't dare try anything.

This thought brought on another problem. What if the man in the camo gear and ski mask was Barton? And what if he was now here posing as a member of staff? Or was Barton too big and fit-looking and much too muscular to pass as a nurse or a doctor should he try to impersonate one? In spite of his restricted condition, he began to relax.

Moving only his eyes from left to right, he could see three beds on the opposite side of the ward. His gaze fell on the one farthest away and he saw the face of the youth staring at him. This gave birth to yet another shock that hit him like a bolt of electricity. Was this the young guy he had hired to plant a gun on the Barton property? The one who'd knifed him on the stairs to his flat? Or was it the deaf boy he had attacked by mistake? Lorinna was hoping for the latter. The resemblance was scary, like they could be identical twins. The only way to be certain was to watch for signs of the youth's lack of hearing. Because of Lorinna's mother having the same disability, he knew he would be able to spot it instantly even if the youngster was good at lip-reading.

<u>CHAPTER 27</u>

Finding himself on another long corridor at the top of the stairs, Guppy was looking at numerous doors down either side. The three women could be hiding in any one of them. A good hard kick at the first failed to budge it. This was an old building with solid wooden doors. After a few more solid kicks, it gave way. Half an hour later, after attacking all the others and rummaging through the rooms, he burst into the last one. Carrying the gun ready to fire, he came face to face with two middle-aged women standing at the far side of a double bed, their eyes full of fear and hands covering their mouths. That was his last scene. In that instant, he felt something crashing onto his skull, sending a lightning flash through his vision. Soon, excruciating pain shot through his entire body, and his surroundings began to spin. The laminate flooring came up to meet him, and as he lay on the cold wood, a strange blackness enveloped him. Trying as much as he could, no amount of fight could dissolve this overpowering floating sensation.

He wasn't sure what had brought him to. Was it the searing pains from his skull or the sensation of being dragged by his ankles? Guppy opened his eyes and was looking up at a ceiling of cracked plaster and passing light bulbs. The movement stopped; a door creaked; and, soon, he could feel himself bumping down steps, his head and shoulders thumping off every one of them. Above, the scene had changed, and he was looking up at a rough stone arch. Now, the only light came from a dancing torch beam from behind.

When he was at the point of almost passing out again, the bumping stopped, and he could feel himself being dragged across flagstones. In a natural reaction, Guppy tried to twist his body, hoping the grip on his ankles would break free. This resulted in a hard slap to the side of his face. The slap was a stinger, but he was determined to fight his way out of this situation and carried on kicking and struggling with his upper body.

A dull light came on, and the dragging stopped. His feet fell to the floor. Next, hands gripped the back of his jacket collar, and he was being lifted into a seated position. Towering over him were the three women, one holding the ArmaLite and pointing it at him. Although his head still thumped with throbbing bouts of pain, he managed to grin. "I hope you know how to use that," he said to the weapon holder.

She was the tallest of the three. Her still greying hair hung over her mature features. Her brown eyes glaring down at him, she grimaced. "There's one way for you to find out."

Holding up submissive hands, Guppy replied, still retaining his grin, "What's your game? Where is this place? Why didn't you leave me for the police to find me?"

"You ask a lot of questions," her companion standing on her left side snapped.

With his eye fixed on the weapon, Guppy was too slow to avoid the slap to his bald head by the heavily built woman who had been standing on the other side of her taller companion.

The slap landed on Guppy's injured area, now a large lump. He yelled and tried to get up, but the weapon was pushed into his jaw, forcing him back down. "I hope you fucking cunts intend to kill me, for if you don't, I'll kill you."

The weapon holder backed off but kept it trained on him while the other two stepped round behind.

"What's going on now?" Guppy shouted, watching her join her companions. Rolling over onto his knees, he watched them walk backwards through the low arch entrance. Before he could get onto his feet, they slammed the heavy wooden door, and the locking mechanism operated noisily.

Left in blinding darkness, he rushed in the direction where he thought the door was and came crashing into it. The impact sent him reeling backwards, and he landed painfully on his rump. Finding it difficult not to get into a state of panic, he crawled, this time towards the door. When he could go no farther and he could feel the rough wood, he stood up. Banging at it with his fists and kicking it, he got no response. He shouted until he became hoarse and could muster no more from his vocal chords. A few minutes later, the sneezing fits started, every sneeze causing a bolt of excruciating pain inside his head, forcing him to sit on the cold slabs and wait for it all to subside.

Using his hands, he felt his way around the cold stone walls and concluded this must be a vaulted cellar. Remembering the style of the hotel building, he thought it could be about two hundred years old. It soon came to him that the only way out of this place was through that enormous door.

Finding himself in a damp corner, he slid down to the floor and hoped the three ladies would return. His second hope was that they couldn't operate that ArmaLite. They would need to use the torch to come down the stairs. And surely he would be able to see some light from it through the crack at the bottom of that door, thus giving him some warning and time to make an attack.

—ɯ—

Realising the two constables who had escorted Vesta into the hospital ward would still be there, Barton made up his mind that the only thing left to do was to walk to the police station and wait outside for them to release her. Walking along the footpath leading to the main road, he still hadn't gotten over the shock of seeing that man driving that police car and his female colleague sitting next to him. It was a close call he must never let happen again. Or was it too late and they were already onto him? Was he meant to hear that conversation? At the police station, he crossed to the opposite side of the street and stood behind a group of people waiting for a bus. His reasoning was still in turmoil, his mind's eyes taking him back to the scene in the hospital canteen. Seeing them driving that police vehicle, with Vesta in the rear, made it obvious he wouldn't be talking to Lorinna soon.

Being so full of drifting thoughts, Barton hadn't paid any attention to the bus pulling up and the people filing in, leaving him standing on his own. A soft punch on his shoulder brought him back to the real world. She stood at his side, frowning into his face. "So, they let you go," was all he could think of saying, shocked by her unexpected arrival.

"Only just," she replied, gripping his hand. "We'd best get away from here. There's a big identikit picture of you on the notice board, facing you as you walk in the doors."

Barton put up no resistance to her pulling at his hand. But at the same time, he didn't want to draw attention to them being in too big a rush.

When they got to a safe distance, she relaxed to a normal stroll.

"Where are we going?" he asked.

She stopped, released his hand, and stared up into his eyes. "Have you not seen the news?"

Uncertain where this was leading, he shook his head. "I haven't had time or been anywhere near a television."

"Some bloody idiot has been running around with a gun shooting at the caravan park. Three dogs were shot, and two people were injured. And in that hotel we had a meal in, three employees were shot. According to the report, the hotel job looks to have been a robbery. They seem to have found the safe opened. It looks like you're their number one suspect."

"Well, you know that's not true," Barton cut in. "I was with you when we heard the shots from the caravan park."

Holding up her hand to silence him, she continued. "I'm not finished. Three men were found lying in the long grass at the side of that road leading to that hotel. The report says they were members of a criminal organisation. It seems my fiancé was one of them. That's why I had to go back to the station. He must have been carrying a photo of me in his mobile. A vehicle was found a short distance away. The report went on to say those men were shot inside it and dragged to the side of the road."

Feeling stunned at what she had just told him, he said, as she was about to carry on walking, "You're well informed. It seems you've learned a lot in the short time you were with the police."

Ignoring his comment, she started walking. "Did you manage to get your bed delivered?"

Catching up to her, he said, "Not yet. If you give me your phone, I'll get it arranged."

Without stopping or looking round at him, she pulled her mobile from her hip pocket and handed it to him. "I need to know if Gilbert was among the dogs that got shot."

"The police will still be there. We can't just walk in there and ask. Showing your face like that could get you further involved. And as you say, I'm their number one suspect. I can't go near either."

"I know one of the guys who lives there. I'm friendly with his girlfriend. I've already phoned him and arranged to meet in a pub about a mile from here."

"What time have you to meet this guy?"

"I still have about an hour," she replied, glancing at her watch. "Time enough for you to get that bed delivered." She nodded at her mobile in his hand.

Having made the arrangements, Barton handed her phone back. "We need to get wheels and pick it up. The guy who's storing my things says his van is knackered."

"In that case, we'll need a van," she replied with a grin. "I know the very place where we could get one." Without warning, she did an about-turn and crossed to the other side of the road, leaving Barton standing puzzled.

He quickly caught up with her and took hold of her arm. Pulling her to a stop, he swung her round, facing him. "I don't even know your name."

In that moment, she looked puzzled, giving the impression she was trying to think of one. A quick glance at her body language confirmed it. "Vesta … just call me Vesta. And you are?"

"I think you already know my name. The police would have given you it when they showed you my picture."

Pulling her arm free from his grip, she said, "Well, they didn't. And they didn't show me your identikit picture. It was stuck up on the notice board for all to see. It didn't have a name on it."

"OK!" he said, but giving her the impression that he had strong doubts. "You can call me Richard. Now let's go and get that van."

Giving him a doubtful grin, she resumed walking and soon turned down a footpath. This led to another busy road. Barton followed a few steps behind her as she made a risky attempt to cross. Facing them was a filling and service station that looked as though it had seen better days. She held out a little hand palm upwards close to his face. "I need some cash to pay for it."

Barton grimaced, digging the bundle of notes from his pocket and noticing it was getting a lot thinner. Guessing what was to come next, he peeled off a few notes, and she snapped them out of his hand.

It happened as he assumed. A grubby little man in oily overalls stepped out the door. She stopped before approaching the service station, and Barton almost ran up her heels. "You stay here and stay out of sight."

There weren't many places where he could stay out of sight, so he began pacing down the pavement, all the while keeping an eye on her as she approached the little man. Barton turned in time to catch them entering through the door. Continuing pacing, he passed the station and heard an engine starting up. He stopped a few yards from the entrance and could see a large blue van pulling out onto the road, leaving a cloud of black smoke in its wake. She grinned as she pulled the vehicle up next to him.

"I need to go and pick up my things from Donnie's flat first," she said as he climbed in the passenger's side. "I've not had a chance to change my knickers in the last two days."

"You're not leaving yourself much time. Remember you have a meeting with that guy about your dog."

She nodded and pulled the van out into the flow of moving traffic. "We can go there after I get my things and then collect your stuff."

"After all *that's* been done," Barton replied nervously, noticing her driving skills weren't too good, "I need to have a word with that guy the police took you to identify in hospital."

She did a last-minute left turn into a narrow street and later into a council estate, stopping sharply in front of one of the houses. She jumped out, saying, "Slip over to the driver's seat and get ready to move the minute I get my stuff and jump in."

Barton would have loved to admire her shapely hips inside her tight jeans as she swayed her way along the path to the front door, but he knew better and kept a keen eye on his surroundings. Up ahead, a group of youths stood smoking. They stopped in mid conversation to ogle her, shouting comments and whistling. The moment she entered the house, the attention of the group turned towards the van. Barton became aware—when, after a brief conversation, they all grinned and nodded—he needed to be ready. He had seen this tactic before and knew what was to come next. He rammed the van into gear as the gang spread out and confidently headed towards him.

Holding the vehicle on the clutch, he waited until they were about a yard from him. Then ramming his foot down on the accelerator, he simultaneously lifted his foot swiftly off the clutch. The van jumped towards the youths, scattering them. Barton felt the bump and knew he had hit at least one of them. In his side mirror, he saw the group collect around their injured mates. He jumped on the brakes and put the lever into reverse. They quickly dispersed as he steered through them again.

With a black bin liner and a plastic shopping bag, she ran out the path and just managed to get in the passenger door before Barton continued on reversing the van out of the street. Concentrating on his rear-view mirror, he had no idea they were chasing after them until she shouted, "For fuck's sake, get this thing to go faster. They're catching up on us."

Instead of going faster, he jammed on the brakes, thumped the vehicle into a forward gear, and soon scattered them again.

"That bastard's a loony. Get the fuck out of here," Barton heard one of them shout.

"I think he could be right," Vesta cried, frantically trying to fasten her safety belt.

"Well, we got safely out, didn't we?" Barton said, wiping the sweat from his forehead.

"Now you understand what I meant when I said I had to live in my caravan when Donnie was away."

She directed him into a parking place behind a small church. Jumping out she said, "You wait here. I don't think this will take long." Finger combing her long dyed hair, adjusting her jacket, and puckering up her breasts, she headed for the only other vehicle parked there. She climbed into the passenger's seat, and the car instantly pulled away.

Daylight was beginning to fade when the car pulled in. She jumped out and trotted towards him.

"That took a lot longer than you must have estimated," Barton complained as he drove the van out the parking area onto the street. "Did you get info about your dog?"

A broad smile beamed across her face. "Yes, he's fine. The police found him under the bed. They have him in a compound. I need to go and claim him soon." She reached her hand into her hip pocket and pulled out a handful of twenty-pound notes. "I noticed you counting the cash you have and decided we'll need money to live on for a while, and you may have to pay for the storage of you stuff."

Shaking his head and driving at the same time, he said, "You didn't need to do that. I'll soon get some money."

Turning her head sharply, she stared at him, holding up her hand. "I didn't have it long enough for it to mark my finger, so why hold on to an engagement ring that a dead man gave me. I didn't have any feelings for him. I was frightened of what he would do if I turned him down."

Pulling the van up in front of the storage place, Barton couldn't shrug off the feeling of guilt over having assumed wrongly how she'd gotten the money. Yet at the same time, he felt elated. Jumping out of the van, he smiled, secretly thinking, *This girl is beginning to grow on me.*

"I could almost bet," she said, poking at his ribs with her elbow at the warehouse door, "that your taste in furniture is typically a man's—basically functional."

Before pressing the buzzer on the large double doors, he gave her a sideways glance. "Did you notice if any of those yobs were badly injured?

I'm sure I must have hit at least one of them."

"I wouldn't waste your concern on any of that lot. If you hadn't done what you did, I doubt we would be in a fit state to be standing here. Did you not notice they all had knives in their hands?"

Nodding his head and at the same time pressing the buzzer, he replied, "I did notice a couple of them with knives."

Warren Blackhurst grinned at the sight of Barton standing at his door. The same height as Barton but a lot slimmer and gaunt-looking, he stared straight into the visitor's eyes. "You've finally moved into your place?" His grin widened at the sight of the young woman standing next to Barton. "You've left it a bit late. If I was with her, I'd have moved in ages ago." After a glance along both directions of the street, he opened the double doors. "Back your van inside. I'll keep this lady company while you're doing that."

Taking Vesta's hand, Barton eased her back to the van, saying, "I'll manage to do that and reverse inside at the same time."

This resulted in a giggle from them all.

With no assistance from Warren, they finally got all Barton's furniture in the van and were driving the short distance to his flat. Luckily, the flat was on the ground floor, and within another hour, they had everything inside. They both flopped down on the sofa, breathing heavily. Barton put his arm around her shoulder, saying, "For a little girl, you're a strong one."

"Living with Donnie, I had to be," she said, resting her head on his shoulder.

"That man the police took you to see in hospital, I need to have a few words with him."

Shrugging herself away from him, she stared into his brown eyes. "Why? What's so important you have to risk going there?"

Following a long moment of deliberation, he said. "My parents have been abducted, and I'm positive he's involved."

Vesta jump to her feet, gazing down at him. "If you couldn't get info out of him when he was nailed to that floor, you'll have little chance getting it from him in a hospital bed, with other patients looking on."

"He was in no fit state to get anything out of, and he had been sedated."

"The police say he's claiming to have lost his memory. That's why I had to go there to see if I could identify him. They had checked his fingerprints and DNA and could find no record of him."

"Do you think he could be fit enough to abscond from the hospital?"

She shook her head. "Not in his condition. He has monitors and tubes attached all over him."

"Time's running out for my parents. They've been gone for over a week now. The more time I waste, the less chance I have of finding them alive."

"We need to get someone else to visit him," she said, settling herself back down beside him.

CHAPTER 28

Trying to persevere with the throbbing pains in his head and the shivering damp cold, Guppy was nearly at the stage of panic. He was thinking those old women might leave him here to die. The sneezing had started, this was the last thing he needed. He had to stay alert should they return. The first sign of them approaching would be the beam of light coming though the crack at the foot of the big door. Thinking they would have to use a torch to descend the stairs, he figured that would give him time to get prepared.

He crawled towards where he thought the door should be. In the sheer darkness, it would make no difference if his eyes were open or closed. After two attempts, his palm finally touched the rough wood. Running his fingers down it, he felt a space at the bottom. Although it wasn't wide enough for him to push a finger through, it was sufficient for him to see the light of a torch through it. His most important advantage was that he remembered this old door opened outwards. Positioning himself close to the door, he crouched ready to pounce.

How much time had passed, Guppy had no idea. His legs were beginning to cramp. His shoulders and arms were aching to the point where they could no longer support his weight. At the point where he needed to lie down and rest, a faint light caught his eye from under the door. This brought new life to his body and thoughts, and once again, he was alert. He repositioned himself, ready to make his attack.

Although he couldn't hear if they were nearing the bottom step, the beam of the torch got brighter, and he guessed the big old door would soon be pulled open. In a sudden realisation, he knew the moment that happened, he could be blinded by the light shining directly at him. A quick change of tactics had to be put in operation. His timing had to be spot-on. Letting about three seconds pass, he charged with all his weight. His expectations that the door would be opened at the moment that his body impacted was way out of sync. The vision came at him like a flash. It was the day of his twelfth birthday, and on his way home from school, he darted out onto the road, anxious to see what he had gotten for a present. The speeding car came at him, headlights on full beam. It had been his shoulder that had taken the brunt, knocked out of its socket. Now, the same had happened, and he felt the same excruciating pain. The old door stood solidly as he slid down it to the flagstone floor.

Strong hands lifted him from his underarms, sending even more pain shooting through his shoulder. Guppy realised he must have passed out. He screamed, but the lifting and dragging persisted. Tilting his head back, he first saw through the beams of bright torches that danced from his own body to the walls of bare stone a figure wearing a black ski mask. As if by magic the floor beneath his dragging heels changed from ragged flagstone to a smooth wooden surface. The next sensation was the comforting heat, and even through the pain, he felt relief and light-headed.

Rubber gloved hands touched the back of his neck. Guppy realised he was being stripped; he could feel his jacket being peeled off. Once again, he couldn't control his screaming as the sleeves were pulled over his dislocated shoulder. Again, the strong hands gripped his shoulders, and other hands took hold of his feet. The agony intensified when he felt himself being lifted. Relief came sooner than he had expected when he was dumped onto a padded leather chair. The masked face towered over him. Expecting a blow to the head, Guppy braced himself and closed his eyes tightly. A good few second passed, and the assault didn't happen. Blinking his eyes open, he found himself looking up at a ruddy face. "What's going on?" he managed to say, his voice sounding like a croaking frog.

A broad smile dawned across the tanned features, the blue eyes piercing into Guppy's. "I'm quite surprised at a big man like you—taken by three old ladies."

Struggling to get up, Guppy soon gave up when the throbbing pains from his shoulder intensified. Slumping back on the chair and breathing heavily, he said, "At last you show face?"

"You brought me into this, and I've had a lot of trouble and expenses ever since you asked me to grab the Barton couple. I want more cash from you."

Turning his head to the side to watch the slim figure in combat clothing turn and walk away caused considerable pain. "I paid you what you asked for. What have you done with them?"

Stopping and turning in military style, the figure grinned, waved his arms around the room, and nodded over Guppy's shoulder, "They're in here with you."

Ignoring the pain, Guppy twisted his head to see the elderly man kneeling down next to a plywood crate. He returned his head to see the figure walking out and closing the door. Like in the cellar, there were no windows. But at least there was light from a bare bulb attached to the wall above the door.

"Who are you?" The shaky voice came from behind.

Without turning, Guppy replied, "I was about to ask you the same question." Using only his feet, Guppy managed to bump the chair around, so he was facing the oldster. It took him a while to focus on the old man through tears of pain. Although he knew the answer to his next question, he still asked, knowing that, even against this old man, he was defenceless. "How long have you been here?"

Shakily and cautiously, the oldster approached and stared down at him. "My wife and I have been here for a week or so. I'm not quite sure. I've lost track of time."

Twisting his eyes from side to side, Guppy asked, "Where is your wife?"

"That bastard nailed her inside that crate. Said he was going to deliver her to our son. It must not have worked, for he brought the crate back with her in it."

"And she's still inside it?"

The oldster nodded his head. "I can't get the nails out. I need a claw hammer or something."

At the point of replying, Guppy noticed the old man's head quickly raise and his eyes gazing towards the door. Before Guppy got the chance to turn the chair, the figure in combat gear was pushing the oldster away. With a hypodermic syringe in his hands, the figure turned and jabbed it into Guppy's thigh. With only one hand to defend himself, Guppy took a wild swing, but it got easily warded off. The last thing he saw was the figure backing away and grinning.

—⚍—

Gazing into Vesta's blue eyes and on the verge of getting aroused, Barton jumped up. "I don't know anybody I could persuade to do that for me.

She grasped his hand, attempting to pull him back down beside her. "I do," she said. "But he'll want paying. He's a pro, thief, and a good con man."

Helpless to resist her tugging at his hand, he eased himself down beside her. "I'm not too sure about that idea. My dealings with con men always seem to end up with me being the loser."

"That won't happen," she assured him, easing herself closer. "This one's my half-brother, and he knows better than to try conning me."

Putting his arm around her shoulder and pulling her closer, he said, looking into her blue eyes, "OK! I think I can trust your judgement. How soon can you set this up?"

Easing herself up, she dug her mobile from the hip pocket of her jeans. "I'll call him and set it up now." Getting up onto her feet, she edged her way into the kitchen, talking into her phone as she went.

A few moments later, she returned with a look of shock on her face.

Jumping to his feet, Barton rushed towards her, taking hold of her arm. "What's wrong?"

She switched off her phone and placed it back in her hip pocket, saying in a shocked voice, "He's already in that hospital and in the same ward. And he's lying in bed looking at that man."

Stepping back from her, Barton gasped. "Did you not notice your half-brother when the police dragged you into ID Lorinna?"

She shook her head in response to his question and took a sudden step back, astonished. She gazed at him, her eyes wide, her mouth open. "So, that's his name? You do know that man?" Throwing her arms up, she turned her back to him. "Why is it that every man I get to know turns out to be a crook?"

"I told you he's somehow involved in the abduction of my parents."

"Please tell me it wasn't you who nailed him to that floor?" She slowly eased around to read his reaction.

It was Barton's turn to shake his head. "Why would I do that?" he said, taking a step closer. "When I found him, he was already nailed to the bloody floor and was out cold. All I could do was get help for him in the hopes they would take him to the hospital and that I could get in to visit and get some answers. I realise how silly that sounds, but it was my only chance."

Holding up her arms and shaking her head, she said simply, "I don't want to know any more. I'm already involved. And the less I know, the less chance I have of getting into trouble."

Remembering the life she'd talked about having with her fiancé, her words struck a deep painful chord, and he couldn't resist the temptation to embrace her. She reacted by turning round and folding her arms around his waist and resting her head on his chest. "I'll do everything I can to keep you out of this mess," Barton said softly, resting his chin on her head, "even if it means I have to visit Lorinna myself."

Stepping back, she looked up at him. "That's too risky for you. The police are watching him, and I've no doubt they won't be far away from my stepbrother. He said they escorted him in after he was beat up by one of his victims. He has a record a mile long. He's been in and out the nick since he was thirteen."

"Maybe I could go in disguised as one of the staff."

She gave him a mirthless laugh. "The only disguise you could get away with is the invisible man. But I could. I did some medical training when I was younger. I could get hold of a uniform. If I'm approached, I'd say I was from another ward and was sent to assist because of staff shortage. I could pretend I was checking on his progress."

"I'm not too sure that would work. The nurse at the station would simply get onto her computer and check you out. And that would be contrary to you not wanting to get involved any farther."

This time, her smile was that of a naughty schoolgirl, "I won't report to the station," she went on, her smile widening. "I'll simply walk past with an air of authority. The nurses will be only too pleased with any help they can get."

"You say the police are there. What if they recognise you from your previous visit?"

Again, the naughty smile. "By the time I've made myself up, they won't."

With an inquisitive grin, Barton asked, "How are you going to get hold of a nurse's uniform?"

Touching the side of her nose with a finger, she replied, "I have my methods." She picked up her plastic shopping bag and trotted to the toilet, leaving Barton trying to get his television to operate. When she finally joined him, he was shocked at the difference in her facial appearance. With a grey wig and thick-rimmed glasses and the previous slight tan almost invisible beneath a film of white foundation, Barton had to give her a second look to be sure she was the same person. "Bloody hell!" he exclaimed. "Have you had a stroke or something?"

"Do I look that bad?"

"You look twenty years older."

"If you didn't recognise me at this short distance, I doubt if those coppers will."

Abandoning sorting Barton's furniture out, they got into the van, with her driving heading out to the country.

"Where are we going? he asked after about two miles of silence.

"Not far now," she replied, grinning.

Suddenly, she swerved off the main road onto a small narrow lane. After a few hundred yard a large mansion came into view ahead of the vehicle's headlights. She pulled up at the front arched double doors and jumped out, shouting, "You stay here. I'll be about five minutes."

Watching her climb the wide set of steps and bang on the door with her fist, Barton wondered what was about to go down next. Was he letting this woman take over his life? One side of the doors creaked open a few inches, and a blade of light hit Vesta, once again shocking him at the change in her appearance. A few words were exchanged between her and the person inside. The door opened wider, and she stepped in.

The five minutes dragged on to ten. The cold was creeping up on him. He started up the engine, turning on the heater to full blast and was glad that he had done so, for at the same moment, the door burst open, and she came running towards him. Barton quickly opened the door, and she dived in the passenger's side, shouting, "Get us the fuck out of here." He turned to see a group of what looked like inmates from an asylum all dressed in long white nightshirts and armed with brushes and other cleaning tools chasing after her.

By the time he had got the van into gear and engaged the clutch, they had surrounded the vehicle, banging on the windows and sides with their makeshift weapons. He succeeded in edging his way through the ones at the front, but they chased, still thumping on the rear doors. When he turned the van onto the main road, he looked in his rear-view mirror and decided they had given up the chase. He sighed. "What was all that about?"

"A few years ago, my stepbrother took a mental breakdown. He was admitted in there. I visited him and noticed that the staff wore identical uniforms as the NHS nurses. I got friendly with some of the staff. That's why I got in out of visiting hours tonight. I chatted with some of them for a while until I saw one that was about my size. I took the opportunity when I was alone with her and thumped her and stripped this off her." Vesta held up the garment. "Now, pull in somewhere, and I'll get changed."

Watching her get changed stirred up a familiar emotion. He reached over, placing his hand on her bare knee. She instantly slapped it, saying, "We've no time for that now."

Barton withdrew and got the van moving the moment she had completed her disguise.

"You're an insatiable bastard," she said, whilst adjusting her grey wig and, at the same time, glancing in the rear-view mirror at her side.

"Not really. Just making up for lost time," Barton replied, noticing her regularly glancing in the mirror. "Are you expecting them to chase after us at this speed?"

She shook her head. "No. But I could bet the police will have been called in to assist in rounding up those inmates, and the head nurse will be reporting the reason they escaped and giving them a description of me and this van."

"Why did the inmates chase after you?"

"They must have heard the ruction of me attacking that nurse and got excited and saw me running out the door and chased after me."

As he pulled the van up close to the hospital doors, she got out, saying, "Park this up in a dark corner and watch for me coming out. And get over here pronto."

Giving her a mock salute, Barton grinned. "Yes, boss."

She delayed a moment and glanced back, saying, "If I was your boss, I'd have fired you long ago."

Before driving away, Barton delayed a moment to admire her hips swaying in the loose-fitting uniform as she walked casually through the glass doors.

Finding a suitable dark place to park up and still be ready to quickly get over to the hospital doors wasn't so simple. The car park was well illuminated and busy with cars crawling around, the drivers looking for a vacant spot. Also, the length and height of the van made it stand out from the other vehicles, and he judged it wouldn't fit into the spaces. In the end, all he could do was keep driving around in the hopes he would be close enough when she appeared.

CHAPTER 29

Weaving through visitors, nurses, doctors, and porters, Vesta proudly strutted her way to the ward. Her plan wasn't what Barton had instructed her. Instead she headed to the bed where her stepbrother lay playing with a mobile phone. Young Andy dropped his phone at the sight of this grey-haired nurse looking down at him. "Hi, shit arse," she said in greeting and sat on the chair by his bedside.

A broad grin dawned across his young features, and his whole demeanour seem to relax but only for a few heartbeats. He sat up, pulling his legs up close to his chest and knocking his phone out the side of the bed. With staring eyes, he muttered, "What's all this about, sis? Why are you dressed up like an old woman?"

"Shut up and listen." She scowled. "You claim to be able to spot a copper a mile away. Are there any wandering about here?"

With a slight tilt of his head, Andy whispered, "Don't look towards the door. One of them is looking in at us. There are two of them. They are to escort me to court in the morning."

"Why doesn't that surprise me?" Vesta said in a muffled voice. "Now listen carefully. That man in the second bed from the door, are the police still interested in him?"

"I think they must have given up on him, knowing in his state he's not going anywhere."

Remembering the tubes and monitors that surrounded Lorinna, she asked, "Is he communicating with them?"

Andy shook his head. "Guys like that don't say much to the coppers. I wouldn't mind a few moments with him myself."

"Why?!" The word came out louder than she'd intended it to, but the thought of her stepbrother knowing this man shocked her. In a more hushed voice, she said, "Why do you want a few moments with that man?"

"It doesn't matter," Andy replied, reaching down and retrieving his mobile. "Why are you here all dressed up like that? I saw you earlier with two uniforms at his bed. I ducked under the covers so you wouldn't see me. What was that all about?"

Standing up and bending over him as if taking his pulse, she said in a faint voice without looking at his eyes, "I need you to take one of your mental breakdowns and cause a distraction outside that door."

Andy didn't need to ask any more questions. With a nod and a wide grin, he swung his legs off the bed and walked out the room, closing the door. Vesta seated herself and waited for the disruption to happen. And it did a lot quicker than she had expected. A cold high-pitched scream shattered the comparative silence. Footsteps stampeded along the hallway, followed by voices yelling, and within a few minutes, nurses and porters were involved in a struggle outside the ward door. Vesta rushed to Lorinna's bedside. She slapped his face until his eyes opened. "I have a syringe here. I'll jab you with it, and in a second, you're a dead man."

Attempting to get up, Lorinna felt a hand on his mouth pushing him back down. "What do you want?" he managed to say, through this woman's fingers.

Still holding him down and glancing around the ward in case they were being overheard, Vesta was relieved to see the that the other patients were more interested in what was going on outside the ward. "I want to know who abducted the Barton family and where they are being held."

"I don't know what you're talking about."

Grinning close to his face, she withdrew her hand from his mouth. "Goodbye, Mr. Lorinna."

Failing to read what was in this woman's eyes for the light reflecting off her glasses, he cried, "OK. I don't know who it was that abducted them." He squirmed. "All I can tell you is that a guy they call Guppy hired someone to do it."

"Where do I find this guy, Guppy?"

"I don't know … You'd need to ask Boss Man that."

Squeezing one of his bandaged hands, she pressed. "Who's this Boss Man? Where do I find him?"

Realising he had little to lose and in a great deal of pain from her grip, Lorinna told her everything he knew about the organisation. But he couldn't give her any more information on the whereabouts of the Bartons.

"It looks as if you're in the shit from all sides," Vesta said, standing up and gazing into his drug-induced eyes. "With your cooperation I know someone who can help you get out of reach of the mob."

He tried to shake his head and cringed with the pain that it caused. "There's no way out of the reach of this organisation," he replied through tear-filled eyes.

The ward door burst open, and in popped four men carrying Andy, two of them holding each of his kicking feet, and the other two, his upper body. Realising now that the interrogation of Lorinna was over, she discreetly walked out the ward with her head lowered. People were still pushing their way in and out of the main exit door, and she became concerned how she was going to attract Barton's attention. She needn't have worried, as the moment she stepped out, his big hand gripped her upper arm, steering her towards the van.

Seated in the cabin of the van, he studied her. She looked deep in thought. When he could no longer hold back his frustration of wanting urgent info from her, he said, "What went down in there?"

She gazed into his brown eyes in the dim cabin light and placed a cigarette between her lips. Soon, the flashing from her plastic lighter illuminated her made-up features. After taking a deep drag of her smoke, she said, "He's a man who knows he is doomed. He has nothing to lose, and he poured his guts out to me."

"So, what did he tell you?" Barton said, impatiently drumming his fingers on the steering wheel.

"What I can gather is he is an outcast from a criminal organisation."

"Fuck, I guessed that."

Ignoring his comment, she went on. "Another member of that organisation named Guppy hired someone to abduct your parents. According to Lorinna, it had to be someone from special forces; they had learned you were in that force. This person had to be good enough to get into the house and out without you realising it. Who that was, Lorinna didn't know. He said to ask someone called Boss Man."

"Did he say why they abducted my parents?"

"He was having trouble pronouncing some of his words because of the pain and drugs. What I did gather is that it was something about a vendetta against you."

"I've never heard of this Boss Man," Barton snarled. "What have I done to him for him to want to have a vendetta against me? I don't even know where his operations are based." For a long moment, he leaned his elbows on the steering wheel and rested his head in his hands. "The only thing I can think of is we go back to your dead fiancé's house and search through it to see if we can find any info on this Boss Man. It's obvious your Donnie was one of his goons."

Tearing the grey wig from her head and tossing it on the dashboard, she cried, "Are you fucking mad? That bunch of thugs will rip us apart after what you did to them."

He shook his head and grimaced. "Not if they don't recognise us," he said, lifting his head off his hands and watching her readjust herself by wiping the white foundation from her face. "First, we need to take this van back and get other wheels. We go back to my place until about 3.00 a.m. We need to park a few streets away and walk to Donnie's house, hoping those thugs will be tucked up in bed."

Vesta snorted, gathering up the wig from the dashboard and the tissues she used on her face and dropping them into her plastic shopping bag. "I don't think those bastards ever go to bed. They can be seen prowling about at all hours. That's why Donnie had that big brute of a dog, not that it was any good, and why I moved into my caravan when he was away."

Starting up the van and getting it on the move, Barton shouted over the noisy engine, "When we get another car, you can stay with it, and I'll get into Donnie's house. Is there a back door?"

She nodded. "But I don't have a key for it. I can't remember Donnie using his back door."

"That's not a problem. I'll get in," Barton assured her. "When I get the other wheels, you can drive this back to that guy you got it from. I'll follow you."

"OK," Vesta replied, placing the bag between her legs. "But I'm coming in there with you. You don't know where to look. I know all Donnie's hiding places. I'm going in there with you. It'll save a lot of time."

—⟋𝔪⟍—

Choking on water stuck in his windpipe, Guppy felt it stopping his breathing. This brought on one of his recurring nightmares—from an incident in his childhood when his young mother had tried to drown him in the bath. Who had intervened and saved him, he was too young to remember. But he was old enough to remember his mother holding him under the hot soapy water. Jumping up, he found he was bound to a heavy padded chair with broad silver duct tape; the chair came up with him, causing him to lose his balance. Pinned down on the floor, unable to move, he looked up at the tall figure towering over him and holding a red plastic bucket.

"While you were out," the figure said, "I banged your shoulder back into place. I was trained to do that in the forces on a first aid course. I hope you haven't knocked it back out with that fall."

With a final choking cough, Guppy wriggled his shoulders and could no longer feel the pains. With a slight grin, he managed to say, "What's your game, mate?

The slim figure, dressed in disruptive pattern combat clothing, stepped around him. Guppy felt himself being lifted, and the chair was soon back on its feet with him still secured to it.

"My game is simple," the man said. "You hired me to abduct that couple." He jabbed his thumb over his shoulder, where Tom Barton stood next to the crate. "The cash paid me wasn't enough. I encountered extra expenses. I need it now.

"I don't have any cash on me, and you didn't deliver the old woman to her house."

"I know. I've already searched you. And I told you before why I couldn't deliver her. So, now you can lead me to where the cash is."

"I need to go to the top man, the guy who runs the organisation and get it from him."

From the side pocket of his jacket, the figure flicked out a P226 Sig Maremont pistol and pushed it under Guppy's nose. "You know what will happen if you play silly buggers."

Shrugging his head back the few inches it was allowed by the chair back, Guppy grinned. "I'll take you to him. But I can tell now, you won't get out of that building alive."

Holding the weapon in one hand, the figure produced with the other a flick knife and began cutting at Guppy's bindings. "I don't intend going into any building. In the boot of my car, I have a hand-held missile launcher. If you don't come out with my money in ten minutes, guess what!"

Guppy got stiffly up out of the chair. He noticed the man step back out of arm's reach, still aiming the pistol at his face. "You'll never get away with it." Guppy grimaced. "Too many witnesses. The building is near a busy shopping area. You'd have to carry your launcher through a precinct where hundreds of shoppers will see you take it out of whatever you're carrying it in. Then you will have to load it and aim it."

The flash from the muzzle blinded Guppy. The pressure of the blast sent him backwards onto the chair. It took what seemed to him hours for the red blotches in front of his eyes to fade away before he regained his normal sight, and soon the burning pain began from his left ear. Feeling the hot fluid running down his neck, he brought his hand up and howled when he touched raw flesh. When he saw the blood on his fingers, he held his hand up to the figure. "Did you have to do that?"

While Guppy was struggling to get up off the chair, the figure picked up the spent casing from the floor and placed it in his pocket. He pushed Guppy back down on the chair, saying. "Any more playing the silly bugger, and the other one gets it." He pointed the pistol into Guppy's face. "I'm not stupid. I know where your boss's headquarters are."

"If you know where the organisation's headquarters are, then you'll know you won't get near the place." Guppy gazed up at the man with a grin, exposing his badly stained smoker's teeth.

"I won't need to get near the place. The launcher has a range of about half a mile."

"That area has buildings all around the HQ. How can you be sure of hitting the target?"

The tall figure sniggered and grinned. "I inserted a device up your arse while you were out of it. The missile will find you and *bang*."

"Then you won't get your money."

"When you tell your boss about what's up your arse, he'll soon give you the cash."

"In ten minutes, he'll be out of that building and, in a car, flying out of the area. He has an escape route in case of a police raid."

"Well then," the figure replied, "I'll have to cut your time down to five minutes."

With the man at his back with his gun in his hand, Guppy was directed to where the figure had parked his vehicle. When they were standing next to it, the four-way flashers came to life. "Open the boot," he was ordered. When the interior lights came on, Guppy was looking down at a rectangular green plastic case. "Lift the container out," came the voice from behind, "and place it on the back seat." Guppy reluctantly agreed. "Now get in the boot," came the final order.

Guppy swung around, seeing the man was about six feet away and realising the distance was too great to attempt to jump this man. He said, "And if I don't, are you going to shoot me? The noise of the shot will get the attention of those people standing outside that pub." He nodded his head in the direction of the smokers.

The figure grinned and extracted a two-inch tube from his other pocket. In a blink of an eye, he had it attached to the muzzle of his weapon. Guppy knew it was a silencer and hastily climbed into the boot.

Before closing the lid, the man said, "If I hear a sound from you, I'll stop and blow your stupid head off." He handed Guppy a packet of tissues. "Hold that to your ear. I don't want your filthy blood on my car."

Knowing that it could be a good half hour's drive, Guppy lay curled up, feeling every turn and bump, which disturbed him from planning his next move. And what that move would be was dependant on how far he would have to walk from where the man dropped him off, and everything would be down to timing. He knew there was no way Boss Man was going to believe he had a device up his arse and knew he would never hand him the cash on such a stupid excuse. Now, it was down to self-preservation and fuck Boss Man.

The vehicle had made a few stops. Guppy realised it was because of traffic queues and lights. But he knew this one was their destination. The boot lid opened, and the man grabbed his arm and pulled him out. Shocked at how easily this man was able to do this, Guppy realised he was dealing with a superfit guy—the kind who could kill with his bare hands.

Taking a few steps away, the figure whipped out his gun, covering it with a dark cloth. "Your five minutes starts now."

On wobbly legs, Guppy turned. Realising he had about a hundred yards to cover before reaching the door, he staggered around a truck and a few cars. Inside, the long corridor that faced him had doors on either side. He barged into the first one on his right, knowing this was the toilet. Two vacant cubicles faced him with open doors. Not taking the time to close the door, Guppy quickly dropped his pants and got sat on the plastic seat. Luckily, he had an easy bowel movement, and he was soon wiping his arse. Worried at what time he had left, he still chanced a look down into the bowl. He cursed himself for his thoughtlessness at not taking a look in the bowl before tossing toilet tissues in on top of his faeces. Quickly flushing it all away, he gambled that the device would travel down into the sewage pipes and out of the building. He had no other choice or time. All he could think of doing was getting to Boss Man, hoping he would be scared and hand over the money.

Shouldering past the goon standing at the door, Guppy almost toppled a chair as he entered the large board room. Sat halfway down the long table, two gang members were debating on what they were looking at on a laptop. Knowing the goon at the door would have informed Boss Man of his unexpected visit, Guppy stood staring at the door the little man always entered through.

Silently watching Boss Man getting settled in his usual seat at the top of the table, Guppy could feel a fit of sneezing about to attack, and it did a lot sooner than expected. The two goons stopped in the middle of their argument to look at him. The little man waited impatiently, grunting and sighing.

"What's the meaning of this intrusion?" came the gruff voice from the other end of the table.

Finally getting his fit under control, Guppy explained all that had gone down with the man, only leaving out the part where he had been taken down by three old ladies.

The response from the little man was far from what Guppy had expected. Instead of Boss Man getting into a mad panic, he burst into a fit of laughter. The two goons soon joined in. "You stupid idiot," Boss Man howled between bouts of giggling. "A device like that would have to be about the size of a bean tin, if such a thing existed. You would know if it had been stuck up your arse, and it would have been painful trying to pass it.

The laughter burst out again, bringing on another fit of sneezes from Guppy.

"Be sure you don't sneeze it out your nose," Boss Man added, kick-starting the laughter again.

When the merriment died, and Boss Man took on a more sombre expression, he said, "Where is this guy who says he has a missile launcher?"

Chancing his luck, not having been invited, Guppy sat on the chair he had almost toppled. "The last place I left him was behind that old filling station on the main road."

The signal from Boss Man's little hand towards the tinted mirror at his back was enough to let Guppy know it was time to get out and meet up with some goons and seek out this man with the launcher.

There were only two goons at the door when Guppy stepped out. "Fuck," he snarled, "is this it? We need more bodies to catch this bugger."

After the two goons had been given a description of the man they were to roust and been gunned up, they spread out, arranging to arrive at the filling station at the same time. Taking a longer route than the other two, Guppy was expecting them to wait for him. His plan was that they would jump this man together. Standing at the corner of the nearest building to the station, he couldn't see any life about the place. After a few minutes of looking around in search of the goons and failing to find any sign of them, he started to walk slowly, expecting them to join him from their hiding places. This never happened. Guppy stopped a couple of yards from the forecourt. He realised he was on his own and very much out in the open. He made a quick dash to the glass front door, expecting shots to be fired at him. He sighed, panting and supressing a sneezing fit, and leaned his back on the plateglass door. For a while, he listened for movement that never came.

Around the back of the station, expecting to find the figure's vehicle, Guppy was shocked to see it was gone. The only cover he could see close enough to reach was an old square metal fuel tank painted black and built on top of a few layers of bricks. He ran towards it, darted down behind it, and was surprised he had reached it without shots being fired at him. As an afterthought, as he crouched down on his knees, it occurred to him the sound of gunshots would attract attention from the people living in the flats that surrounded the filling station. This guy in the camo suit wasn't stupid enough. But the two goons were, and if they had spotted this guy, they would have blasted off a few rounds.

Having no timepiece on him, Guppy had no idea how long he had crouched there and decided to get up and search inside the building. He was surprised to discover the rear door was unlocked, surprised and shocked. With his fingertips, he gently pushed it open. But at this stage, he didn't put a foot inside. In his wave of thoughts, this was an obvious trap. Letting the door swing creakily to its extent, he charged in, hoping this would be the last thing the camo man would be expecting.

He found himself in an abandoned kitchen, with mugs and cutlery scattered over a dust-covered table. Under a steel-meshed window, a large white square sink half full of slimy water offended his nostrils as he squeezed past it. Beyond this, Guppy concentrated on the door that faced him. Putting his ear to it and getting no sound from inside, he once again finger pushed this one. On the floor, facing upwards, lay the two goons.

No way was Guppy, remembering the last assault on him by the three old ladies, going to walk into that trap again. Silently and as quickly as he could, he about turned and headed for the rear door. He couldn't remember closing it but was glad that he had, for as he neared it, he noticed the handle being turned gently. Being the impulsive type, he quickly pointed his gun and fired three shots through it. He stood silently for a long moment, hoping to hear a painful cry or a moan, but the silence continued. Finally, when his patience ran out, he stood at the side of the door with his back against the wall, and using his fingertips, he turned the handle.

The old door slowly opened but only halfway, as it got jammed on the loose floor covering. Easing his head around the framework, he stared down at the man in camo gear—who was crouched over, his head now leaning on the half-open door. A pool of blood covered almost half of the steps where he lay.

Guppy didn't need to examine this man to know he was gone. But to make sure, he stepped over his crouching body and put another round into the back of his head.

CHAPTER 30

Staring wide-eyed at him, Vesta gasped. "You're not going to buy a car off *him*." She followed Barton's gaze after he had parked the van close to the yard with the neglected wire mesh fencing and twisted tube-framed gate.

Grinning, Barton leaned over and clasped his hand over hers. "So, you know Jimmy Stitch. I'm not going to buy one. I'm going to nick it."

It was Vesta's turn to grin. "Does he have anything worth nicking?"

"We'll soon find out," he replied, getting out the van door and saying, "Get in the driver's seat. When you see me crashing though that gate, get ready to follow me back to that guy you got this van from."

"I don't like following," Vesta protested. "I always manage to lose the car I'm supposed to follow. Why can't you follow me?"

Watching her climb into the driver's seat, he said, "With one of Jimmy's cars, I'm guaranteed to run out of fuel. That way, if that happens, you can get some for me." With a wave, he turned and was soon climbing over the gate and then out of sight behind a large wall at the rear.

Shaking her head as she watched Barton stumbling over broken car parts, Vesta remembered the day she and Donnie had come here to buy one of Jimmy's cars; they'd only gotten halfway home when the engine blew up. She'd had to pull Donnie off him before Jimmy got killed. From inside the yard, a dog barked, startling her out of her revelry, and she quickly started the engine. Moments later, the crash of an old car ramming through the gate made her ram the van into first gear. In her mirror, she saw Barton at the wheel as he swerved around the van. She engaged the clutch, and the vehicle jumped forward and was soon behind the stolen car. She kept it just a few feet from the bumper.

As had been previously arranged, in case the place might be closed when she returned, she drove the van around the back of the hirer's building. Barton parked at the front, waiting for her. When she appeared, she marched up to his window, and he wound it down. "You've no fucking rear lights on that piece of shit," she shouted. "The first patrol car we pass will come after us."

He shrugged his shoulders. "It's not far, and I'll keep to the side streets. And that's not the only problem. We're running on fumes. If we run out, we'll have to leg it."

Leg it they did, but luckily, they didn't have too far to go. They soon came to the back lane that led to Donnie's backyard. In the darkness, she lit her mobile as they stumbled their way over toppled wheelie bins. They passed numerous wooden gates, and Barton had to stop and ask her which one was Donnie's.

"I'm not sure. I've never been down here before," she replied, the light from her phone exposing her confused expression.

Following a few more cautious steps, they came to a broken gate that lay on its back. "Try this one," Barton said, stepping over the wooden remains.

"This is it," Vesta whispered. "I remember looking out the back window and seeing the state of the gate and the garden."

The back door proved not to be a problem, and they were soon walking through a small kitchen. "Where do you think Donnie kept his diary or whatever he kept some kind of records on?" Barton whispered.

"I know where he kept a gun and some knives," she replied, walking past him and opening a door.

Following her through it, Barton found himself in an L-shaped lounge. In the light from an outside streetlamp, he could see it was overcrowded with fifties-style furniture. There were no curtains on the widow, and Barton knew why this was. He, like this guy, liked to have an all-round vision of what was going on outside, who was loitering in the area, and what cars were parked close to his house.

He leaned closer to her ear and whispered, "Donnie was a bit old-fashioned with his taste in furniture."

Getting down on her knees, she pulled a box out from underneath a sideboard. "This was his parents' house. They died suddenly when he was a teenager. He's lived here ever since." She lifted the wooden box and placed it on the table.

Thinking it looked heavy, Barton attempted to help, but she had placed it down before he could get a hand on it. Seeing her struggling to get the lock open, he intervened with his knife and soon flicked it open. She gasped at the sight of what was inside and stepped back. Barton was equally shocked at the number of guns and knives inside. There were even a few grenades and sticks of dynamite. Looking closer, he could tell they had been cleaned and were ready for use. "You looked a bit shocked when you saw this,"

Barton said. "I thought by the way you pulled it out you knew what was inside that box."

Now sat back on the old sofa, her eyes and mouth were wide. "I knew of the box. I'd always wondered what was inside but couldn't get a chance to open it. I was only here when Donnie was here with me."

Closing the lid and tucking the box back under the sideboard, Barton turned to her. "That's not what we came here for." He held out his hand and helped her back onto her feet. "What other secrets does he have hidden?"

"I know where he stashed some drugs." She pointed her finger up at the ceiling and opened another door. Sensing him close behind, she climbed a steep set of carpeted stairs. At the top, she opened a door. "This was his bedroom." She grimaced.

Barton looked up at a small attic door above their heads. "How do we get up there?"

"I think Donnie used a chair."

Stepping behind her through the open door, he found himself in a small bedroom with a king-size unmade bed. She pointed behind. He turned and found the chair. He had to lift it high above his head to get it past the bed and out the door. Placing it under the attic entrance, he hoisted her onto it and admired her shapely hips as she eased herself through the small opening. He followed her up but had trouble squeezing his bulk through the space.

She had located the switch, and a blinding tubular light shone above their heads. Barton noticed the surprise in her face as she gasped in awe at the sight that faced them. He was surprised himself at the conversion that had been made. The attic looked like a control room, with numerous computers on a long desk down one side. A smaller desk sat at the far end. Behind this was a large black padded leather chair. Barton turned to see a large plywood sheet on an easel that was plastered with photographs. The first thought that came to his head was, *This is some kind of operation room.* "What the fuck's been going on here?" he gasped.

Below the long desks were numerous drawers. Vesta began pulling at the handle of the nearest. Finding it locked, she held out her hand for Barton's knife. Barton held back and asked, "Just how much did you know about your Donnie?"

She looked up into his brown eyes with confusion written all over her features. "It seems not a lot by the look of this place."

He waved his arms around. "Look at all this equipment. How did he manage to get it in through that small attic door? There has to be another way in here."

Shaking her head, she stepped away from the drawer. "I only ever saw him use that chair once."

"Look around you," Barton said, still waving his arms. "This is some kind of operation room. And by the amount of ash trays and the butts in them, a team has occupied this place." He pointed at the tall stools that were place in front of computer monitors. "There has to have been at least three operators working in here." Reaching over and picking up a half-full mug of coffee from the long desk, he sniffed at it and dipped his finger in, finding it cold. But it looked as though it had been used within a few days. "How could you have lived here and not known about this?"

Again, she shook her head. "I knew Donnie had something going on up here, but I had no idea what."

"Didn't your curiosity get the better of you to at least ask?"

"I was too afraid to ask."

"You must have seen a team of operators arrive and climb up here."

"As you said, there has to be another way in here," she replied, holding out her hand for his knife.

While Vesta got to work on the drawer with his knife, Barton searched for another entrance and soon found it, hidden behind a large plywood board. He knew the door would be locked. Nevertheless, he had to try it. His assumption was spot-on, and he discovered it was an expensive-looking device remotely connected to an alarm. He backed away, not daring to put too much pressure on the handle. He turned at the sound of Vesta's exited cry. He was surprised to see she had managed to open one of the drawers.

Pointing her finger at it, she said, "Every one of them could be crammed with plastic bags full of white powder like this. I don't think we're naive enough not to know what that powder is. There has to be a street value of around a million quid if they are what I think they are."

He placed a comforting hand on her shoulder and looked deep into her blue eyes. "You know what I think. Donnie got himself involved with a big-time dealer and offered him this place to hide the stuff. He must have underrated the enormity of the operation. And when things started to get out of hand, and when this operation got too serious, he wanted a bigger share of the profits.

"That could be why he got killed. Maybe the other guys were the team that operated in here," she replied.

Steering her towards the attic door, he said, "We'd best get out of here, or we could be next." He helped her down onto the chair. When he got his bulk through and the hatch door into place, he stepped down beside her, saying, "We need to search in here. He might have left some kind of clue as to who the Boss Man is or even where his organisation's HQ might be located."

Entering the living room, Vesta stopped at the sight of the wooden box below the sideboard, and Barton nearly ran up her heels. Swinging around, she found herself inches from his chest and stepped back with a look of horror on her face. "To think I lived in here with all this going on."

He could do nothing but stand there staring into her blue eyes, feeling the same dread she had telepathically shared.

Turning away from him, she stepped around the sofa, saying, "How could I not have suspected as much? I never at any time heard movement from the attic. To think, I would lie in his bed, and all this was going on above us."

"How regularly did you stay here?"

Shrugging her shoulders, she said, "Quite regularly—until Donnie said he was going away. Then I would move into my caravan with Gilbert."

Thinking back to the time they shared in that small caravan, Barton couldn't visualise her staying in those cramped conditions for any length of time with that big dog. He remembered how they'd laughed when she'd fallen over Gilbert on her rush to the toilet. Also, there had been a hesitant moment when she'd had to think where the spare bedding was stored. Not the actions of someone who lived there quite regularly.

Was this him letting his feelings for this girl cloud his judgement? How did she know where to locate the light switch so quickly up in that attic? She was also quick at locating the chair Donnie used to climb up on. Was this his old paranoia taking over?

CHAPTER 31

Pulling the body back from the door by the collar of his combat jacket and leaving it lying face up, Guppy searched through the pockets and found the keys to his car. As a bonus, he pulled out the man's wallet and retrieved most of the money he had previously given this guy but could find no means of identification. His next find could be even better than ID. And for the first time in the last few days, Guppy smiled, stuffing the man's mobile into his hip pocket. The smile soon disappeared when the thought struck him that all those shots he had fired would have been heard, and in a matter of minutes, armed police would arrive, sent for by the neighbours living in the flats that surrounded the filling station. He guessed that, if this had happened, eyes would be on this place. And if he rushed out, he would be spotted and even videoed by someone's mobile.

Leaving by the front entrance, which would mean crossing the forecourt, was a definite no. The traffic on the busy street at the front was too noisy for him to listen for the sirens. Realising his time was running out, Guppy slunk back to the cover of the square fuel tank. Leaning his back against it and focusing through the darkness, he searched for a way out. He noticed a gap in the chain-link fence, and he only needed to cover a few yards to reach it.

He had to crawl feetfirst through the gap, lying on his stomach. In a final push, he ripped his jacket to get his upper body free. That was when the beam from a powerful torch shone above his head. Ducking down and rolling over, he felt himself falling and sliding down an embankment and failing to grip onto dark-shaped bushes.

Only for a split second did the ice hold his weight before it cracked noisily, and he was sinking in freezing water. When only his head and shoulders remained above the water and his feet had hit the bottom, panic began to take over. Guppy knew he had to get out of this before hypothermia set in and stiffened his limbs into a paralysis that would soon take over the rest of his body and his life.

Although Guppy cursed his disability of sneezing fits, he learned later that it was this that attracted the attention of the police armed division, who pulled him out of the freezing water and rushed him to the hospital.

Although now in the hands of the law, he at least still had his life. Not that it would amount to much once they investigated the criminal organisation he was a part of and the murders he had committed. He determined he must somehow get out of this hospital, though he realised that the police would be here guarding him to make sure that didn't happen.

Had it been the intensive heat that had aroused him from what he decided could have been a coma? Lying on this bed, he could feel every tissue in his body ache. His limbs were stiff and unworkable. How long would this go on? Memories of the icy water and the stiffness of his limbs and the sinking feeling of drifting into unconsciousness swept over him. *Is this how it all ends?* he remembered thinking. In a flashing vision, the faces of the people who had meant nothing to him who he had killed all stared at him, each pointing an accusing finger and laughing. "I was ordered to ... I was ordered to."

Realising he must have been screaming, he discovered he was sitting up on the bed when a group of hospital staff crowded around him, all fighting him back down. Exhausted and feeling his eyes getting heavy, he knew he had been injected. But his limbs were so numb he never felt the needle. An overwhelming surge of panic gave him a little strength to put up a feeble resistance when his last thought entered his head, *I am now in police custody.*

Opening his eyes slowly at the sound of distant voices, his vision was blurry. Je could make out shapes of faces, but the features were out of focus. As if he were lying under the branches of a tree, they all seemed to hover above him. "What's happening?" he heard himself say, his voice sounding alien.

"You're in hospital," a high-pitched male voice declared. "The police rescued you from the water of a frozen pond."

Attempting to get up, Guppy felt sets of hands restraining him. "How long have I been in here?" he asked, surrendering to the force that held him down.

"Not long," another voice from behind the first said. "We need to know who you are—we couldn't find any identification on you—so we can inform relatives."

Still not recovered fully from almost being a hypothermia victim, Guppy couldn't recover the sharp workings of his brain and could only think of the obvious. "I don't know who I am. I seem to have lost my memory."

"We seem to be getting a lot of your kind in here lately." This came from a female, who forced herself to the front of the others. Guppy could now distinguish her features as she bent over him, her face a few inches from his. She unblinkingly gazed down at him with watery blue eyes. A broad grin dawned across her pale face, which contrasted with ruby-red lips. Holding up a finger she said, "Follow my finger without moving your head."

The test only lasted a few minutes. The woman stepped aside, and her face was replaced with a black man's. "Get his clothes. He's coming with me." In an instant, a set of handcuffs got clamped on Guppy's wrist. "We know who you are." The black man grinned triumphantly, exposing a set of pure white teeth Guppy thought was rather small for a big man. "We found a mobile phone close to where you were rescued."

Before realising what was happening, he was hoisted onto his feet, looking down at another man, who was struggling to pull trousers up his legs and another who was jamming a pair of trainers on Guppy's kicking feet. "That mobile phone's not mine," he shouted as they dragged him towards the door. Before they managed to get him out of the ward, he noticed the man who was lying in the next bed. It was only a fleeting glance, but it was enough for him to recognise Lorinna. "You bastard," Guppy shouted, struggling to free himself to get to Lorinna. "You're a fucking dead man."

Hour after hour, the black detective and his colleague interrogated him in a small interview room with grey walls and a two-way mirror behind them. Guppy sat back on the padded chair and was glad to have been uncuffed, while the detective sat leaning over the table with notebooks and pens and a recorder in front of them. All he needed to answer was, "I can't remember."

"You remembered the mobile phone wasn't yours," the colleague shouted for the umpteenth time.

"Did I? I can't remember."

"I would have thought, with us saving your life, you'd be more cooperative," the black detective cut in.

"I can't remember."

The colleague gritted his teeth and stood up. "I'm going for a piss."

"I'll join you," the black detective said, getting up and following his colleague.

"Don't be playing with each other's dicks," Guppy shouted and grinned as they slammed the door. "I'll just piss on the floor." He laughed and stuck up a two-fingered gesture at the mirror.

Expecting a long boring wait, Guppy stretched back on the chair with his hands behind his head and grinned at the mirror, knowing he was being studied by the personnel behind it. Unexpectedly, the door flew open, and in marched a tall white-haired man, wearing a green tweed jacket and corduroy trousers finished off with a pair of brown highly polished boots. Guppy place him on the farm, rather than in a police station. He was followed by the same two detectives, the colleague carrying a chair. The big man sat opposite, while the other two placed themselves at either end. Guppy knew the drill. This was a tactic to make him feel vulnerable and also for them to study his body language.

The big man cleared his throat and slapped a large manila envelope on the table, "Have these two introduced themselves?" he said, waving a hand at the detectives at the end of the table.

Still retaining his grin, Guppy shook his head and sat forward, leaning on the table like the big man.

"I'm DS Tragg. This is DC Meldrum." He pointed to the black detective. "And his colleague is DC Jarvie. They tell me you claim to have lost your memory. That's understandable, since you were very close to death by hypothermia; maybe some of your brain cells haven't fully recovered."

"That's if there were any there in the first place," DC Jarvie added, and both he and Meldrum laughed, while Tragg ignored the comment.

Tragg dug his big hand into the envelope and pulled out the mobile in a sealed transparent plastic bag. "This is the phone in question. Are you sure it's not yours?"

"I'm not sure," Guppy replied, shaking his head.

"So, if you're not sure, there's a chance it could be yours?"

"I'm sure it's not mine," Guppy shot back, staring into the big man's intensive blue eyes beneath his overgrown eyebrows.

Digging his hand into the envelope again, Tragg pulled out another plastic bag. Inside this one was Guppy's pistol. "Is this yours?"

"I've never seen one of those, never mind owning one." Guppy replied, making sure he held this man's gaze and keeping his body still.

Replacing the bags back into the envelope, Tragg stood up, saying, "We'll send this lot to forensics, and you can hope your prints are not on any of them … Oh, by the way, we found a body lying on the back doorstep of that old filling station and another two inside. They had all been shot." Leaving his words resonating through the room, he and the other two detectives walked out, with Jarvie deliberately making an issue out of slamming the door.

Sitting on a slab that represented a bed, Guppy lay listening to drunks and junkies shouting they wanted a lawyer and other nasty threats through the steel doors. The cell was a comfortable temperature, and he lay back, wondering what the results of his legal phone call would be. Only he hadn't called a lawyer. He called Boss Man, who informed him he was a lucky prick to be in a safe cell and that the mob's goons "are after *you*" for the missing drugs.

CHAPTER 32

A thorough search of Donnie's house gave them negative results. "What now?" Vesta asked as she followed Barton out the back door. He said nothing as he slunk over debris and the broken gate. Crouching down on his knee, he waited till she approached and whispered, "We need to go back to the hospital and find out from that guy where this Boss Man's HQ is."

She shot up onto her feet and shouted, "Are you fucking crazy, after the disruption from our last visit?"

"I'll go in this time," he replied, jumping up and scouring for signs that she might have been heard.

"You can't, you great stupid lump." She punched him on the arm as he began sneaking along the lane with bent back and head down towards the busy street. Adapting the same posture, she chased after him and caught up with him standing under a streetlamp. "We'll head back to that old banger and get my bag; I'll soon get changed," she said, carrying on walking in the direction where they had abandoned the car.

Shrugging his shoulders and shaking his head, he replied, "If you insist, boss." And he followed behind her. "If we can get some fuel for the banger, we could use it to get around quicker."

Just as the words left his mouth, she stopped at the corner of the building close to where they had abandoned the car and gasped, pointing along the street. Barton edged around her to see a carrier hoisting the banger up the ramp onto its deck.

She turned, dropped her hand and shoulders, and let out a deep sigh. "What now?" she demanded.

Watching the driver securing the car, Barton suggested, "I'll keep the driver talking and distracted. You can get onto that truck and grab your bag out of the banger."

Patting the driver's vis jacket on the man's shoulder, Barton asked where he was taking that old car. The driver shook his head, saying he had been instructed to take it back to his depot. "The reason I'm asking," Barton replied, "I'm busy restoring one of the same make. If you had any idea where you will end up taking it, I'd be grateful for that information." Barton flashed a few twenty-pound notes under his nose, and the driver hastily took them and gave him a few addresses where he would eventually dump it.

When the truck pulled away, she was standing in front of him holding up her bag. She stepped over, grinning. "You're a crafty bastard."

Nodding and grinning with her, he said, "Where do you intend getting changed?"

"In the hospital public toilet."

Leaving Barton sitting at the back of the waiting room, his head buried in an out-of-date magazine, Vesta entered the lady's toilet and, a few minutes later, came out reformed, looking like a middle-aged nurse. Unlike her previous visit, she was carrying the plastic bag with her own clothes, something neither she nor Barton had given thought to. The only thing she could think of to discard it was to risk walking among the rest of the waiting visitors and leaving it down beside Barton's feet. Noticing a few other nurses talking to visitors, she didn't hesitate to approach Barton and leave her bag.

After a few words with him that had nothing to do with their situation, for the reason of not looking out of place. she smiled and walked towards the wards as he picked up her bag and placed it on the seat next to him. Anyone noticing this would think he was a patient waiting to get a lift home.

She stepped back with the shock of finding another patient lying on the bed Lorinna had occupied. She scoured the room looking for him, hoping he had just been moved to another bed. Some were empty, but it looked as though patients could be in a restroom. When she asked an elderly man sitting on a chair if he knew where the restroom was, he gave her a toothless grin and pointed a gnarled finger at the door.

Noticing a man leaving through a door at the end of the corridor, she guessed that was the restroom. A wide-screen television was the first thing she noticed when she entered the darkened room. The flickering exposed the features of the few people sitting with their eyes glued on the program. It was the bulky bandages on his hands that she noticed first, and she took the empty seat next to him. Nudging him with her elbow, she asked quietly, "Do you remember me?"

He turned his head slightly towards her and quickly returned his attention back to the program on the tele. She followed his gaze and was shocked to see the news presenter reporting about the gangland killings that were taking place in the area. Pictures of the victims came on the screen. She counted seven in all, and what shocked her most was the mugshot of Donnie. "I could have been one of them," Lorinna mumbled.

"What's all this about?" she leaned closer, whispering into his ear.

"Drugs, big time. I'm talking tons."

"The last time we spoke, you mentioned a guy you called Boss Man. Tell me where I can locate him, and I could solve your problems."

Again, he turned and looked into her eyes for a long moment as if trying to read what she had to gain from this info and how she could solve his problem. "Are you some kind of undercover cop, or what?"

Shaking her head, she replied, "Nothing like that; just trying to help a friend."

"Must be a very good friend for you to risk asking questions about this mob." He nodded towards the screen. "You and your friend will finish up added to that list."

"Are you going to help then?" Vesta asked, a little louder than she had intended.

She noticed a slight grin playing on his thin lips. "You need to keep your voice down; nurses are not supposed to raise their voices at a patient," he mumbled. Leaning his head closer to her, relishing her perfume, he said, "I need you to help me first."

"How am I supposed to help you when you're in here?"

"I need to get out of here. They won't discharge me if I haven't got someone to help me get on with my everyday life." He held up his heavily bandaged hands. "I can't feed myself like this. Can't even wipe my arse."

"So, you want me to tell them I'm willing to care for you until your injuries heal?"

He shook his head, making him wince in pain. "No. That won't work. They'll ask for names and addresses, and the coppers will have to check them out. That's the last thing I want to give them. You, dressed as a nurse, could get one of those wheelchairs and wheel me out of here, saying you're taking me to another ward if you're questioned."

"So, when I get you outside, what then?"

"You can drive me, and I'll take you to the Boss Man."

With a quick look around the room, she said, "What about the police? Aren't they watching you?"

"I think they've decided, with this lot"—again he held up his hands —"I'm not going to get far. Now, they only check on me by phoning the nurses."

"I need to speak with my friend," she said and stood up. "You do realise the risk we're taking if we do that?"

Returning his attention to the television, he replied through the side of his mouth, "It's me who's taking all the risks. Boss Man has a contract out on me."

When she had finished informing Barton the conditions Lorinna had laid out, he was left with no other choice but to confess. "I've had dealings with this guy. If he sees me, he'll shit himself and want you to return him back to the ward."

"Well, we'll just have to make sure he doesn't see you." They stood inside the main hospital door sheltering from a heavy snow fall. "You'll have to put your talent at nicking cars to use," she went on, "only this time you'll have to nick two, one for me to take him to this Boss Man and the other for you to follow in."

Fastening his leather jacket and pulling up the collar, Barton stepped out the door with her arm hooked around his. He held out the plastic bag to her, saying, "You'd better get something warm out of that. It's going to be chilly night ahead of us." Passing lines of snow-covered cars, he led her into the nearest bus shelter, where they stood behind passengers waiting for a bus that might never turn up in this weather. "He's a devious little shit," he said, leaning close to her ear. "Why don't you just wheel him out here. I've an idea how to get the truth out of him. I'm sure that's his plan—to get you to push him out, and the minute he's out that door, he'll jump at the first opportunity to run."

Pulling her jacket out of the bag and wrapping it around her shoulders, she gazed up at him with a shocked look in her wide-set blue eyes. "On a night like this? Only wearing a hospital gown? Surely, he's not that stupid."

Seeing her shiver, he put his arm around her waist for body heat. "Oh! He's not silly, but he's desperate to get himself lost. On one side, the law is observing him, I've not doubt looking for a reason to charge him. On the other, according to what he's told you, the mob is out to get him. He has no intentions of taking us to this Boss Man."

Mulling over what he had said, she finally looked up at him. "We'll have to do something if you're to get your parents back soon. They could be locked up in a cold house, even a shed somewhere. They'll be freezing."

"If you had let me finish telling you my plans," Barton said, pulling her tighter into his body. "I'll nick a van. I'll crouch down in the back of it, let him think you're on your own, get him into the front seat beside you. With his hands bound up in all that dressing, he'll not be able to open the door and jump out. I'll soon let him know I'm in the back, and with a gun at the back of his head, he'll soon take us to this Boss Man."

An extended period of silence followed as they watched a bus pull up. The passengers got boarded before they were on their own and she replied. "As you say, he's not stupid. He'll realise, if you shoot him, you won't get to this Boss Man."

"Oh! I won't kill him, and he knows that. But I could inflict a lot of pain."

"What if he decides you're bluffing and don't have the balls to hurt him."

"As soon as he realises who's holding the gun at his head, he'll know I'm not bluffing."

Holding each other in the bus shelter, they waited until the snow eased off, and then went on the hunt for a suitable van. Getting the type of vehicle Barton had in mind proved to take a lot longer than expected, and wading in the snow didn't help. All the way, Vesta cursed and swore like a building site labourer. He had to support her most of the way, cursing at the shoes she wore, bloody trainers in this weather.

Jammed between a truck and a car, he saw a small Astra van. "Ideal," he said to her. "Now all we have to do is get it out of this tight squeeze." Getting it started wasn't a problem, but it took them a good few valuable minutes to bounce it out. Finally, with Vesta driving, they entered the hospital parking area. She was lucky to find a spot close to the doors. As planned, Barton got in the back and waited.

Although he felt quite cramped inside the rear of the small van, he managed to twist himself into a position where he could watch the front doors through the rear window. Barton wasn't feeling too good, and his cursed claustrophobia was gradually taking over. And if that wasn't bad enough, his legs began to cramp up. To crown it all, the snow began again, this time with huge flakes. Visibility was getting poorer by the minute. As the time dragged, the windows began to steam up, and his phobia drove him almost to the point of jumping out. When he could see nothing through them, it happened. The hazard lights flashed, and the passenger's door opened. Although he was expecting this, it startled him. He was even more startled when the cabin light came on, and the person who climbed in wasn't Lorinna.

—ⱴ—

His confidence was quickly diminishing, and waves of panic set in. Boss Man sat in his usual seat, his breathing apparatus in his hand ready for use as the three suited men entered. His only defence was the three goons behind the mirror, and he knew that, by the time they got in here, he would be dead meat. He had been informed about the fate of the four goons and had rushed to see the broadcast about the incident on his television. With Donnie dead, thanks to Guppy, there was no way of recovering the missing cocaine—now that Donnie's house had been bombed.

Splitting up, two of the men took seats on his left side next to him, both smiling as they silently gazed at him; the other walked round behind him and stood behind him. Boss Mann could feel the man's eyes piercing into the back of his head. "You know why we're here?" came the voice from the rear.

Boss Man attempted to get up, but a huge hand clamped on his shoulder. "I know." He whimpered. "I've explained to your bosses and have dealt with the bastard responsible."

"So, you say," said the man sitting closest to him as he stroked his Van Dyke beard with his fingers. "But we're here to collect the missing cash or the goods."

Clamping the oxygen mask to his mouth, Boss Man gulped in the air a few times before replying, "I don't have the cash or the drugs here."

"Maybe you didn't get the message," the bearded man snapped. "We're here to collect, now."

Making another attempt to get up and finding himself anchored down by the goon behind, Boss Man began swinging his arms. The three men behind the mirror were relatively new recruits. They were armed with double-barrelled twelve-gauge shotguns but hadn't been clued in on the proper hand signals from the little man. They all fired at the same moment.

The explosion from behind Boss Man sent thousands of shards of tinted mirror flying rapidly at everything in its path, imbedding itself in walls and furniture, gouging and tearing at the faces and bodies of the three suited men. Boss Man knew he had only a split second to get under the table from the moment he gave the signal but was expecting the three goons to rush into his rescue. He discovered he wasn't injury free, as blood started blinding him, and soon he felt stabbing pains from his head.

He lay under the table, still expecting the goons from behind the mirror to come in. This never happened, and eventually, he crawled out. He was sickened at the sight that confronted him, his pride and joy totally wrecked. His own specially designed conference room was a total bomb site. Stepping back from it, he almost tripped over the goon who had stood behind him. This man's head had been severed and lay between his legs. The one who had been closest to him had a large shard of glass imbedded in his face. The third man lay face up on the floor, his arms spread and his white shirt matted in blood, with some of his intestines exposed through a gaping hole in his stomach area.

Gagging and vomiting, Boss Man staggered out the room heading for his private apartment. He plunged his head into the toilet bowl and brought up what was left in his stomach. He now understood that the three clowns who were behind the mirror had just started a mob war. Drying himself after a cool shower, he idled into the lounge. And using his mobile, he booked a flight to France. Discovering he wouldn't get one for two days, as baggage handlers were engaged in an industrial dispute, he packed all the cash he could carry into a suitcase, intent on driving to London.

CHAPTER 33

"You!" young Andy cried and made to get back out the van door.

Barton managed to grip hold of his arm and pull him back in. Punching his pistol into the back of his head, he shouted "Sit."

Just then, the driver's door opened, and Vesta climbed in. "What's going on?" she shouted.

"This thug and I have a history,"

"What kind of history?" She turned gazing at Barton, her eyes glaring in the dim cabin light.

"It's a long story," Barton replied. "We don't have time to discuss it. Where's that guy you went in to get?"

Pointing a finger at the youngster, she replied, "He's gone. But Andy knows where this Boss Man's place is."

Giving her a surprised glare, he said, "You give me the impression you know this creep," and pushed the gun deeper into the back of Andy's head.

"This is my stepbrother. I've told you about him."

"Get this thing started up and get out of here before the copper's come looking for that guy."

"It was the coppers who took him away." The youngster squirmed. "Two nurses came and bundled him in one of those wheelchairs, and two uniforms pushed him out."

While Andy had been talking, Vesta got the van moving. "Where are we heading?" she asked as she turned onto the busy street.

Barton had relaxed his gun hand and was resting against the side of the van. After a slow hour's drive, in busy traffic, she pulled the vehicle into the forecourt of a closed-down service station. And as Barton was about to open the rear door, the van jumped forward and was back on the main road before Barton had recovered his balance. "What was that all about?" he shouted.

"Round the back of that garage is packed with police cars," Vesta cried over her shoulders.

"Pull into one of the side streets, and we'll walk. It's not far from here," Andy said.

On stiff legs and aching back, Barton followed them from a dark side street onto a busy residential area. At the end of this, Andy stopped and pointed to what Barton thought had once been a church hall or a community centre. "That's where I followed that guy to," the youngster declared.

"It doesn't look like the kind of place a criminal gang would operate from," Vesta said.

"That's what you're led to believe," Barton interrupted. He had begun walking towards the building when he felt a hand grip his arm. He turned and came face to face with Andy.

"Something's not right," the youngster said and led them into the shadows at the corner of a block of flats.

"What do you mean?" Vesta asked.

"I've been here a few times hoping to nick some of the drugs from the pushers. Normally, there's always a car parked at the front with a couple of thugs in it."

"Not today," Barton said as he viewed the building. What he did see was a slightly built man rushing out the door carrying a suitcase. "Who's that?" he asked the youngster, pointing at the figure heading round the side of the building.

"According to some of the descriptions I've gathered listening to some of the goons involved, that could be Boss Man."

"We'll soon find out," Barton shouted over his shoulder as he rushed out after the little man.

Being burdened with the heavy case, Boss Man couldn't move fast enough and was caught by Barton as he was about to the throw the case into the boot of a small car. The moment they faced each other, Barton recognised him. "Well if it isn't lieutenant Boris Manning, the little shit I caught raping and knifing a young Asian girl. I thought they had put you away for life?"

"The spoils of war," Boss Man said. "She was just a peasant girl, not worth a shit."

"What war?" Barton gripped him by the neck and pushed him against the vehicle. "We were there as peacekeeping unit."

"What do you want, Barton?" Boss Man squirmed, his arms and legs punching and kicking but not hitting the target.

"I want to know where my parents are and who's holding them."

"I don't know."

With his free hand, Barton grabbed his gun from his pocket and pushed it against Boss Man's groin. "If you don't tell me what I want to know, your family jewels will be splattered against your car. And if that's not enough, your feet will be joining them."

"You're not right in the head, Barton. If the clowns who work for me had done their job, you'd be dead by now."

The click of the safety catch was enough to make Boss Man choke and gasp for air in panic. "I don't know where your parents are being held." He whimpered between gasps.

At that moment, Vesta and her stepbrother arrived, panting.

"What's he saying?" she asked, while Andy began forcing the case open.

"Not much," Barton replied. "But if he doesn't start, he'll be missing a few of his vital organs."

It was the loud gasp from Andy that caused the distraction. When they saw what he had discovered inside the case, even Barton was distracted long enough for Boss Man to jump out of Barton's grip and pull a pistol from his jacket.

Barton reacted fast but not fast enough, and the shot rang in his ears. He heard that familiar *thump* of a round smacking into a body. At a glance, he saw Andy fall back, and Barton's natural reactions took over. Before the little man chanced a second shot, Barton's pistol exploded before he had a chance to aim. The round grazed Boss Man's shoulder, spinning him around and smashing his head against the boot lid. Before the little man fell, Barton gripped his injured shoulder, pulling him clear of the vehicle.

Having been under this little man's command in the services, Barton knew he was a tough little shit, and the only way to get information out of him would be to put pressure on his wounded shoulder; and that might take a while. Time was running out. The residents in the flats would have heard the shots, and the police could be on their way. "Tell me what you know about the abduction of my parents, or you're a dead man," Barton shouted and put more pressure on his injury, pushing him over the bonnet of the car. It wasn't the anticipated scream that offended Barton's ear but, rather, another shot from behind.

She stood a few feet away, her legs apart, holding Boss Man's pistol two-handed like a pro. The smoke was still drifting from the barrel. She stared wide-eyed at Boss Man's body as it slid from the bonnet and crumpled at Barton's feet. He stepped away, shocked at what he had just witnessed, his eyes darting from her to the corpse at his feet. "What made you do that?" Barton shouted at her.

"I've just put an end to one of the biggest criminal gangs this area has ever seen," Vesta said, letting her arms drop. The pistol clattered to the ground. Still holding the tissue she had wrapped around it, she extracted a green plastic lighter from her pocket. Holding it up, she lit the tissue, letting it fall with the flames still rising from it. Satisfied it was destroyed, she ground it down with her foot. Now with her eyes fixed on his, a grimace developed on her expression. She waved a hand at the case. "There has to be about a million in there, money that can no longer be used to finance drug smuggling."

Feeling shocked at the sparkle in her eyes and unable to read her intent with this money, Barton eased past her and flicked the suitcase lid closed. Without turning, still gazing down at it, he muttered, "What are you? Who are you?"

Grabbing his attention, she stared into his eyes, her wide grin remaining. "Come on, Richard. Don't be so naive. I thought you might have tumbled onto who and what I am."

He shook his head, holding her gaze. "I'm not sure who or what you are." Reluctantly, he raised his gun and held it against her forehead. "If my guess is right, then you can't afford to let me live."

Stepping back a few paces, she peeled off the grey wig. Her grin faded. She stopped and dared him to shoot with beckoning hands. A long silent period dragged by as they held each other's eyes. Eventually, she couldn't resist the smile that dawned across her face and said, "You're not a cold-blooded killer, Richard. Yes, you've killed but in self-defence. You've assaulted people, always in defence or for a good reason."

"I still don't understand who you are and what your game is. Why did you kill that little piece of shit?" Barton pointed a thumb over his shoulder at Boss Man's body.

"That, you will never get to know, now that Donnie's out of the way."

Still showing and feeling confusion, he asked, "What does Donnie have to do with all this?"

Spreading out her arms, she said, "Don't be so naïve, Richard. You saw our operation up in that attic. I thought I could get you in on it. When I saw that shocked look in your eyes, I knew you wouldn't be interested, that you were genuinely trying to get your parents back."

Pointing at Boss Man's weapon lying a few feet away, Barton said, "If you're one of the mob, why go to all that trouble wiping his weapon? Why don't you just take it with you and get rid of it later?"

"I need that gun to make his murder look like another mob killing."

"Well, isn't that what this is? How about the body of your stepbrother? The coppers know him and know he's not in any mob."

Grinning with confidence, she nodded towards Boss Man's body. "Andy somehow got involved. Maybe to save himself, he shot at Boss man, wounding him. Then all hell broke out—a typical mob war." Pulling another tissue from her pocket and handing it to him, she instructed, "Wipe your gun and put it in one of Andy's hands and make yourself disappear."

After doing what she had suggested, Barton asked, "What are *you* going to do?"

"Disappear." She picked up the case and began jogging back to the van.

Confused, Barton stood there, watching her struggle and trying to prevent the heavy case from bumping into her legs. In the distance came the sound of sirens, making him jump into action. He caught up with her in time to see her slamming the rear door and jumping into the driver's side. He managed to grip the passenger's door handle and struggle in beside her as she began to drive away. He wrenched up the hand brake, and the drive wheels spun, creating a cloud of blue smoke at the front. Finally, she turned the engine off and gazed at him. "What now?"

"You little bitch," Barton shouted. "You were about to piss off with all that money. What are you, just another dirty little thief like your stepbrother?"

"What I am has nothing to do with you. We need to get out of here before a squad of coppers arrive." She had noticed that he'd removed his hand from the brake lever, and she hastily restarted the engine, released the hand brake, and drove off.

Nervously, he sat, stamping down on the pedals that weren't there as she darted in and out of the traffic, exceeding the speed limit, a few times missing oncoming vehicles by a fraction of an inch. "Are you in a hurry to get somewhere?" he shouted.

"We need to get back to Donnie's house and get those drugs down from the attic."

"Fuck the drugs. How am I supposed to find my parents now with Boss Man dead and the guy from the hospital in police custody?" he shouted, simultaneously throwing his hands on the dashboard as she jumped a red light. A truck had to swerve, and when Barton looked behind, he saw that it had toppled over, shedding its load of steel pipes.

She took a last-minute left turn into a back street close to Donnie's house on two wheels. "Fuck your parents," she cried. "Let the police find them."

"They could be dead by then," he shouted and was thrown forward, his head thumping off the windscreen when she jumped on the brakes in the lane leading to the back of Donnie's house.

"You sit there and keep an eye on that case," she said and got out, gently closing the door.

Jumping out of his side and standing in the open door, he shouted, "How are you going to carry all those drugs on your own?"

The only response he got was a wave of her arms as she stepped over the broken gate and was soon out of sight.

Settled back in the van, this time in the driver's seat, he prepared himself for a long wait and was about to tune in the radio when she came running out. Barton got the engine started, thinking that the thugs had spotted her and were chasing after her. She dived in the passenger's seat, shouting, "Get this thing moving."

Luckily, there were no other vehicles travelling nearby when he reversed onto the back street, his foot flat to the floor. At a crazy speed, Barton drove down the back street, narrowly missing parked cars. At the end of it, he pulled up. "What the fuck's happened? What the fuck is going on in there?" Again, before she could answer he had the van moving, throwing her back against the headrest.

"I don't know," she cried, her voice trembling and her head in her hands. "I didn't get in the door. I heard a man shouting, 'Get the fuck out of here.' I realised he wasn't talking to me, so there must have been someone else in there with him. I panicked and ran."

At a reasonable speed, Barton drove along a dual carriageway, not knowing where he was heading and not paying too much attention. With his mind racing in turmoil, he firstly tried to work out who this woman sitting beside him was. His next crowding thought was, Where was his family being kept? And were they still alive? The headlights illuminated a big P sign, telling him he was approaching a layby. Pulling in behind a truck and still keeping the engine running, he turned on the cabin light. Staring out the windshield at the back doors of the container in front, he gripped the steering wheel tightly. "Are you going to tell me what's going on in your head, who and what you are, and what all this drug dealing and killing is about? And are you involved?"

After a moment of zero reaction from her, he turned and came face to face with the barrel of a Sig-Hammerli 240 pistol only an inch from his nose. "Get out," she shouted, "or I'll let you have it here, right now."

Grimacing, he moved his head back. "You do that, and that truck driver will hear the shot, alerting him. And you'll have to drag me out. He'll witness you doing that through his mirror."

It was her turn to grimace. "That driver will be in his bed. And by the time he gets up to investigate the shot, I'll have kicked your body out and be on my way. And anyway this little peashooter doesn't make much noise. So, get out."

Remembering her stance and how she'd handled Boss Man's weapon, Barton assumed she had been trained in the use of firearms and decided to comply with her demands.

"Leave the door open," she shouted when he was halfway out. "And step back a couple of steps."

Once again, he complied with her demands, watching her climb into the driver's seat. All this time, her gun hand never faltered, and her eyes never left his. He hoped that, at some point, she would have to reach over to close the door, giving him time to make his next move. In an instant, the vehicle shot backwards, the open door striking him on the arm and twisting him around. By the time he had regained his balance, the van had shot out of the layby, sideswiping a passing car and causing it to swerve across to the wrong side of the road into the tracks of an oncoming truck. Its brakes screaming, tyres burning, and spewing blue smoke in their wake, it ploughed into the car with a deafening crash, causing it to roll over and land in the ditch at the opposite side of the road.

In a natural reaction, Barton had dived in behind the container truck that had been parked there when they'd pulled in. After recovering from the shock, both he and the driver rushed to the car in the ditch, with little hope of finding the occupants alive. They were joined by the driver of the truck involved but only got to within a few yards when the car exploded, sending a huge blade of flames skyward. The power of the blast blew them back against cars that had been forced to stop.

In a few moments both sides of the road was totally gridlocked, with cars, trucks, and buses. Barton noticed the driver from the truck involved on his mobile and knew he was too late. He guessed the people who had also witnessed the accident had already phoned the emergency services. He decided now was the time to disappear and slowly turned away, finally walking at a brisk pace along the road, trying not to attract too much attention from the motorists stuck in the queue.

In spite of her deceit, he couldn't get her out of his mind as he stumbled along the rough grass verge. He realised she had played him all along, that she must have known about the cocaine in Donnie's attic but needed a clown to help her move it. The money in that case was compensation for the loss of it in that explosion.

Although there was plenty of noise going on around him, with drivers blasting their horns and sirens from the emergency services, he could hear a slight whimpering over to his left side. Being mindful of his footing, he stepped towards it and, in the light from the stationary vehicles, found himself looking down into a steep embankment. Halfway down it, almost hidden by shrubs, he noticed the red taillights of a vehicle. This had to be the Astra van. He scrambled down, finding it on its roof. Sliding on his buttocks and the soles of his shoes, he got to the driver's door. After a few failed attempts, he pulled it open. She lay under the steering wheel, her upper body through the smashed windshield under the bonnet. Strangely enough, the headlights were still shining, and he attempted to assess her injuries, at the same time trying not to slip on the muddy slope. Judging by the position her head was lying in comparison with her torso, Barton knew she had broken her neck and maybe a lot more bones. And her internal organs, he dare not think about. She would have only a few minutes left. Staring at her face, still covered in the white foundation, he was startled when her blue eyes opened. She uttered one word and slowly closed them. Her body jerked a few times and then slumped.

Knowing there was nothing he could do for her, he stumbled and slipped his way to the rear of the upturned van. Finding the door half open, his hand soon came in contact with the suitcase.

CHAPTER 34

Slipping the suitcase under his bed without the thought of opening it, Barton strolled into his living room, got settled on the sofa, and turned on the television. The news was about the accident. According to the presenter, six people had lost their lives, and the police were trying to contact the driver of a white Corsa van. *So!* he ruminated. *They haven't found her.* In his mind's eyes, he could see that white foundation on her lovely face and that last look in her eyes and hear that single word she'd spoken—*hospital.* He had thought there and then she was asking him to take her there. Now in hindsight, he realised she must have known she was about to die. *So, why ask to be taken to hospital?*

He woke with a start, realising he had dozed off on the sofa. That last word Vesta had spoken was still ringing in his mind. She wasn't asking to be taken there. Was she telling him that was where his parents were? Surely not, he decided, and got up off the sofa and headed for his kitchen, which was not yet set up. Finding his kettle and filling it with water, he contemplated. *How would she have known they were in hospital?* These thoughts came scrambling through his mind. In the end, he decided she was a part of the mob who'd arranged it. *When she saw that cash in the suitcase, she knew the only person stopping her from getting it was Boss Man.* That name brought on another sobering thought. Why hadn't the head of a criminal organisation had his goons with him for protection, especially when he was carrying all that cash?

Pinning his hopes on the assumption that Vesta was part of the mob that had set up the abduction of his parents, Barton headed for the hospital. He was glad he had put on a heavy cotton duffle coat with a hood when he stepped out. The snow was falling, and a strong wind was driving it into his face. The weather made for a good excuse for hiding his identity without attracting attention.

Wiping the snow from his coat and hood, he pushed his way through the glass doors and headed for the reception kiosk. Three young women were sat around an L-shaped bench-type desk. Barton approached the one closest. "I believe my parents were admitted, and I'm not sure what ward they're in." He answered all her questions about his parents. The difficult part came was when she asked for the date of admission. This took some time. She had to spend a lot of time on her computer going through all the dates and times. She came back at him, saying there were four of the same name over the past month, but she couldn't find either name in any recent admissions.

Resigned to the belief that he had misread Vesta's message, he thanked the girl and was about to walk away when she said, her eyes still on her monitor, "An elderly couple was admitted. It seems they were unconscious, and there was no means of identification on them. It would be helpful if you could ID them."

"I can do that," Barton readily agreed. "Could you give me more information on how they were brought in?"

She took her eyes away from her monitor and slowly shook her head. "Not until you Identify them as your parents ... I'll get someone to take you to them"—she pointed to a row of chairs—"if you would like to take a seat."

It felt like he had sat there for an hour watching people approaching the reception and walking to a directed area somewhere in the bowels of the edifice before a tall woman in a white jacket approached carrying what looked like a file envelope.

"Are you Mr Barton?" she asked with a thin-lipped grin.

Nodding, Barton stood up and returned her grin. "That's me."

"Follow me," she said and turned, striding towards a sign that read, "Intensive care."

As instructed, Barton followed, admiring the sway of her shapely hips. She held a door open for him, and when he entered, she ushered him to a bedside. The shock of seeing his mother lying there hit him. Her complexion was a bluish grey, her sunken eyes were closed, and tubes were inserted into her nostrils. Her thin bare arms were bruised, and a cannula in her small hand was attached to a tube feeding fluid into her frail body, which hardly created a crease on the bedding. He could only stand, gazing at her pale face and couldn't control the tears flooding his eye. "That's my mother," he finally said and could feel the woman's hand gently holding his arm.

"Your father is in the next room. We've only just been able to get a response from him. If you would like to see him, I'll take you to him."

Seated next to his bed, Tom Barton, with his head in his hands, got up on unsteady legs when he saw his son enter the room.

"What's been happening?" Barton asked, helping his father back down on the chair.

With tear-filled blue eyes, Tom looked up at his son. "It was all my fault. I thought I was doing you a good turn, helping you get some sleep. I told your mum to slip a couple of her sleeping pills into your tea."

"How was it your fault? You weren't to know someone was about to break into your home and abduct you." Barton sat on the edge of the bed and put his hand on his father's shoulder. "How's mum? Is she going to be OK?"

Shaking his head slowly, Tom sighed deeply. "I don't know. They say it could leave a lifelong scar on her mental health."

"How about you? Are you going to be all right?"

"I'm OK. The bastard nailed her into a wooden crate. She was in there for three days before I managed to find something to open it with."

"Who nailed her into the crate?"

Shaking his head and leaning forward Tom replied, "I don't know who he was. He wore a ski mask and was in an army outfit—a tall guy with, I think, a London accent. He held a gun at your mother's head and ordered us out and not to make a sound. He cable tied our hands behind our back and bundled us into the back of a van. I've already given all these details to the coppers."

"Can you remember how you got here?"

"At the sight of seeing your mother crammed inside that crate, blood and shit all over her, I must have passed out; the next thing I knew I was lying in that bed with tubes in my arms."

Barton was aware time was running out. Soon, the police would want to know more about what had happened now that his father was recovering. He also didn't want to stress him out further by questioning him. He left after saying, "When you're discharged, you need to come and live at my flat—until I know it's safe for you both to return home."

Before leaving the hospital, he visited his mother and was confronted by the tall woman in the white coat, who took a gentle hold of his arm and led him back out the room. "The doctors say she has a few physical injuries. But mostly, it's mental. It's going to take a long time for her to recover from what's happened, and she might need months of psychiatric treatment. It would appear she's had a slight stroke, maybe brought on by her ordeal."

Barton thanked the woman and left with one thought on his mind—he would get this guy in the combat gear and make him suffer for what he had done to his parents. The snow had eased off but was ankle deep as he trudged his way to his flat. As he was about to turn into the street, a car pulled up beside him at the kerb. The electric window slid down. Barton's thoughts were that this car hadn't travelled far, as the snow was still on the roof and on the windscreen where the wipers couldn't reach. Bending over and looking inside the vehicle, and in the glow from the headlights reflecting off the snow, he recognised the grinning face of his old army mate Ex-Sergeant Tommy Marvell.

"Hi! Richard," Marvell said, "get in out of this snow, and I'll drop you off where you're going."

"I'm OK, Tommy. I live just down the street," Barton replied.

"Get in," Marvell demanded. "I need a few words with you."

"Fair enough," Barton replied and opened the car door and got in. "We can talk in my house."

Marvell was seated on the sofa when Barton joined him with two mugs of coffee. "What do you want talk about?"

He cringed after taking a sip of coffee. "You always were a lousy coffee maker, Richard. He placed the mug down by his feet and gazed into Barton's brown eyes with a serious expression and holding both his hands out as if surrendering to something. "Do you remember Corporal Harrison?" He went on when Barton nodded. "I've heard he has been killed. Or should I say executed."

"I'm sorry to hear that. He was a good lad and a good soldier. Is that what you wanted to talk about?"

Marvell grimaced. "I believe that, when he got demobbed, he got mixed up with some criminal organisation in this area."

Taking a sip of his coffee and cringing, Barton said, "I'm sorry to hear that. But what does that have to do with us?"

"When I got out," Marvell said with some hesitation, "I applied for a private investigator licence and took on a job with insurance companies. It seems that Harrison's family had put in a claim on his death." He delayed a moment to see what reaction he was getting from the big man. "It turns out that because of his criminal activities, the company wouldn't pay out—"

"Where is this all leading to?" Barton interrupted.

"The police have a guy in custody. And according to the information I was given, they suspect Harrison was one of this guy's victims.

Shaking his head and grinning, Barton said, "You've lost me. I still don't know what this has to do with me."

Holding up his hand, Marvell said, "Let me finish. And by the way, I'm telling you this in confidence. The police have found weapons with this guy's fingerprints on all of them, and ballistics reports confirm that one of those weapons was used to kill four members of that gang, the same automatic weapon that was used to kill three dogs in a caravan site." Again, he delayed and noticed that Barton was showing a lot more interest.

"Does this guy have a name?" Barton also put his mug at his feet.

Shaking his head slowly, Marvell replied, "I didn't get a name. My informant was killed in a road accident earlier today."

Jumping up, Barton gazed down at Marvell. "Was your informant a woman? And was she driving a stolen van?"

"Yes, and she was driving the same van that was used to abduct your parents." Marvell gazed into Barton's brown eyes for a long thoughtful moment and grinned. "By the way, it was me who took your parents to the hospital."

"I couldn't begin to thank you for that. Do you know who it was that abducted them?" Barton shouted down at him.

"Calm yourself down, Richard. It's all over." Marvell stood up and handed Barton the empty mug, saying, "Try and improve your coffee making skills." He grinned and watched Barton slump down on the sofa and left, closing the door softly.

Gazing into the empty mug, Barton finally tossing it at the door. He watched the fragments disperse over the floor before springing to his feet. "It's not over," he shouted, "not by a long shot."

As he bent down, picking up the broken crockery, she came to mind. Who was this woman Vesta? What was she? And how did she fit into this? In spite of the confusion, she was causing, he couldn't get her out of his thoughts. Dropping the broken mug pieces into the wastebin, he decided the only way to find the answer to all these questions was to go back to Donnie's house and get up into the attic. The more thought he put into it, the more he began to feel like bloody a naive idiot. How could she live in that house with Donnie and be ignorant of the action that must have been going on above their heads?

Dressed in his heavy hooded coat, Barton headed out to hail a taxi. This proved to be difficult because of the lying snow. In the end, he finally got into one, the driver saying, "You're lucky, man. I was heading home. I'm the only cab on the road."

Barton thanked him and told him to drop him off at the nearest point to Rapper Street.

"I'm glad you didn't ask me to drop you off in that street. That's a no-go area for us," the driver said when Barton paid him.

Carefully placing his footing over the broken gate, now covered in snow, Barton remembered that one wrong step could mean a large rusty nail into his foot. A sudden flash of light made him duck and crawl behind the fence. He was certain it had come from within the building. Was it a torch? Or maybe a car headlight reflecting off one of the windows? Taking no chances, Barton stayed down, focussed on the rear windows of Donnie's house. Being aware he stood out wearing a black coat against the surrounding snow-covered debris, Barton relied on his army training, knowing it was movement that most often gave you away. Fortunately, he didn't have to crouch there long before confirming it was a torch inside Donnie's house. Whoever it was in there, was doing a lot of moving about. Barton's immediate thought was a burglar. And from what Vesta had said, there were plenty of them on this street.

Deciding this has to be a burglar, judging from the amount of movement that went on from room to room, Barton slowly got up and crept towards the back door. He'd managed only a few steps when the figure from inside burst out, running towards him. Barton threw a punch at the small man as he charged past, catching him on the chest. Barton was wrong-footed and was swung around, landing on his rump in the snow-covered debris beside the man. He threw out a hand, gripping the man's arm and dragged him closer, landing another left-handed blow to the man's head.

Getting onto his feet, he lifted the man with him. He was about to head-butt the smaller man when the ground beneath shuddered. A split second later, it happened—the deafening force of the blast throwing Barton and the man out onto the alley. The man landed on top of Barton. This, he realised, was what saved him. With both his hands on the man's shoulders, Barton attempted to push him off. But all that happened was his hands continued past the man's torso when the man's shoulders dislocated.

By wriggling and twisting, Barton finally freed himself from the charred body. Sickened by the stench of burnt flesh and clothing, he scrambled to his feet and started to run on wabbly legs—legs that gave way after only a few steps. He stumbled, falling to his knees when it happened again, forcing him facedown on the snow.

This time, the blast lit up the sky in a blazing white flash. Soon, debris from the building began falling around him. Covering his head with both of his hands, Barton began to crawl like a grub through the snow-covered alley. But before he reached the street, a third blast happened.

At the first blink of his eyes, the blinding white light sent excruciating shocks of pain. He tried to cover them with his hands and panicked when he couldn't move them. A shadow blocked out the glare, and a face came into focus, a face he first thought was a stranger. And again he fought to move his arms and failed. A hand gently held him by the shoulder, followed by a gentle male voice, a voice he had heard before.

Gradually, his eyes came into focus to see his father looking down at him. "Lie still," Tom Barton advised. "You're in hospital, they found you crawling about close to where an explosion happened."

Trying to get up, Barton found himself being restrained by more shadows towering over him. "What's going on?" he heard himself cry, his voice sounding alien and distant.

"You've been caught in what is thought to have been a gas explosion," One of the silhouetted figures explained. "You've sustained minor injuries physically, but we have to keep you in for twenty-four hours for observation. You have a slight concussion."

"How long have I been in here?" Barton asked, struggling to hear his own words through increasing ringing in his ears.

No reply came, and one by one, the shadows faded. He struggled to keep his eyelids from falling and finally succumbed to a deep dreamless sleep.

Stabbing pains in his shoulder and a vision of someone driving a bayonet into him woke him. He jumped up to see hands gripping his upper arms and lowering him back down. Barton found himself looking up at a ruddy face with grey eyes and a long thin hooked nose. A thin-lipped grin dawned across the face as it moved away.

"I'm DS Tragg," the man said. "They tell me you are being discharged sometime today, when that happens, I'll be here to assist you and take you to a private establishment for an interview." *A private establishment for an interview.* These words reverberated through Barton's head as he tried to understand what it could mean. *Not the words that an arresting officer would use.* "What kind of interview?" was all he could think of saying.

No reply came, the big man had stepped back out of his vision. Barton turned his head in time to see him step out the door. Soon after, a young girl in uniform stepped in to take D.C Tragg's place at his bedside. For a long moment, Barton studied her as she sat on the wooden chair close to his bed. Their eyes met, and she smiled, and soon she began playing on her mobile.

"I would like to see my father," he said, returning her smile.

Without taking her eyes from the mobile, she shook her head. "I can't authorise that."

"Can you get someone who can?"

She twisted her head and spoke a few words into the radio on her shoulder. Then she stood up and reached for the door, pulling it open. In walked DC Tragg. His build and the way he carried himself gave Barton the impression of a gentleman farmer. He wore a green Harris Tweed jacket and brown corduroy trousers and, to finish off the fashion, a pair of polished brown boots on what Barton judged to be size twelve feet at least.

Tragg stood at the foot of the bed, one hand in his trouser pocket the other pointing a large plump finger. "Get dressed," he ordered. "I'm told your fit to be discharged."

CHAPTER 35

Escorted by two uniformed officers, one on either side, with Tragg leading the way, Barton found himself being bundled into the back of a hardtop Land Rover, typically used by farmers. One officer climbed in beside him. The other, Barton guessed, was driving. And Tragg would be sitting beside him as passenger. The big tread tyres were making a noisy whine, amplified by the metal canopy as they cruised along on the M6 motorway. The only window Barton could see out of was at the rear, making it impossible to work out where they were heading.

No sooner had the vehicle got onto the motorway when it turned off and was soon on what he reconned was a B-class road. The going here was slow, and Barton could see faint tracks on the snow telling him very few cars had travelled along here. They came to a sliding stop close to old buildings. The view through the window was something he thought looked like an abandoned farm. Barton heard the doors at the front slam. Soon, the rear door opened and the driving officer stood facing them. His colleague jumped out and stood next to him, a tactic, Barton decided, to make sure he didn't do a runner.

The driver waved him out, saying, "Put your hands behind your back."

Barton nodded and climbed out, conforming to the order, and felt the other officer fastening cuffs on his wrists. They jumped into the front of the Land Rover and drove off, leaving him standing and watching at it as it disappeared around a bend on the road.

Long after the vehicle had gone, Barton began to feel the cold creeping into him, and he started to pace back and forth, stamping his feet. He turned at the sound of hinges creaking. and there was Tragg standing in a doorway waving. Barton trudged through the ankle-deep snow toward him. "What the fuck's going on?" he shouted at the big man.

No reply came from Tragg. Instead he shot a big hand out, grabbing Barton's shoulder and guiding him inside the dark building. No words were needed when Barton spied a narrow blade of light at the opposite side of the interior and allowed the big man to steer him in that direction.

Opening the door and, at the same time, moving his hand from Barton's shoulder to his upper arm, he guided Barton on a chair next to a rough wooden bench and released the handcuffs. Tragg pulled up a seat and perched himself opposite and leaned over on his elbows, his grey eyes fixed on Barton's. "I've enough on you to put you away for a very long time."

Holding his gaze, Barton grimaced, "If that's your intent, why did you bring me *here* to question me?"

Sitting back on his creaky chair, Tragg replied, "Because what I'm about to say is only for your ears and better not come out your mouth; I know for sure this place isn't bugged."

It was Barton's turn to lean on his elbows across the bench. "How about those two uniforms? It can't be that big a secret. They'll scream when put under pressure. Your superiors will want to know why you ordered them to drive us out here."

Holding up his big hands, Tragg grinned. "Let me worry about those two. This is off the record. I want you to give me a little help to bring down a mob that is operating in the city centre."

"How am I supposed to do that?"

"I'm sure they know your reputation. If not they'll soon find out. I want you to get in with that mob. Get as close to the head men as you can—"

"So, you want me to be a grass for you?" Barton quickly interrupted.

Nodding his head and smiling, Tragg added, "The choice is yours. You do this, or you spend a lot of years in the can."

www.ingramcontent.com/pod-product-compliance
Lightning Source LLC
Chambersburg PA
CBHW032033310726
48972CB00002B/656